PLAYING WITH HELLFIRE

SIN DEMONS

MILA YOUNG

HARPER A. BROOKS

Cover Design by Jervy Bonifacio | Phoenix Design Studio

Visit our books at
www.milayoungbooks.com
https://harperabrooks.com

DEDICATION

For Tania.
-Harper A. Brooks

For Krys.
-Mila Young

CONTENTS

SIN DEMONS SERIES

PLAYING WITH HELLFIRE

The devils aren't in the details. They're in my bed...

When my warlock foster father trades me to demons for his outstanding debts, I find myself in Hell on Earth. I'm thrust into a supernatural underground crime ring I can't get out of, eternally bound in a contract I never made.

Three hot-as-hell demons stand in between me and my freedom.

A tattooed, brutish Hellhound shifter. An incubus with the power to bend wills on command. And the heir to Lucifer's throne—the original sin demon, Pride, himself. I have to find a way out of the deal before they devour me, body and soul.

But I'm no angel. There's something inside me, something that craves the chaotic darkness these demons possess.

Escaping may mean giving in to Hell's more sinful temptations. But playing with fire only hurts if you get burned...

CHAPTER ONE
ARIA

"Hell is empty. All the devils are here." William Shakespeare.

My foster father once told me that everyone was born with the ability to be kind. I call bull.

Murray's known to spew some random philosophical sayings, usually ones that go against his own actions. It's kind of his thing, and for some reason, that one comes to mind now, while I'm dangling from a rope fifteen feet off the floor inside the town's most popular antique store. It's an ancient building, the oldest in all of Glenside and most likely haunted.

But right—back to my foster father's words of wisdom and the reason I know without a shadow of a doubt that he is wrong. The answer is simple—Sir Surchion. The old fart who owns this store is the most vile person I've ever met. When the man looks in your eyes, he peers into your soul.

As cliché as it sounds, it's damn true. In his presence, I feel unease in my bones, so I don't harbor a thread of guilt as I break into his store. He'll walk over anyone to add to his collection of dusty antiques. Plus, the prick just fired my best friend after he made a move on her and she kneed him in the balls. Did I mention he's three times her age?

Down below me, the warehouse is quiet, and darkness shrouds the large room. Only one door leads into the main store, and the place reeks of mildew, dust, and mothballs. Four rows of metal shelving are packed to the rafters with artifacts of all kinds. Vases, clocks, things dating from back in ancient times, and dozens upon dozens of wooden crates with God-knows-what stored inside. Magical pieces are his favorite, but if it holds value, Sir Surchion wants it.

Yesterday, Joseline told me about this new item Sir Surchion shipped in. He tried to keep it secret, but his infatuation got the better of him. He called it the 'Orb of Chaos,' and it supposedly contained the waters of Hell's River Styx. Of course, like any good story, the facts are exaggerated, but I don't care. It's apparently worth six figures, and that's what interests me more than anything else.

It's going to bring in quite a bit of money when I sell it on the magic underground market. Even in the dingy little city of Glenside, there are enough supernaturals living among the humans that extra levels of precaution are put into place to keep us all secret. One being a secret and magically protected market in the city's basement.

I lower myself in slow motion, scanning the warehouse below. If I were a dirty old man with a hoarding problem, where would I store a prized relic? I try to remember everything Joseline told me during our previous conversations. She'd mentioned it being stashed back here somewhere, but not much else. And since I was doing this without her knowing, it's not like I could just ask her for more details without sounding suspicious. So, it looks like I am on my own from here.

Closing my eyes, I quiet my thoughts and try to picture the orb in my mind using Joseline's description. A circular glass sphere the size of my fist with silver liquid inside. Like a crystal ball the fortune tellers from the movies use.

Nothing happens at first, but then a flutter of tingles start at the base of my spine, telling me the object is definitely in the room. The sensation creeps down my left leg and ends in my pinkie toe. I flip open my eyes and look down to my foot, which is now pointing to the back right-hand corner of the room.

Perfect.

Don't judge... I may not know exactly what I am, but I like to think I'm special. In my own odd little way. I'm not Wonder Woman by any means, and I can't conjure up fireballs or predict your future, but I've never met anyone else who can detect magic so easily. Spells, charms, hexes—anything touched by magic, I can feel out. Objects are my specialty, and the darker the magic, the better. The evil stuff just likes me I guess.

And right now, this Orb of Chaos is feeling pretty dark to me. The familiar sensation continues to rocket through my body, my Vans pointing in the direction I need to go like a compass's arrow.

So far, so good. I just need to propel down, grab the thing, and sell it before tomorrow night when I hit eighteen and my foster dad loses legal guardianship over me. Will Murray actually kick me out? That's a good question. He threatens to all the time, but all my other foster siblings left immediately on their eighteenth birthday, and now I'm the only one left. They figured braving the world on their own was better than living with empty cabinets, roaches, and no heat in the winters. And with the winter months fast approaching, taking a chance was sounding better and better to me too.

I pull at my harness and descend to get this over with, but a few feet from the floor, a faint shuffling sound comes from up ahead. I freeze and jerk my gaze as the door leading into the main store pushes ajar.

My breath wedges in my throat. Sir Surchoin isn't supposed to be here. He never lingers after closing. I've been watching this spot for days to work out his routine, and as Joseline said, he leaves at 6 p.m. on the dot and returns at seven in the morning. Locks and security make the front and rear entrance hard to enter, but the skylight window is always open for his pet crow to come in and out.

A dark form pushes through the door, walking on all fours. Black as the night with a long tail, I watch the animal trot into the warehouse. I squint for a better view, trying to make out the form in the light of the bright green exit sign. A dog. I had no idea Sir Surchion kept guard dogs. Well, that explains why he doesn't have a security system. Joseline never mentioned any other pets besides the damn bird.

The door pushes wider, and a second animal enters.

Oh, hell!

I wait, dangling and not making a sound, biding my time. If I'm completely still, there's a chance they'll leave. Then I'll hop down and use something to block the door, giving me plenty of time to grab the orb and get the heck out of here.

Fifteen minutes later, and the harness's straps are chafing between my thighs and digging into my legs, while my fingers are stiff from gripping the rope for so long. The mutts pace the front of the warehouse before making themselves comfortable on the floor. Right in the middle of the aisle where my built-in magic detector points to where I need to go.

Bastards.

Sick of hanging around, I curl my hands into fists and concentrate for my next parlor trick.

Come out, Sayah.

Seconds is all it takes for the familiar icy pinpricks to glide across my skin, like being caressed by a ghost. My shadow stretches out from me, elongating and changing shape on its own. Horrifying to witness from an outsider's perspective, I'm sure, but I've grown used to it. Sayah is part of me and my dark little secret. I've even given her a cute name, meaning 'shadow.'

A simple link is all that's needed to keep us bound. A strand of darkness from my feet that connects her spirit-like essence as she leaves my body and manifests in the real world. She's her own entity—full of attitude and all—but she listens when I need her to.

She slides along the floor and up one of the shelves, mimicking my shape... mostly. The wisps of her hair, though, float around her as if manipulated by water, and her limbs are a bit longer than what's natural.

Sayah skitters across the room. In a flash, she rounds the edge of the shelves and dances right in front of the dogs. They leap to their feet and try snapping their jaws at her, but she's too quick. As she zooms toward the door, the dogs howl and give chase into the main store.

Good boys.

Frantically, I pull at the ropes and lower myself. My feet touch the floor, and I unlatch the harness. Dropping the equipment down, I sprint to the door and slam it shut. I reach down and flick the lock. The shadowy cord between me and Sayah shifts back and forth under the space beneath the door as she teases the mutts. Booming barks and nasty snarls come from the other side, so I don't waste another second.

Knowing exactly where to go now, I run down to the end of the last row of shelves. Now that I'm on the ground, my skin crawls with the strong pulses of magic all around me. This place is full of things touched with the stuff, but the strongest and darkest one that vibrates above them all is the one I want. The Orb of Chaos.

I glance over my shoulder just to make sure I'm alone. I am. It's just paranoia at seeing those hounds. Several wooden crates sit against the wall, but they look unopened, so I doubt what I'm here for is in there.

Pivoting toward the shelves, I pull the small flashlight from my pocket and flick it on. Rapidly I scan the artifacts, searching past the Greek tea set, the figurines of animals that are salt and pepper shakers and quite cute.

No, Aria. Don't take the cute piglet set. Even though it's adorable. Following the rapid tingles, I crouch low, and through the darkness something gives off a faint, pulsing glow from the back of the shelf. I direct the beam back there and discover a circular orb. It sits in a miniature wooden basket lined with red velvet.

Bingo.

I grab the orb, the surface round and smooth and cold to the touch. Inside, the silver liquid looks like mercury, and the way it swishes and flows is mesmerizing.

The object hums in my grasp, almost vibrating. This bad boy is going to bring in a lot of money. Water from Hell or not. It's special. I can tell just by the way it feels in my hand.

"No idea what you are, but you're going to make me a hell of a lot of money," I whisper to the thing like it can understand me.

Tiny waves inside begin ebbing and crashing into the glass, reminding me of the unruly ocean right before a storm.

I stand and stuff the orb into the satchel on my hip, then turn and run toward the rope two aisles down.

A hissing sound surges in my ears, buzzing across my mind like a swarm of angry cicadas have taken residence in there. Seconds later, the door to the store flings open and rebounds against the wall. My heart jumps into my chest, and I skid to a halt.

Two guard dogs stare at me from the doorway.

The twist in my gut turns into a shiver.

Shit!

This close, they look like feral things. Black ears plastered to their heads, sharp fangs exposed from peeled-back lips as they growl viciously.

Sayah returns, snapping back into me. Our link allows me to feel her general emotions too, if a shadow can feel such things. And right now, it feels like she's disappointed she let me down.

My anxiety shoots up a notch, the danger more real. If I don't get out of here, I'll become dog food in moments.

I spin on my heel and dart in the opposite direction, racing down the corridor between the wall shelves.

Paws thump the stone floor behind me, claws click-clacking as the dogs close in on me. Panic claws up my throat. I sure as hell don't want to end up found mauled to death by dogs in this place.

Feet pounding the floor, I run for my life.

I careen around the shelves and dart past the next parallel aisle. I swing into the second lane where my rope dangles about fifteen feet away.

Sprinting for it, I glance back. The savage hounds make the turn, teeth snapping and snarls ricocheting through the warehouse. The rope's close but feels miles away. The dogs are upon me in seconds, their hot breaths practically on the back of my legs. I spin last minute, and a sudden snap of jaws comes inches from my calf, the wind fluttering against my jeans.

Son of a bitch.

Heart racing, I run up a set of crates near the shelves and catapult myself up toward the dangling rope. Snatching it mid-air, I swing violently and hold on for dear life. I pull my knees up high so they reach my elbows and wrap the rope around my ankles. Working quickly, I use it to push myself higher. My muscles scream in protest, but the immediate danger has me scrambling for more height.

A sharp, excruciating pain tears right into my calf. It comes so fast and hard that I cry out.

The dog jerks its head, teeth scraping down my pants and tearing skin. The pain is so intense I almost let go, but instead I thrash to force myself into a wild swing.

"Fuck off!" I slam my other foot into its face to dislodge it.

It whines and lets go, squealing when it hits the ground.

Frantic now, I scale up the rope like a crazy squirrel, moving on pure adrenaline. Higher and higher I climb above the hounds that are jumping up after me and tugging on the cord.

My pulse thunders in my ears, and I hate how damn terrified I feel.

Perspiration runs down the side of my face, and halfway up and out of reach, I pause, gasping for air.

Down below, the damn things are snarling and making a racket, enough to wake the neighborhood. A sudden tug on the rope has my grip slipping. These dogs are relentless! I slide down and a scream escapes past my lips. Frantically,

I grasp the rope and jolt for a hold, my palms burning, knuckles white.

Fuck!

Snarls echo through the room while agonizing pain digs deeper into my leg from the bite. I swear, if I get rabies, I'm coming back for revenge.

I resume my escape, dragging myself up by my sore arms, my feet twisting around the rope for leverage and pushing myself up. I hate to admit this isn't my first breaking and entering attempt, and with my funds absolutely abysmal currently, it probably won't be the last. I try not to make it a habit, especially since things always seem to go wrong—like with the teeth marks in my leg, for example.

The dogs continue to jump and bark ferociously at me, but I'm too far up to catch now. That doesn't slow me down any though. With all the ruckus, I'm waiting for the police sirens next.

The windowpane in the ceiling sits half-open from where I left it, and just as I reach for the edge, something bursts inside and flutters right past me.

I shudder and flinch, my heart nearly bursting out of my rib cage.

"The fuck!?" I look back down to see Sir Surchion's stupid crow landing on top of a shelf. It tilts its head, beady black eyes studying me.

Damn bird. Damn dogs. It's a freaking zoo in here.

Clumsily, I grab hold of the edge of the open window and haul myself out. Sitting there with my legs dangling inside, I gasp for each breath, trying to calm my raging pulse.

This night has sucked, but at least I got the orb. I heave the rope and harness up, away from the dogs. They snap at it a few more times before giving up and rushing back into the store as if knowing they've lost this battle. Or maybe they heard another sound?

Right now, all I want is to get the hell away from this store before any more craziness happens.

I shove the rope and harness into my satchel as fast as I can and head across the flat roof to the overhanging tree, hurrying to get down. When my feet kiss the ground, another hissing sound from the orb threads over my thoughts. It stops me in my tracks. Last time it did that was just before the dogs burst into the warehouse. Like it had been warning me.

And now... now I don't want to find out what danger waits for me.

As I half-limp, half-run home through the dark, my skin crawls like I'm being watched.

CHAPTER TWO
ARIA

The sounds of dishes clanking and cabinet doors slamming wakes me. I sigh, aggravated, and roll over to find my cell on the nightstand. After a quick tap on the shattered screen, the time glares at me. Not even six in the morning yet.

"Not again," I grumble and rub my eyes. I'd only gotten to bed three hours ago, and after the fiasco at the antique shop, exhaustion still clings to me. Murray really has to get his drinking and gambling under control. These early morning wake-up calls are getting ridiculous.

Remembering what day it is, hope flares in my chest, making me jut upright and scramble out of bed. The moment I stand, pain races up my calf and I wince, leaning back against the mattress. I'd bandaged my bite mark last night, but it still hurts like crazy. I'm lucky to have gotten away with minimal injuries after those two dogs attacked, even if I don't feel that way right now. It could've ended a lot worse.

I sweep my gaze to the corner of the room where my satchel lies, the orb tucked safely inside. One dusty, old object is going to change things for me. These injuries will be worth it if the payout is huge.

I'm tired of having no money for school stuff, of the bare kitchen cabinets. Having to barter or scrounge for food will be a thing of the past, along with Murray's addictions. I won't have to worry about a lick of it after tonight. After selling the orb at Storm's market and the clock hits 11:30—my exact time of birth—things are going to change for me. I just know it.

I glance at the stripped twin bed on the other side of the room where Joseline used to sleep. She's one of the lucky ones. Like our other foster siblings, she'd gotten out of this hell hole on her eighteenth birthday and was now couch surfing at friends' until we could meet up again.

Soon. Very soon.

The Orb of Chaos is our golden ticket to a new start. Maybe even an apartment, if I can find the right buyer and squeeze enough money out of them. And that means traveling into the secret part of Glenside, a magical subterranean the supernaturals call Storm, where most folk venture for all things mystical, powerful, and rare. Specialized crystals, fortunes told, or ways to chase off pesky spirits, Storm's got it all.

While most of Storm is fine, the markets aren't what you would call classy or glamourous by any means; they're where the lowest of the low crawl and deal, a swap meet for those looking for anonymity. A quick buy or sell without the paper trail, if you know what I mean. Just follow the umbrellas and the sound of rain, and they'll lead you to the market—hence the name.

My cell phone vibrating on the nightstand catches my attention. Peering over, I see a chat bubble pop on screen. It's a message from Joseline.

"Today's the day! Happy birthday!" it says.

If she knew what I did last night, she'd kill me.

That's why I was taking the secret to the grave. Right along with my shadow. *Right, Sayah?*

She shifts lazily inside me, still half asleep herself. I roll my eyes.

The memory of my close call with the dogs has my heart racing again. And that hissing sound...

I shiver. Just another reason to get to Storm and sell this thing.

More crashes from down the hall and hurried whispers. A desperate shout.

Uneasiness wiggles up my spine. This doesn't sound like one of Murray's typical drunk endeavours. Something else is going on.

Pushing away from the bed, I quickly dress in skinny jeans and a black sweater, then step into plain sneakers. Believe it or not, Joseline's need to hound me for my clothing choices is something I'm looking forward to again. *Too dark*, she'd always say, since pretty much everything I own is black. With my dark hair and eyes, it helps me blend in, which comes in handy when you've got a sketchy record and an unheard of, freakish gift. It suits me just fine.

I make sure to grab my satchel before heading out towards all the ruckus, not trusting it being left behind even for a second.

As expected, Murray is there in our small dining area, but to my surprise, he's not alone. A stranger in a hooded cloak has him pinned against the wall. The stranger looms over him, growling menacingly. The kitchen table has been flipped over, and there's a new hole in the wall near my foster father's head.

Fear churns in my gut. When the stranger's head whips my way, the first thing I see is his shockingly pale eyes.

"Beewwaarreee!" a scratchy voice hisses in my head, making goosebumps rise. I twist around, swearing someone has leaned in behind me.

"That's—that's her," Murray stammers and nods my way. His short gray hair is messed up, and a purple bruise paints the skin under his eye. "She's the one I told you about."

My gaze flicks between Murray and the man, and I clutch my satchel closer. Is he here because of the orb? Had I slipped up again last night and there'd been cameras?

Moving away from Murray, the man's back straightens. He pulls his hood down to reveal long white hair and translucent skin. Obviously not human, but what kind of supe exactly, I'm not sure. His nostrils flare as he inhales deeply, as if taking in my scent, and I instantly remember my wounded calf from last night.

Shit.

On cue, his pupils dilate with hunger. My pulse thunders.

"Ssmmeeellllsss bbllooooodddd," the voice whispers in my ears again.

The hell? I seem to be the only one who can hear the voice. No one else reacts to it.

The terrifying stranger stalks over to me, towering over me, his shoulders broad and every inch of him intimidating. But instead of seizing my satchel, he grabs me roughly by the arm. I try to yank myself free, but his hold is iron tight.

"Let go!" I shout, staring up at him. "Let me go!"

Ignoring me, he begins to tug me toward the door, his strength overpowering mine by a mile. I lock my knees to slow him down, but it does nothing. He's a mountain, and I'm a pebble.

"You better hope the Lords approve of the trade,

warlock, or I will be back for your soul," the man calls over his shoulder at Murray.

By now, my heartbeat is a thundering echo in my ears. Lords? Trade? "What's going on?"

Desperate, I look at Murray for help.

His gaze is full of regret, but fear locks him in place.

"M-Murray?" I stammer.

"Beettrraayyeed," the terrifying gravelly voice scrapes across my mind.

Panicked, I do everything I can to loosen the stranger's grip on me. I punch his arm and thrash with everything I have, but that only has him glaring at me with the promise of death.

"I'm so sorry, Aria," Murray murmurs from behind me, his voice choking. "I didn't have any other choice."

I can't believe what is happening.

The man tugs me again toward the door, and I stumble while my world flashes before me.

"Come on! Come on!" he says, aggravated. "It'll be less painful if you stop fighting me."

"You don't want me!" I shout. "I'm nothing. Just an ordinary!" It's the lie on all my social work documents, the one I tell every day. An ordinary—a person born into the magical world, but who presents no magic themselves.

The stranger hesitates for a second and glances at Murray for reassurance. I take the chance to slam my sneaker into his leg. He growls, flashing fangs at me in warning. "She's more trouble than your debts are worth, old man."

With those words, all my thoughts of this being about Sir Surchion and the orb vanish, and I'm smacked in the face with the truth of what's happening. Murray—the man who's supposed to take care of me, the one who's been responsible for me for years—is bartering me away in his place. As payment for his debts. He's sold furniture and other belongings to pay off his dues, let us go hungry and cold when he gambled away his paycheck—but this is a new low, even for him.

I twist toward him. "How could you do this to me?" Rage unlike any I've ever felt before pushes through me. My entire body shakes with the force of it. "How could you!"

I've never been anything more than an object to him. He never cared at all, did he?

His face is two shades paler, but not even the sorrow glinting in his eyes can bring me pity for him. "Aria, just do as he says. It'll be easier—"

I snarl at him like a caged animal, and he jumps back. Sayah stirs from my anger, rustling inside my chest and wanting out, but I can't reveal her. Not yet. I'm not even sure what she can do to help me now. This is a man, not a dog; he wouldn't be distracted by a measly shadow.

"Are you sure she isn't an ordinary?" the man asks cautiously, wanting to be sure.

Murray nods. "She has a temper, but she might be of use." His voice trembles. I can't believe I ever felt sorry for him when his wife left him. "Don't let her fool you."

"Have you ever seen her use her power?" the stranger pushes. "What is she, then?"

"I'm not sure exactly, but she's powerful. Trust me."

The mention of my power baffles me. No one knows about Sayah. She's a secret I've kept all my life. From everyone.

He has to be lying—trying anything he can to get out of his deal. There's no way he knows about my shadow.

"She's a very pretty girl. I'm sure they'll find *something* to do with her." The white-haired man laughs.

Disgust curls in my stomach at his suggestive words.

They're going to serve me up like meat. Make me a meal or a slave or....

How could Murray do this to me?

I should have run away when Joseline left, like I'd wanted to. Why had I listened to her and stayed?

The man's long nails bite into my arm. "Stop fighting me, girl!"

One more glare at Murray and tears well in his eyes. As I continue to do everything I can to resist my captor, shoving against him and kicking him, the man grunts and reaches over. I respond too slowly as he presses two fingers to the curve of my neck.

The voice in my head bellows again. *"Beewwaarreee!"*

"Enough of this!" There's a sharp pinch, and heat floods me. Suddenly, darkness rushes forward, feathering the edges of my eyes, and I lose sense of my body.

I cry out, but it's no use. Whatever he's done has me spiraling into unconsciousness. The last thing I see before sleep takes hold are eyes, which are now almost completely swallowed by black.

His words echo in the void. "Enjoy your nap."

CHAPTER THREE
ARIA

My mind drifts back to me from a far and distant place. I'm uncomfortably warm all over, sweating. My stomach roils and my muscles ache. I groan.

What the heck happened?

My foggy mind struggles to recall my last moments awake, but when I feel Sayah scrambling inside me in worry, the memories snap into focus. Murray. Being traded for his debts. The orb. And that voice in my head. The hooded man who dragged me out, then somehow knocked me out with a quick pinch of his fingers…

I've been kidnapped.

Panic gripping me, I sit up. So where am I now? I quickly take in the room and what I see astounds me. I'm in a bed, surrounded by lush pillows and a comforter of royal blue and gold. There's a roaring fireplace across from me. No wonder I'm sweating.

My gaze continues to sweep the room. There's a bookshelf, a quaint little chair and table, a dresser. Everything looks expensive and old, like the designer had a strange love for Charles Dickens novels or something. Victorian-chic.

Bizarre. But at least it isn't a prison cell or someone's grimy basement.

There's a beautiful, tall, stained-glass window that takes up most of the wall on my right. Through a few clear panes I can see the gray sky outside, foretelling of a thunderstorm rolling in.

How long have I been out of it?

I glance at the door, wondering if it's locked. I swing my legs off the bed and touch down on the wood floor. Instantly, my head and stomach whirl in different directions, and I'm afraid I might go down again. Or worse, barf.

Whatever the fuck that creepy white-haired guy did to me, it really messed me up. All with a simple pinch of his fingers. I've never heard of a supernatural species that could do that.

Leftover raw anger for what my foster father did to me sweeps through me, too. If I ever see that asshole, I'm going to tell him exactly what I think. Of course this shit had to happen on the day I was finally going to be free.

As I wait for the dizzy spell to pass, I realize I'm no longer wearing my normal jeans and sweater. Someone has changed me into a silky sheath nightgown that leaves very little to the imagination. Even my shoes and bra are gone. My wounded leg has a fresh bandage, too.

The thought of a stranger's hands on me—especially that hooded man's—makes me cringe. I've never felt more violated in my life.

I need to get out of here. I scan the room once more for my clothes. Nothing.

"Sayah," I whisper, and my shadow seeps out of me on command. I can sense her restlessness through our tether.

She's worried for me—for us—as strange as that sounds. "Is it safe to leave out that door?"

Understanding me, she zips along the floor and slips under the door to investigate. While she does that, I creep to the window and peer out. Wherever I am, it's surrounded with rolling hills and a thick forest, which isn't too uncommon in Vermont. I can't see much else though, besides part of a long stone driveway that disappears behind more trees.

I remember the hooded man saying something about the "Lords" being pleased with this fucked-up transaction, so that means there's more than one person to watch out for during my escape. But there aren't any cars parked, as far as I can see. Maybe I'm lucky and I've been left alone?

Right. Me, lucky? I almost laugh out loud at that one.

I run a hand over the stained glass to find it isn't like a normal window that can slide or crank open. It's merely a decorative piece, which means I'd have to break a pane and squeeze myself out. From the height of the room, I'd say I'm about three stories up, so that makes jumping out of the question. If I had my satchel and my rope, I might be able to climb down most of the way and jump the rest.

Oh shit. My satchel! The orb! I'd had them before.

My pulse quickens. Where are my things? Did someone take them?

I'm about to move to search the dresser when Sayah skitters back into the room, her movements jerky as if startled.

"What is it?" I ask in a rush. My anxiety spikes. Not many things can disturb a shadow.

Her chin lifts up as if she's looking at the door. A warning. One that doesn't come soon enough, because the door opens and a man steps in. Sayah quickly dives back inside me, making me stumble from our forced reuniting. It's like a punch to the chest.

The man pauses mid-step, and my breath catches. I'm sure he's seen Sayah. He must have, but he doesn't say anything. Only stares at me with eyes that are a hypnotizing shade of blue and a scowl that creases his brows.

For the first time, I look at him—really look at him—and my heartbeat races for another reason. He's outstandingly handsome. No, *he's gorgeous,* with dark hair cropped short and styled away from his face, a square nose, full lips, and a strong jawline lightly shadowed by facial hair. He's dressed in a midnight-blue collared shirt and dark pants. Both had to have been made for him specially, and it only adds to his overall commanding presence.

But what strikes me the most are his eyes, which I can't seem to look away from. Besides their intense color, I can't help but feel like he's seen a great deal, holds a lot of secrets and power. It's intimidating. Even as he stands there, not saying a word, I find myself backing slowly toward the window.

My ass hits the sill, and I know I have nowhere else to go. He hasn't moved a muscle, yet he's backed me into a dead end.

His frown fades into a look that appears more bored than anything else. "It's a long way down," he says. His voice is as steely and refined as his looks, with a deep accent that swirls around the ends of his words.

I force myself to look away, momentarily breaking eye contact.

Get it together, Aria. Stop ogling.

I suck in a deep breath, hoping it'll be enough to clear my head. Then, forcing bravado into my tone, I ask the only question I can think of at the moment. "Where are my things? My bag?"

He blinks, as if that was the last thing he'd expected me to say.

Suddenly conscious of the nightgown and my lack of modesty, I fold my arms over my chest. "My *clothes,*" I make sure to add. Although the idea of this stranger having his hands on me paints a very different picture in my mind than the white-haired man who'd brought me here.

"Anything you came with has been put away." He gestures toward the dresser. "In there."

I glance that way and instantly hear the familiar buzzing of the orb in my head. Softer now, since it's buried somewhere in the drawers, but relief floods me at the sound. I praise my luck no one's found it. If I can get out of here, then I can still sell it at the market and start my new life with Joseline. Like we'd always planned.

Suddenly, the handsome man stalks closer to me, closing the distance between us, and I press my back against the window. Orange and red light from the fireplace dances across his face as he stares down at me with a scrutinizing gaze, and my heartbeat gallops.

"Why are you here?" he asks. No—he *demands.*

"I-I—" I stammer, taken off guard by his sudden nearness. He's so close now, I can smell his masculine cologne.

The muscles at his temples jump as he clenches his jaw. "Well?"

Inside me, Sayah paces, not liking how this man is trying to bully an answer out of me. Anger stirs, and this time when I meet his gaze, I don't falter.

Why am I here? What did he think? That I had a choice in the matter?

"Why don't you tell me?"

His lip curls, obviously not used to being talked to this way. "I've been told Ramos brought you here in exchange for another's debts. A warlock."

Ramos had to be the white-haired guy who'd knocked me out.

"If you mean kidnapped me, then yes. I guess so."

"Ramos has been with us for quite some time. He may be just a dhampir, but he has a special set of skills that have proven handy when it's time to collect payment."

Just a dhampir? Half human, half vampire, they are considered rejects, the effect of what happens when the blood-exchange ceremony goes wrong. They're rare, though. Most are killed for being abominations, so I'm shocked to have met one at all.

Like their full-vampire counterparts, dhampirs crave blood, but unlike full vampires, they can walk in the sun without turning into a pile of ash. I still have my neck intact and all my blood... why hadn't Ramos bitten me? Instead, he'd pinched me with his fingers and somehow that'd been enough to knock my lights out. Some kind of pressure-point voodoo or Jedi mind-trick?

Still, my mystery visitor doesn't move away from me; he only continues to study me with a piercing gaze. Could he be a dhampir, too? I'm not sure... Everything about the man in front of me is different. More controlled. More powerful. More everything.

"Ramos also said you have great power and could be useful to us," he says. "That you're special."

"He lied," I say, holding my chin high.

His brows raise. "Oh?"

I've piqued his interest now, but I'm not sure that's a good thing.

"Yeah," I reply. "I'm just an ordinary. I told your dhampir friend the same thing." If I can keep up this facade and make him believe I'm nothing special, he could report to whoever's in charge that there's no reason to keep me here. He could free me and go after Murray instead.

"An ordinary." He emphasizes each word as if he doesn't believe them.

"Yep. Nothing special here. I'm plainer than sin."

Slowly, the corner of his mouth lifts, amused. "Plainer than sin, you say?"

Is there an echo in here?

My insides squirm under his look. It's as if he knows my secret but is waiting for me to slip up and reveal it myself. Like he's playing a game with me that I can never win. I hate it.

I may be pressing my luck, but I have to try. "Afraid so." When he doesn't reply right away, I add, "Since there's been a misunderstanding, I'll just go. Then Ramos or whoever can collect the debt with Murray. Like it's supposed to be."

"Let you go? But the warlock traded your soul in place for his as payment. He *is* your legal guardian, correct?"

Soul? That's an odd way to say it, but okay. "Well, yeah, legally, but—"

He cuts me off. "And you are under eighteen?"

"Only for a few more hours, technically."

The smirk never leaves his handsome face. "We own you then."

My stomach flips. So this guy is one of the Lords I've been brought here for. But he looks so young. Maybe mid-twenties, at most. How could he be the leader in some underground supernatural crime ring?

"But-but—I don't belong here."

"What a coincidence," he says simply. "Neither do I."

A chill snakes up my spine. When I meet his gaze again, I find his eyes have changed. The cool blues and whites have been completely swallowed up by blackness.

I gasp, terror icing my veins. I've never seen a supernatural do *that*. Even a vampire.

For a few seconds, I'm frozen in place. Chest heaving as I struggle to take in air, I can only stare.

"You see, the three of us are quite the experts on *sin*," he says against my stunned silence. He's grinning now, thoroughly enjoying my reaction. "We are demons, after all."

Demons.

"Fuck..." I rasp. I'm in more trouble than I thought.

This is bad. Really, really bad.

The demon's hand shoots out and grabs my chin—hard—forcing my face closer to his. With his eyes still inky black, I can't tell what he's looking at, but his mouth is so close to mine, I wonder if he's going to kiss me. My heart hammers behind my ribs.

"You have quite the wicked mouth for a young lady," he whispers.

Wanting to help, Sayah pushes for release, but I internally shove her back in place. That's what he wants. He's trying to tempt me, scare me into revealing myself. I can't give in.

Instead, I give him a sickly-sweet smile. "Why thank you."

He holds me like that for another long moment, his lips hovering over mine, his strong grip on my face unwavering. Then, unexpectedly, the blackness of his eyes slithers away from his natural icy blues and he releases me.

Seeming disappointed, he steps back, turns on his heel, and walks away, slamming the door closed behind him as he leaves.

Alone again, I rub the pain from my jaw and try to make sense of what just happened. My racing pulse is still a thundering echo behind my ears.

Demons... My captors are demons? Like, from Hell? I've heard of them, but I've never seen one. All I know is that they prowl the night, making deals in exchange for souls to devour. It's what gives them their power. And with that power, they are feared by all.

And now, I'm their prisoner.

Shit. Things just got way more complicated.

CAIN

Aria has power. It's so strong that it buzzes under my skin, and I can taste it under my tongue. Something dark and familiar, but I don't know what. Not yet anyway, but I will.

Whatever is inside her, it calls to me and that definitely wasn't what I was expecting when Ramos brought a woman to our home instead of the warlock that was promised. He claimed to have smelled something in her blood, but I had to judge for myself. What I'd found only confused and aggravated me. And, if I was being honest, *intrigued* me.

After living on Earth for over a century, not much surprised me anymore. But this woman... this Aria... she did.

Ordinary? She was anything but.

She was unmistakably beautiful, with inky black hair and matching dark eyes, but those things could be overlooked at first. The world is full of delectable women, and I've had my share of the spoils over the decades. But when she dared challenge me, despite the obvious danger she was in, it became clear I'd misjudged Ramos's decision to take her.

The clang of the dresser opening and closing in her room echoes even out here in the corridor. Whatever power she possesses can be of value to us. The potential danger is just as exciting as the rest of her.

Tonight we were meant to feast on a warlock's soul. The power would have been incredible. I don't know yet if we gained a fair exchange with Aria, but time will tell.

I make my way down the main staircase to the front parlor where I know Dorian will be. The entire way I am tortured with images of my fingers curling around her silky, raven hair and exposing her throat as I plunge into her. If she stays, that's where we'll end up and there is too much to be done. She couldn't have come into our lives at a worse time; I can't afford distraction.

The blaze in the fireplace crackles and spits into the metal grid, roaring like a dragon. I find Dorian where I expect him to be, lounging on the leather sofa in front of the flames. Two of his latest victims sit on their heels near him, completely naked and awaiting his orders. As an incubus, or lust demon, it's not uncommon to find him occupied by a woman that he's lured in to temporarily sedate his unquenchable desires. Unlike him, I'm tired of the repetitiveness of it all, and their presence does nothing but annoy me.

"Leave this place," I bark at them, my voice echoing against the stone walls.

As if snapped from a spell, their heads jerk upward, panic scribbled over their faces. Seconds is all it takes for them to scramble to their feet and rush down the hall.

"You spoil everything," Dorian murmurs at me with a boyish pout. "I would have let you have one if you asked nicely."

"We need to talk." I stand by the fireplace. Heat envelopes me, and I bathe in its presence. I miss our home, the scorching heat of the underworld, where I'm meant to rule. It's where I should be now, sitting on the throne my wretched father still occupies. We should be in control of all of Hell now, of every damned soul, not lurking in the shadows of the living.

Our failure pinches. Even after all this time.

Dorian reclines, his arms stretched out on either side of him along the back of the couch as he crosses one leg over the other. "It's about our new plaything, isn't it? I told you to let me go see her first if you wanted her to obey."

I clench my fist on the mantel, sick of his shit. "We don't need you hypnotizing her into another one of your sex puppets."

"If she's really that powerful, why don't we just dine on her? Absorb that power?"

"No." It comes out too fast, and I instantly regret it.

Dorian leans forward, eyes wide, suddenly interested. "She's done something to you," he says and then laughs, slapping a knee. "My word, she's baffled you. I never thought I'd see the day. The great Cain, son of Lucifer. Demon of Pride himself, and she's got you smitten. A woman."

"Don't be idiotic," I snap. "And she isn't just an ordinary living woman. She's... different."

"Different? What do you mean?"

"There's something else to her, something I can't work out. A darkness in her aura... I can feel it."

Brows furrowed, Dorian places his elbows on his knees. "So what is she?"

"I've never seen this before, and that is what has me..."

"Captivated," he finishes.

"Curious," I correct. No one has ever bewitched me before; I'm not about to allow it now.

"Ramos said he sensed a power in her, but I assumed she was a spellcaster. Or shifter. The usual," Dorian says.

Clenching and unclenching my fist, I think about her

face in my hand and what would've happened if I'd given in and kissed her like I'd wanted. Maybe then I could have deciphered what she was by tasting her.

No distractions, remember?

"Maybe you ought to go pay the warlock a visit and find out," I force myself to say to push away temptation.

Dorian's on his feet. As usual, he's shirtless, and his leather pants are tight enough to hide nothing, especially his boner. Blond hair lazily sits half over his eyes as he stares my way. "Or, we just put her through a binding ritual."

A memory of the last binding ritual Elias conducted back in Hell—the one that landed us all in this shithole called Earth in the first place—rises to the surface of my mind. "You want Aria bound to us for eternity? You haven't even met the girl."

He barks a laugh. "And? I grow tired of looking at your ugly mug all the time. And Elias is always down in the basement or in the woods brooding, so why the hell not? We get to sense what she is, and if it doesn't work out, then we have ourselves a feast on her soul. How does that sound?"

"We find out what she is first. I don't want us tied to another fucking problem like last time."

Dorian narrows his eyes. "Shit, man, you're still going on about that. It was a mistake none of us saw. Get the hell over it."

I scoff at his words. "I'm starting to wonder if you actually like it here."

The corner of his mouth quirks up in a smirk that makes him look much younger than he actually is. "It does have its perks," he says, then flicks his head back to drive the hair out of his eyes. "You know the difference between us? I'm an opportunist. I make the best of where we are. You've had a stick up your ass since we got here."

"Fuck you," I growl coldly. He didn't lose as much as I did—my birthright, my title, the majority of my power. He'll never understand. Not fully. Being banished has been torture for me, not a vacation.

"Only if you ask nicely," he teases before blowing me a kiss and sauntering toward the door.

"Where are you going?" Irritation pulses in my temples.

"To jerk off since you sent away my toys."

I growl under my breath and push away from the fireplace. It shouldn't surprise me his solution is always the quickest and easiest—for *him.* What he doesn't understand is that every new power we encounter might be an answer to our problem. And unlike him, I can keep my dick in my pants if it means a chance to get us home.

CHAPTER FOUR
ARIA

My clothes and satchel are exactly where the demon said they'd be—in the bottom dresser drawer. I rummage through my bag and find my rope and the dirty sweatshirt I'd wrapped around the orb, which is safe from harm. Thank. God. My cell phone is completely dead—doesn't even turn on when I hold the button, so there goes any chance of calling for help. The thing was on its last leg, anyway. But at least with the orb there's still hope that I can move on from this. My first step is finding a way out of here.

Quickly, I throw on my bra, jeans, sweater, and sneakers, instantly feeling better in my own clothes. I take another glance at the darkening gray skies outside. My plan is an easy one. Once the storm hits, I'll wait for the rumble of thunder and break one of the windowpanes; hopefully that will be enough to mask the sound of glass breaking. Then I'll be hauling ass down the rope as fast as I can and running for my life under cover of the storm. Easy. Now to just hope the heavens play nice and pour down.

A knock on the door halts me. My pulse kicks up a

notch at the thought of the sexy, blue-eyed demon returning, and not entirely out of fear. I throw my satchel back in the drawer and slam it shut just as the door creaks open. When a young female steps inside, I ease.

There's an innocence in her hazel eyes and youthful features that makes me think she's around thirteen years old. Fifteen at most. But despite her age, she wears a long-sleeved, high-neck black frock and white apron, like a servant.

Wow. They're really trying to sell the old-timey motif, huh? I'm starting to think I've been zapped back in time.

She smiles warmly at me, and I find myself returning it out of reflex. After being man-handled by so many men these past few hours, it's nice to see another girl here.

"Hello, Miss," she greets me formally. "My Master would like to meet you. I've been told to bring you to his chambers."

"But I've met him already," I start, confused. "He was just here."

"You've met Master Cain. It is Master Dorian who requests your presence," she replies.

Cain. That's what the blue-eyed demon's name is.

Now that I think about it, he had mentioned there being three of them here. My stomach flips at the thought of meeting *another* one. Another demon.

"And what if I decline?" I ask.

Not expecting my answer, the servant blinks rapidly. Suddenly nervous, she stammers through her next sentence. "I-I-I've been given orders to..."

I sigh. Refusing to go with her could mean her punishment, one I'd be the reason for. I couldn't do that to her, even if she is a stranger. It sucks having a conscience.

If Dorian's anything like Cain, I need to watch my back. Who knows what these creatures are actually capable of, what sadistic and hellish powers they possess. That means to get out of here alive, I need to follow along and—more importantly—not die.

"Fine, let's go." I walk toward the door, making her follow close behind me. We pass a tall, bullish man waiting nearby. Uneasiness crawls over my skin as his eyes track our every move down the hall. They'd had a guard at my door? Good to know. I'll have to remember that for my great escape later.

The servant guides me around the bend and down a short set of stairs to the second floor. Noises echo from the door at the far end. They sound like nothing at first, but as we get closer, I recognize them as groans of pleasure. Heavy breathing, gasping, and calls of ecstasy.

I hesitate.

What the heck?

The servant slows too, her cheeks reddening. Still, she waves for me to follow. "This way."

"In there?" Throat tight, I point at the door where the sex noises are coming from. "He's in there?"

She nods.

It sounds like an orgy in there. Or like someone is watching porn at max volume.

"I think your Master is… busy," I say.

Despite her nervousness, she walks ahead of me and knocks. There's a final shuddering cry of release, and after a few uncomfortable moments of quiet, the door opens. A shirtless man steps out, the lean muscles of his chest on full display. He's wearing leather pants, and despite all the moaning, a growing erection can be seen through the skin-tight material. He sweeps gold hair away from his eyes and looks me up and down, grinning broadly.

This has to be Dorian.

Like Cain, he's wickedly handsome. Dangerously so,

with a mischievous gleam in his eye that says he's always up to no good and that it's something he's mighty proud of. But unlike Cain, I can read him easily, and it's clear he's undressing me with his eyes.

Crossing my arms, I shift uneasily on my feet and avert my gaze.

"Well, well. Look at what we have here," he muses. His voice is silky smooth. Slippery. It glides over my skin, making goosebumps rise. "Cain didn't say you were such a delectable morsel."

"Will that be all, Master?" the servant asks with a short bow.

"Yes, Sadie. Thank you." He dismisses her with a wave, and she wastes no time hurrying away from us. With her gone, I suddenly feel like a cornered animal. My heart rate picks up. I'm facing down a predator, and I'm not sure if he wants to devour my soul or devour *me*. Maybe both. Although, if I had a choice, I'd rather the latter.

"Come, join me," he says as he gestures into his room. The command slides over me, the words buzzing in my head, and I feel my feet moving toward him without my command. I try locking my knees and digging my heel into the rug, but I've lost control of my own body.

His lopsided smile never wavers, and fear seizes me. He's compelling me somehow… with his voice.

As I pass him to enter his room, my body brushes against his, and just the brief contact leaves me prickling with heat. Once inside, he closes the door. As expected, his room is larger than mine, but it doesn't hold the same Victorian flare as the rest of the house. The walls are painted a dark blue; the furniture is white and modern; and black, white, and gray accents give it a masculine air, somehow adding to the seductive feel of the room.

It smells like sex, which isn't too surprising, but I'm

shocked to see that we're alone. With all the sounds of pleasure coming from his room before, I thought someone else would be in here.

I glance up to see my reflection staring back at me, and I balk. There are mirrors on the ceiling, over the couches, over the massive bed, over random parts of the room that contain sketchy-looking racks, strappy contraptions, leather doodads, ropes...

I swallow roughly. The feeling of being trapped in a lion's den increases tenfold, and my insides itch.

"Please, sit."

The two words slither over me again, my temples pounding as I try to fight his strange power. But it's no use. I walk over to the modern couch and sit in the middle. Like a freaking obedient puppy dog.

His movements are so graceful, fluid, as if he's very aware of his body and what he's doing to me. He takes a seat on the opposite couch and spreads his arms lazily over the back.

"What is your name, little girl?" he asks.

This time, his voice holds no power. I don't feel the same tingling over my skin or push in my mind. Realizing that my muscles are clenched tight and I'm holding my breath in anticipation, I force myself to ease.

"Aria," I answer on the exhale.

He licks his lips as if tasting my name on his tongue, and for some reason, the gesture makes my stomach flip. "Does that come with a last name, too?"

"It does." But I wasn't about to tell this stranger, especially since he was a *demon.* Mention of my last name would only bring questions about my parents that I couldn't really answer, and I didn't want to get into my complicated history and my bumpy ride through the foster care system.

"Well?" He waits for me to continue.

"I don't think that's any of your business."

One of his brows arches in annoyance. "Tell me your last name," he says more forcefully this time, and like before, the command tingles up and down my limbs and ricochets in my head. Immediately, my lips part to obey him, but Sayah stirs inside me. It isn't much, but it's enough to draw my attention away from the hypnotizing power. It calms the bouncing of his command in my mind.

When I clamp my mouth shut, his eyes widen. The same curiosity and intrigue I'd seen in Cain passes over his face.

He leans forward now, staring at me intently. "What are you?"

"What?" I ask. My knees bounce under his merciless eye contact.

"How peculiar... You're resistant to my charms," he says.

His charms? More like machismo on steroids. "Honestly, you come on a little too strong, buddy."

To my complete surprise, he laughs. "Cain was right. You are a wonder."

At least this demon seems to have a sense of humor.

"And you're not a virgin."

His statement takes me aback. "What the fuck? What makes you think—"

He holds up a hand, unbothered by my outburst. "There's no shame here. No judgment."

Sure, I had boyfriends in the past. Well, I wouldn't really even call them boyfriends, because they never lasted long—a one-night stand; maybe a few dates, at the most. Like everything else in my fucked-up life, I could never find anything stable or permanent.

"As an incubus, it's my job to know," he goes on.

"Incubus?"

He grins. "A sex demon."

My gaze whips around the room again—the huge bed, the mirrors, the playthings... and those noises I'd heard. Yeah, sex demon checks out.

"Is Cain like you?" I ask, curious.

"Ha, no. Far from it. Although he probably could use a good lay. But no. He's an original sin demon."

I'm not sure what that means exactly, but it sounds scary and evil enough. "Original sin demon... Like the seven deadly sins?"

He nods. "It's a big family, yes. He's the oldest. Pride."

That makes sense. With how easily his presence had weakened my knees, Lust would have been my first guess.

"But what I really want to know is what you are," he says. "What are you hiding?"

It's the same type of question Cain had asked me before. Why are they so determined to find out more about me?

I shrug, trying my best to seem nonchalant. "I'm just a girl. Nothing special."

He launches himself at me. It happens so fast, I can't even process what has happened until I'm laying on my back and he's straddling me with his hands on either side of my head. My heart pounds against my ribs as I'm forced to do nothing but look up at him.

His hair drapes over his face and his gaze darkens on me. "Oh, my dear, that's where I think you're wrong."

I wiggle under him, but with his immense weight on my hips and his arms caging me in, I can't move. His nearness makes my head whirl. His rock-hard erection presses against my stomach, and my breaths grow more rapid and shallow. He smiles wide, liking the change in me.

"I need you to be a good girl and tell me what you are,"

he says. His power caresses me like gentle, coaxing fingers, and I tremble as desire surges through me. It's stronger now that he's touching me. The need to give in is overwhelming.

Outside, thunder rumbles and rain begins to beat against the window. Sayah thrashes and tumbles inside me like a hurricane confined in a cardboard box. She's trying to help me fight Dorian's advances, but his pull is too great. I feel the words climbing up my esophagus.

"Tell me what you are." His voice booms with his power, rattling my brain. My pulse slams against my eardrums, and there's a sweet, building pressure between my thighs. Back arching, I squeeze my legs together, trying to focus on anything but his demands.

"Tell me and I'll give you what you want."

I can see our reflections in the mirror above and the sight of him hovering over me only heightens the sensations spinning through me. A delicious pleasure is mounting, and I can't stop any of it. I'm completely at his mercy.

"I-I don't know!" I gasp. My body trembles violently as I wait for the release. "I don't know! Please!"

As if he's thrown a bucket of cold water on me, I'm snapped out of his spell. The pleasure never peaks. Instead, he climbs off me, and I'm left feeling achy and shaken to the core. He'd almost brought me to orgasm by doing nothing but speaking. I couldn't imagine what else he was capable of.

Slowly, I get up. All my clothes are still on, and really, we did nothing, but I feel more naked and vulnerable than ever before. I don't like it.

Seemingly lost in thought, Dorian moves across the room but doesn't say a word. It's like he's forgotten about me completely. Or he no longer cares.

Not wanting to be here a second more, I shuffle toward

the door. His back is to me, and even when I twist the door's handle and pull it open, he doesn't turn. I guess he must have gotten what he wanted out of that.

I slip out and hurry down the hall to my room so I can grab my satchel with my orb and rope. Thank God I carry that rope with me everywhere, because you never know when you'll need it. Case in point—right now. There are no guards or maids around as far as I can see, and with the storm in full swing, now's my chance to leave the demons and this hell.

I need to get out of here before it's too late.

CHAPTER FIVE

ELIAS

I plunge through the forest, the landscape a blur, my heart beating frantically. The storm roars overhead and rain comes down in sheets, drenching me to the bones. My paws pound the ground, water splashing everywhere, and it's only when I burst out of the woods that I skid to a halt. The mansion rises before me like a sentinel high on top of the hill, overlooking the land. Out here we're alone; no one can hear the screams. It's why we selected this home—not to mention it avoids questions from humans on how long we've lived without aging.

Four days of being away from the other two, who constantly argue, isn't enough time, but I trot toward our home for the simple purpose that I hate the rain. It runs down my face and mats my fur. The woods are the closest thing to being in Hell. The shadows back home are filled with menace and blood-thirsty creatures at every turn. And fuck, I crave those days. I miss it with every fiber of my being.

Cain insists we're close to finding a way home soon. Except *soon* isn't good enough when we've been stuck on this damn Earth realm for a century, dealing with human emotions every time we switch on the TV or head into town. It bleeds into me, and I loathe it. This is why getting out is priority. There's nothing here for me... for any of us.

I don't belong here, but at the end of the day, I'll persevere through whatever's thrown at us and bloody my hands with the asswipes who backstabbed us. Rage floods my veins even after all this time. I'm not the kind to forgive easily, and I never forget.

I'm a hellhound who hunts down souls way overdue their entry into Hell. Well, at least I *did,* before we got expelled from the underworld. But *'never give up on your dreams'* the humans say, and all that bullshit. I will do just that. Live up to my name and tear apart the whole fucking world to get vengeance against those who wronged us.

Deciding I'm not ready to return home just yet, I whirl around and lunge back for the thick woodlands. I shove against the ground, propelling myself into a sprint. I make easy work climbing, dodging branches, and jumping over dead logs.

A streak of lightning flashes overhead. Seconds later, an explosive thunder booms, the ground and my jaw vibrating from the sound. Bursting out of the dense woods, I skirt around the manor to the rear entrance. This entry is closest to my room, and I want to get out of this damn rain fast.

Darkness slithers over the land, and a shadow darting across the open grounds catches my attention. It flits out of sight in seconds, merging in the woodlands surrounding our home.

I lift my head and sniff the electricity in the air, the freshness of rain. But beneath it is a prickling of magic, along with something else.

Something sweet.

Something to devour.

Something for me.

A female.

One of Dorian's conquests? Doubt it. Anyone under his spell doesn't run; they beg to stay by his side. No, this is different. I pivot away from the house and prowl in her direction. The storm hides any sounds I make, and the heavy clouds and forest conceal me.

Paws dance across the land, my heart flinching with excitement at every movement. I no longer feel the pellets of rain washing down on me. The chase is on, and I'm captivated. Whoever she is, her scent calls to my animal side. My stomach tightens the longer I search with no sign of her.

Tilting my head back, I sniff the air once more.

There you are.

I snap my head to my right and dive in her direction.

ARIA

My heart jackhammers inside my chest so loudly everyone within a mile is bound to hear it—including the monster searching for me.

My body ripples with power as Sayah hovers before me, spreading herself into a dark blur before me while I crouch low behind some tall grass and thick bushes.

Don't move. Don't breathe. Shit.

Piercing yellow eyes glint with hunger. Lips curled, sharp teeth, an enormous wolf bursts into the woods like a tank. Its head whips my way instantly, and my heart leaps into my throat. Those eyes glint right through my shadow.

With a savage snarl, he rips through the shrubs and creeps closer, like he sees me.

Where the hell did he come from, anyway? One second, I'm scaling down the window, escaping; next thing I know, I have a massive wolf on my heels. I've never seen a wolf that terrifying, that big, that fast. Of course my luck would have me being tracked by some kind of rabid beast. Why would I think escaping would be that easy?

Thanks, universe, for not cutting me any slack.

"Dannggerrr," the orb's voice hisses over my mind. I really need to change its name from 'Orb of Chaos' to 'The Too-Late-to-the-Show Orb' or 'Orb of Stating the Obvious.'

Fingers digging into the soggy soil, I curl forward, tightening my crouching position. I suck in a raspy breath, waiting, praying to whoever is listening for a chance to escape. For anything.

Heavy breaths fill the air, but they're not mine.

I lift my head, and beyond my shadow, infernal, blazing eyes stare right into me. I flinch as acid hits the back of my tongue, and I practically fall onto my side like one of those ridiculous fainting goats.

Great job, Aria. Roll over and show your belly to the big bad wolf who's about to tear you apart.

In the same instant I scramble to my feet, my shadow flicks back into me, while the monster before me seems to be growing in size... because he wasn't big enough already. Except, I'm wrong... he's not growing, he's pushing himself to stand up on two feet. A split second of fur melting away, bones cracking, limbs lengthening, and before me stands a naked man. An insanely gorgeous man with the world's biggest dick...

Sweet Jesus, how is that possible? And why am I

checking out his junk when he was a wolf seconds earlier and coming at me with the rage of a starved predator?

He stands at least six-foot-three. Dirty brown hair dangles past his shoulders, messed up with twigs and leaves. He's made of muscles. Broad shoulders and chest, his waist tapers inward, drawing my attention to the sexy lines in the V shape of his chiseled abs. A faint peppering of dark hair covers his chest and funnels down the center of his stomach, right to the thatch of black hair crowning his dick. Healed scars criss-cross his chest, while tatts cover his neck and arms. If I wasn't shaking and trying for the life of me to come up with an escape plan, I might pay attention to the images. But I remind myself this man isn't a man at all, not really.

Oh, and he most likely plans to kill me.

"Your tricks won't work with me," he growls, the thick timbre of his voice sending shivers down my spine.

My gut tightens, and I blink at him with utter shock. Except, remaining frozen in place makes me an easy meal, and that's not me. I didn't come this far to end up being eaten by a feral beast on my eighteenth birthday.

"I got lost," I lie with ease, despite how my insides tremble. "I'd appreciate it if you'd back off so I can head home."

His pale-yellow eyes take on a darker glow. "You smell of lies and dark magic. Of… home." Thick, dark eyebrows bunch together, accentuating the healed scar across one eye.

This guy is practically covered in healed injuries. How many fights has he been in?

Goosebumps skate down my arms, but I won't back down or let myself willingly be taken as a slave by these monsters. "Didn't your mother ever tell you it's rude to smell a girl?"

My comment takes him off guard and he stiffens, thinking about my words.

I use that sliver of a distraction to whip in the opposite direction. My shadow slices out of me, concealing me. My satchel bounces against my backside with each rapid step I take, while my wounded leg cries out as I zip around trees, running for my life.

Seconds later, he grasps my arm and wrenches me back toward him with the strength of a mountain. A cry spills past my lips, and I swivel around from the momentum, slamming into his chest. Fire curls through me from the heat pouring off him in waves, as if a furnace has been switched on in front of me.

I shove my hands against his chest just as quick, but not before I catch his cock twitching like he got off on being rough with me. Sadistic bastard.

"Don't waste your time trying to escape." His grip is cruel, squeezing my arm.

I grit my teeth.

Even under the tree canopy, fat raindrops fall and drench us, water rolling down my face and into my eyes. He doesn't move at first but towers over me, and even Sayah inside me shies away. I lift my chin and face him—if he's going to kill me, I can't stop him, but I sure as hell am not going down without a fight.

The tendons in his throat flex as he pushes into a walk, half-dragging me alongside him toward the mansion.

Dread races through me as I stare at the looming three-story building made of black stone. I frantically look back into the woods. I could have escaped if it wasn't for this… this… shifter. Okay, maybe not a shifter, exactly. He's definitely stronger and more monstrous than any shifter I've ever seen, and his animal is bigger than any normal werewolf.

But then, what is he? Another demon?

"Look, you don't have to do this." I'm stumbling to keep up with him, my feet catching on tree roots and shrubs, but nothing stops him. "What do you want? Anything, please. I can't go back." I hate begging, but I'm not beyond it.

"You don't have anything I want."

I tilt my head back to look up at his strong face, the slight bend in his nose from being broken too many times, the furrow on his brow.

He cuts me a glare with those captivating wolf eyes. Heat flares over my body. I hate how a simple look affects me so severely. He could tear me apart without a whim, without care, without anyone knowing what happened to me. So it's wrong that coupled with fear, a whisper of delight sweeps over the heat between my legs. Something is completely wrong with me as I stand before a monster and feel arousal rise within me.

His eyes may resemble fire, but something glides over them, an expression I can't work out. His nostrils flare as he inhales the air deeply. Then he grins, studying me with a different intention.

Yikes. That's all it takes. My whole body sparks to life, buzzing for attention, my nipples hardening. As much as I loathe admitting it, his aggressiveness and nakedness are huge turn-ons. But I'll run around town naked before I ever let him know that.

His gaze trails down my body and back up.

"Don't flatter yourself," I throw at him, then shove my fist into his forearm and dig my heels into the dirt, but nothing stops him from dragging me across the yard.

"You're making a mistake! Do this and you'll end up locked up for life."

He ignores me as he hauls me across the lawn toward the rear door of the demons' home.

“Hope you spontaneously combust,” I murmur under my breath.

He kicks open the rear door of the house, and I have a sudden image of myself chained up in a room, never to see the sun again. I’d rather die.

My chest tightens, and I thrash against his hold, locking my knees. One tug on my arm, and I stumble over the threshold and into the dark embrace of my prison.

CHAPTER SIX

DORIAN

Just thinking about Aria's lithe body under mine on the couch has my cock stiffening again. Goddammit. I already had to jerk off after she'd left my room. Watching her nearly hit climax had ignited my imagination, but her ability to deny me over and over baffled me, which only made me want her more.

No one in this realm—and I mean *no one*—has ever been able to ignore my advances. Especially a woman. I am simply irresistible.

Am I losing my touch?

No. Impossible.

This little mysterious Aria No-Last-Name has taken me off my game.

Hmm... I hate to admit it, but Cain was right. There's something to her that we've never seen before.

I walk straight for the rear of the mansion. I find Cain exactly where I expect him to be; in his private office set in an alcove off the library. He is predictable that way, spending most of his time either tending to our nightclubs or in here, poring over his ancient demon texts to find a way to get us back through Hell's gate. Both have become obsessions.

Always business, never pleasure with him. It's a bit sad really.

I twist the handles to the French doors and break the lock with ease. He looks up from his work and gives me a snarl—another thing I expect from him.

"It's locked for a reason," he says.

I ignore him and approach the desk, standing there until he looks up. Eventually he does.

"What the fuck do you want?"

"We have a problem," I begin.

"I'd say so. You don't seem to understand the meaning of privacy."

I slam my hands on his open books and lean over. He doesn't move. "Our *guest* is more powerful than we originally thought," I say.

"What makes you say that?"

"She refused me." It still stung to admit.

That gets his attention. Eyebrow cocked, he sits back in his chair. "You tried compelling her."

I nod. "There was no resistance at first, but then I commanded her to tell me her name..."

Cain was watching me intently now, fully engaged. Maybe he'd found a new obsession in Aria? Seemed so. "And?"

"I only got a first name from her. Aria. She refused to tell me her surname."

"That would help us track her lineage, since the warlock wasn't blood."

"That was my thinking too. But she *refused* me." I emphasized the word again to make sure he understood what I was saying here. "And that's not all. I even demanded she tell me what she was and got nothing."

He blinked, as if the weight of it was really sinking in. "What did she say, exactly?"

"'*I don't know.*' Those were her exact words to me."

"Maybe she doesn't know. Not truly," he suggests, but he's lost deep in thought. I can almost see the gears turning in his head.

"I'm not sure about that," I reply. "She was able to ignore my compulsion before it. Who's to say she didn't do it again?"

Cain is silent for a few moments, his eyes trained on the cluttered desk before him but not really seeing anything at all. I look at the scrolls and books for the first time and see that they are, in fact, about Heaven and Hell's lore and the use of dark magical instruments.

He snaps out of his trance and pushes to his feet suddenly. He strolls to the window and looks out at the storm. "The only known souls you can't manipulate are those from Hell, correct?"

"Are you thinking she's… like us?" I ask.

He pauses. "I'm not sure yet. The darkness I sensed in her did feel familiar, but I still can't put my finger on it. I've been searching for something that can identify her—a hint of an answer—but have found nothing."

Looks like I had been right about his newest infatuation. But after meeting her and seeing what she was capable of, I could also understand it.

Cain turns to me again, his body rigid. "My father may have sent her."

Shit.

My muscles tense at the thought of Lucifer still trying to meddle in our lives. "He already kicked us out of Hell. Why send someone up here? Just to fuck with us?"

"I'm not sure yet."

"Could it be one of your brothers?" I ask. "Maybe someone is trying to swipe the throne for themselves?"

His gaze hardens on me, like it normally does whenever I mention his siblings. I don't trust any of the lot, personally.

"My bet is on Greed," I go on anyway. "That asshole was always doing shady shit. I'm pretty sure he owes me money."

"My brothers would rather I rule than Lucifer. They supported our takeover. You know that."

I shrug. "Then I don't see why they aren't here with us, banished for eternity."

"Enough," he barks. It's almost *too* easy to get a rise out of him these days. "We need to concentrate on the issue at hand. This… Aria. We should send Ramos back to the warlock and retrieve her birth records, see if they can give us any insight on who she is. Until then, we make sure she stays close. Under our thumb."

Or, more specifically, under me as I fuck her senseless.

My pulse picks up at the thought of such a temptress living among us. "We're keeping her then?"

Cain waits a few beats as he considers it himself. Then he sighs, giving me my answer.

Oh, this is going to be *fun.*

"Where is she now?" he asks, walking back to his desk. "In her room?"

"Hell if I know," I reply. "After our little encounter, she ran off."

Cain's anger flashes. "You don't know where she is?"

"She couldn't have gotten far," I say. "We have guards at all outside doors."

There's a loud bang as someone crashes through the rear entrance to the mansion. From the thundering footsteps, it can't be anyone but Elias. The hellhound. He disappears for days at a time doing God knows what, only to come back smelling like dirt and wet dog to eat, sleep, and do it all again. He's more like a wild animal than a man.

When the sounds of a woman's frantic gasps and grunts echo through the hall, too, Cain and I exchange looks and rush into the library.

No... It can't be.

Elias shoves his way inside with none other than Aria in his brutish grasp. Desperate and dripping wet, she punches against his arm and chest. "Let me go, you son of a—"

Unfazed, Elias pushes her forward, and she stumbles between us. She is soaked to the bone, strings of dark hair sticking to the sides of her beautiful face.

"I found this in the woods," he says nonchalantly, standing naked and drenched before us. "Is it yours?"

Smiling despite myself, I glance at Cain. A muscle in his tense jaw tics, and I know he's thinking the same thing. Looks like we underestimated the girl. *Again.*

ARIA

"You can't do this!" I shout, stumbling into my room. I twist around to Cain, who's in the doorway, tall and menacing as sin. With the dark clothes, he could easily be mistaken for the devil himself. "You can't keep me here against my will. I have rights!"

The side of his mouth quirks up in the slightest smirk.

"Maybe you did before, but you're in our world now, and your soul is mine to do with as I please."

I narrow my eyes and clench my fists. Sayah shifts in my chest with unease. Even she thinks picking a fight with him isn't a smart thing to do, but as scared as I am, I have to pretend I'm not giving in to him. "If you don't let me go right now, I'll... I'll..."

"You'll what?" His voice is a deep rumble as his anger pushes forward. Blackness swallows up his irises.

Knowing I have nothing to combat against a demon—a very scary, very powerful demon, Pride himself—I clamp my mouth shut. That's not the way I am going to win this battle.

Cain takes one lumbering step toward me, suddenly seeming much taller and more intimidating. My pulse speeds up. "Challenge me again, Aria, and see what happens next," he warns. "I have no problem devouring you."

An involuntary gasp slips past my throat. Those words... The way he said them... It's like he's talking about something other than my soul. The image of his face buried between my legs as he laps at my sex, bringing me to orgasm after orgasm, springs to my mind, and I shiver.

Slowly, he straightens, appearing pleased he's gotten his message across. Then he moves over to the bed, grabs the rope I'd tied around the post and used to climb out the window, and jerks the knot free with one yank. He lets it fall to the ground below.

"Remember that next time you think about escaping," he says, and with that, he steps out of my room and shuts the door behind him. The clang of a heavy metal lock sounds.

I rush forward, grasp the handle, and wrench at the door as hard as I can. It doesn't budge.

I pound at the wood fiercely. "Let me out! I'm not your slave. Take my foster father, he's the one in debt to you!" I bellow. When no one comes for me, I scream out of pure frustration.

Running back to the window, I stick my head out the broken pane and stare down. My rope lays in a pile on the grassy knoll three stories below. Useless. I wouldn't survive a jump from this high. Looks like I'm trapped. Again.

I slide onto the floor, tucking my knees to my chest. There's so much hatred, fear, and aggravation tumbling inside me, my entire body trembles from the force of it. I despise Murray for what he did to me, selling me like my life is worth nothing to save his own skin. I should have known better than to think someone cared about me. Even a little.

Now these three sadistic demons refuse to let me go. Part of me wishes they'd just kill me and get it over with, but it seems like they'd rather play with me instead. I just don't understand why.

This has been the worst birthday in the history of birthdays.

I think about Joseline and all the plans we'd had for a better future. They seem like stupid dreams now.

It's not long before my anger dies down, leaving me sinking in sorrow instead. Burying my face in my hands, I listen to the fireplace pop and spit while the storm outside my window rumbles. The rain drums against the stained glass. Sayah slithers out and stretches across the floor, but despite her familiar presence, I know that really, I'm alone.

Time passes and night slips over the world outside. I'm not sure how long I stay like that, huddled on the floor. When my ass numbs, I drag myself to my feet. The wind whistles, rattling the window, and a coldness creeps over me despite the fire.

For the first time, exhaustion rattles through me. I crawl into bed and curl in on myself. I pull the blanket over me to warm up, while my heart beats wildly that I've ended up in this awful situation.

My foster father was meant to always be there for me. To protect me. But the asshole barely had food on the table and wasted his time gambling.

Everything about today has sucked. Today was supposed to signify my freedom; it was the day I'd planned to move out and make a new life for myself. Well, that's not going to happen now is it?

Closing my eyes, I think of what it will be like to finally escape for good. To sell the orb and start fresh. Those are the images I conjure in my mind, and slowly the heaviness of sleep comes for me.

CHAPTER SEVEN
ARIA

My eyes flip open to a white ceiling with fancy ornate mouldings and an extravagant chandelier dripping with crystals. It takes me a few seconds to recall where I am. The memories flood over me, bringing an ache to my chest. I'm stuck here. I push myself to sit upright, the morning sun climbing over the treetops outside the window. How long had I slept?

Sliding my legs out from under the blanket, I turn to climb out when I spot a small hotel-like trolley on wheels in the middle of the room with silver lids over three plates. There's also a cup with steaming coffee, by the smell of it.

I slept through someone sneaking in here to bring me food? Looking down at myself, I note I'm still in my clothes, so on the bright side, no one undressed me this time.

I push myself up and collect the cup of black coffee and stumble toward the door. A quick check tells me it's still locked, so I turn to the window. Clouds still blot the sky, but it's stopped raining. Woods are all I see; no roads, no other homes, no signs of Glenside in sight. We are completely isolated out here. Exactly how the demons would want it.

Sniffing the coffee, I decide it smells normal and probably doesn't contain poison. I doubt they'd spike my food, so I sip on the nutty ambrosia, its warmth washing down my throat. It brings forward my hunger, and before I know it, I'm uncovering the plates. Eggs and bacon. Pancakes and cream. Oatmeal with cinnamon and raisins. My mouth salivates.

I don't remember the last time I stared at this much food during one meal. Back home, I'd be lucky to find a slice of bread and the last scrapings of jam in the empty jar for breakfast. Excited, I put the coffee down and drag the whole cart closer to the bed. There, I sit and pig out. I'm not ashamed to say I intend to eat everything... or as much as I can before I burst at the seams.

By the time I'm full, I've managed to eat half the food from each plate. I lick the maple syrup from my lips and head into the en suite bathroom. On the sink I find a new toothbrush still in a plastic wrapper, along with an array of toiletries. More than I've ever owned. On the counter sits a small bundle of folded clothes, including a black lace bra and matching thong. Dear God, are these demons really so arrogant to assume my size? Rolling my eyes, I start stripping and head into the shower made of marble tiles.

Once I'm done and dressed in jeans that hang low on my hips and a blue tee that's one size too small, I grab the brush and comb my hair. To my surprise—and slight irritation—the underwear and bra fit perfectly. I tug down on the top that keeps riding up my stomach and swing back into the bedroom.

What now?

I pace from the door to the window, frustration rising through me quickly. The walls feel like they're closing in around me. I'm a caged wolf in a zoo. This can't be my new future. Locked up. Stuck in a room until demons decide on what I am to do next.

I'll die first.

In the bathroom, I rummage amid the hair brushes and rollers in the drawers.

My fingers scrape over the cold, thin metal of several bobby pins. *There you are.* Seizing two of them, I turn to the door.

For years, I lived in numerous foster homes, left to my own devices, doing what I needed to survive. And right now, what I need is to get out of here. I'm not going to sit back and wait for my soul to be drained... no matter how sexy and alluring the three demons in this mansion are. Those things are illusions. I've heard enough about demons to know they are all smoke and mirrors.

They're monsters who control legions of demons and do the devil's bidding. What am I even doing finding them attractive and feeling arousal toward them? I don't understand my reaction to them, so I focus on what I can control. The door standing in my way.

"Sayah, are there guards outside?"

My shadow shimmers across the floor and slithers underneath the door. A flare of warm energy pricks up my arm—Sayah's own way of telling me it's safe.

Perfect.

I throw myself to my knees and jab the bobby pins into the lock, jiggling it around. I've done this enough times to know it's a matter of perseverance. I keep my concentration on getting out of here and not letting Cain's threat get to me. I mean, if they wanted me dead, I'd be gone by now, right? So, I stick to my plan.

Get out of this house.

Get Joseline.

Get the hell out of town and never look back.

Click.

I smile to myself, pull out the pins, and stuff them into the pocket of my jeans. Up on my feet, I gingerly open the door and stick my head out. Empty.

Sayah bristles on the inside at the implication that I didn't believe her earlier inspection, but hey, things can change in a heartbeat. I look back over my shoulder, my gaze landing on the wardrobe with my satchel. I dart back to grab it, then I slide out into the hallway.

The walls and ceilings are painted crimson. Matching rugs run the length of the flooring, darkening the corridor. Paintings pepper the walls, and it's only when I pay close attention that I note each piece of artwork resembles the masterpieces I've seen in museums. One has a man collapsed on a rock, naked, head low and black wings starting to curl in around him. The next is a savage image of one man kneeing another in the back, while wrenching his head back, biting into his neck. *Ouch.* One after the other, they tell dark stories of battle, of black-winged creatures harmed. Everyone is naked, and with darkness or fire behind them. Are they representations of Hell?

With each step, my ears prick for any sounds. I won't be caught this time. Down a small staircase to the second floor, I quietly make my way through the hall toward the grand staircase, making sure to be as light on my feet as possible. I lean my stomach against the polished handrail as I descend. Once in the grand foyer, I peer down to a marble hallway that I know leads to the library and more unknown rooms. No one in sight so far.

Quickly, I hurry down it, passing an array of disfigured masks on the walls, most likely from various tribes. I speed past the library without so much as glancing inside, just in case one of the demons are in there, and find more doors surrounding me. All closed.

Footsteps echo in the corridor ahead of me, coming my way. Panicked, I swing right and reach for the closest door. I wrench it open to find another set of steps, but these sink into darkness.

I don't have time to second guess it—the person is getting closer—so I hurry inside and close the door behind me. I rush down the stairs, almost tripping over myself to get away. The deeper I go, the colder the temperature gets. I'm going underground to a basement or cellar. But there's a dimly lit hallway at the end, and I rush for it.

More doors line the walls here too, and I'm reminded of a carnival's funhouse or something. This place never seems to end.

I reach for the closest door, and the moment I grab the handle, a buzz zaps up my arm. Flinching back, I cradle my arm to my chest. The sensation comes again at the base of my spine, just like it does each time I sense strong dark magic. It runs down my right leg and to my pinky toe, the little thing twitching, pointing to the hallway to my right.

Freaky toes... Another reason I don't tell anyone about my strange abilities. Last thing I need is to be known as the 'Supernatural Toe Whisperer' and be the butt of jokes. The movies have it all wrong about powers, sparks and fire bombs and whatnot bursting from people's hands. In real life, it's nowhere near that glorious.

Shaking the sensation, I glance at the door, then down the passage my toe is pointing toward. The choice is easy. I'm escaping, and I have my orb with me, so I don't need anything else. I grab for the handle again.

"Ruuunnn!" the orb's grating voice scrapes over my mind.

My skin crawls just as the thumping of footfalls comes

from overhead. The sound of the door opening and closing, and then a shadow struts downstairs. I don't wait a second to see who it is. Instead, I dart down the passage. My heart hammers in my chest, and I follow my toe to avoid going down a dead end in case someone follows. Left and right, I rush down so many corridors that I now suspect a maze might be a better description for this place.

I pause for a moment, gasping for air, while my pinky has a small convulsion which might mean I'm getting close to something. Glancing over my shoulder, the dim light from the wall lamps reveals no one following. Shadows crowd everywhere, and unease slithers up and over my neck and head. How do I even find my way out?

In my experience, following my instinct usually gets me out of trouble, so I pay heed to my twitching toe and follow its direction. Sayah slides along the floor ahead of me, sweeping from left to right like an inverse flashlight, popping into any rooms we pass, but all are empty. By that, I mean no furniture, no decorations, nothing.

Around the next corner, I hear a soft hum. A soft, delicate melody. It's definitely female. I pause and study the area behind me. Nothing. The farther I walk, the more the music fills my ears. Like a wave, it rushes in and curls around me. It carries a soft tempo, almost sorrowful. I follow it as though it calls to me. Sayah glides under a door at the end of the hall, and as if an invisible cord is wrapped around my chest, I'm pulled in that direction. As I stumble forward, the door seems to swing open for me on its own accord.

The room is empty except for a round table sitting in the middle. It holds a dark wooden box, ornate and beautiful, carved with runes. Common sense tells me to leave it alone, that nothing good can come of messing with anything belonging to a demon.

But the music... It glides around me, filling my ears, luring me in. I drift toward the box, releasing each breath heavily as if something is constricting my chest. The melody grows irresistibly sad, a faint humming voice interlacing with the notes. It purrs in my chest, raising deep feelings of longing.

I reach over and delicately lift the lid. A slight prickle of energy dances up my fingers, but I'm captivated by the thing inside.

A thin, golden cord lays on a bed of black silk, curled around as though it were a lasso. There's no handle, and before I can stop myself, I'm picking it up. The music hums in my head louder now, the cord smooth and icy to the touch.

Someone clears their throat behind me so abruptly, so unexpectedly, I flinch and drop the cord back into the box, the lid clapping shut.

I whip around on my heels, heart in my throat, and find the beast from the woods standing in the doorway. One shoulder propped against the doorframe, arms folded over his chest, glaring at me.

"What are you doing here?" he commands, voice deep and clipped.

I hear his words, but the tune still sings in my ears, drawing me back to the box, to the relic.

"Can you hear it too?" I ask, staring into the ceiling as the music slides over me like a lover's caress.

"What I see is a girl who's broken the rules. And that comes with punishment."

I snap my attention back to him—the beast, the demon, the ass who dragged me back into the mansion when he could have let me go back in the woods.

The tune fills my ears again, pulling me back under its spell. "The song is beautiful. I think it's about tragedy."

He closes the distance between us in two long strides and seizes my wrist. His touch is scorching hot. Another zap shoots up my arm and directly to the pit of my stomach. A tingling awakens within me, one that deepens and deepens the longer he touches me.

He pauses and eases his hardened gaze on me. He feels the buzzing, it's obvious by his narrowing eyes.

"What is that?" I ask.

A growl rolls through his chest, and he wrenches me out of the room with haste, then shuts the door with a bang. The music softens, the fog in my head clearing somewhat.

His hold tightens, and I wrench against him.

"Hey, you don't need to be so rough," I say. "What's your name, anyway? Better yet, *what* are you?"

He swings back around, something glinting in his eyes, and in a heartbeat, he has me pinned up against the wall, his body pressed up against mine. He is so large, looming over me. He pitches a hand on the wall over my shoulder, the other gripping my chin as he forces my head back.

Instinctively, my thighs clench together. They shouldn't, but apparently I've lost control of my body when it comes to deadly demons.

"How did you find that room?" he grills me, ignoring my questions and pelting me with his own. His face hovers inches from mine.

I stare into those bronze eyes, at the dark, long lashes crowning them. "I don't know." It's the truth, though he doesn't seem to buy it since his lips quirk into a wry frown.

"Did you hear the music, too?" I ask, confused by what happened in that room. The orb talks to me, and this strange golden string seems to sing. I've never experienced anything like this before. It's bizarre.

Still, he doesn't answer my questions, but I sense the growing erection pressing against my stomach.

Oh. My. God.

I narrow my gaze at him, to let him know I know what he's doing. Of course he'd know, I tell myself. Even Sayah stirs inside me to confirm. I can barely breathe, let alone think logically.

"What-What are you?" I ask again, unable to stop the trembling in my voice.

He hesitates, unsure if he wants to answer. After a long moment, he replies, "Hellhound."

My mouth dries. A hellhound? Those things actually exist?

"Do you have a name?" I'm sure I'm pushing my luck here, but color me curious.

Again, he pauses and thinks before responding. "Elias."

Cain, Dorian, and Elias. The three Hell demons who think they own me.

Good to know.

"See you managed to find your clothes." It's my attempt at a joke, a way to break the awkwardness, but he doesn't seem to be in a humorous mood.

"Beauty lurks in all relics, but so does savagery," he replies. "Is that the Pandora's box you really want to open?"

I blink at him. Those are some profound words coming from him. "What are you talking about?"

He grumbles. "The rooms down here are forbidden. Stay out of them."

There's no mistaking the golden rope I found means a lot to Elias. Something about this string—or *relic*—has rattled him.

"Is it yours?" I ask.

He doesn't respond but holds me in place, his face *so* close to mine. It sends my pulse into a frenzy. Every inch of my body awakens to attention from our bodies plastered together, my nipples pebbling.

I suck in a raspy breath, heat flushing over my chest.

He smiles, his pearly white teeth contrasting perfectly against his tanned skin. His gaze falls to my lips, sending a shot of arousal to the pit of my stomach.

He swallows loudly, his gaze darkening.

Silence.

Burning heat slides down my spine. I shouldn't be looking at him as anything but the monster he is. I should *not* be looking at his broad shoulders, should *not* be admiring his muscular chest and biceps, and I *definitely* should *not* be thinking about the thick hardness growing bigger between us.

"If I catch you down here again, you will be punished."

The warning shudders through me, snapping me back to reality. I shove my hands into his chest. "Get the hell off me then. You're suffocating me with all that testosterone going to your head."

He inches back a smidgen, and it's enough for me to slide out from under him.

My heart races, and I march away fast.

Don't turn around. Don't do it.

I know that if I do, I'll end up doing something stupid. Why am I letting him even affect me so much?

Strong fingers clasp around my arm, and I'm spinning back around in a flash. No warning, no sound. Just me colliding into this huge demon, his other hand clasping behind my neck, firm but tender.

Elias's expression is twisted into a scowl, and for a moment my heart stops, unsure what he's got planned. But then he drags me into a forceful kiss, his mouth crashing onto mine. Butterflies burst in my stomach, batting their wings wildly.

I can't breathe. I'm letting a demon kiss me. But my body seems to respond on its own, and I grasp his shirt and haul him closer, kissing him back. He claims my tongue into his mouth as my knees wobble beneath me. He is huge, towering over me while I push myself onto tippy toes to reach him easier.

I close my eyes and let myself float on the promise he makes in his kiss. Strong hands dig into my back as his hold tightens. Our tongues tangle, and this wicked, taboo kiss is wrong, but I can’t stop myself.

"You smell and taste so good," he murmurs against my mouth when he finally pulls away.

I breathe out slowly, lowering myself back onto my heels. As I come back into my senses, a thread of embarrassment crawls over my cheeks that I let myself fall so easily for his charm.

“We need to go.” Suddenly, he seizes my hand and storms back through the myriad of corridors with me by his side. It’s like the reality of our kiss has hit him as well. I have no doubt he's dragging me back to my room, intent on locking me away.

The truth of what just happened sinks through me too. We are different, and I'm not here to find a boyfriend. He’s my captor. Still… when he kissed me, it was like he was someone starved, and I was everything he needed. There’s something extremely attractive to having a man want me in that way, especially one that looks as rugged and handsome as Elias. I’m lucky if guys look at me in the first place; I’ve never snagged the attention of an Adonis-looking one. And now my lips are swollen and bruised, my underwear drenched.

What is wrong with me? And more importantly, how the hell am I supposed to deal with seeing him again when I can't keep my libido in check?

CHAPTER EIGHT
CAIN

Tonight's dinner is Dorian's idea, even though we have no need for food—at least, not the kind the living prepare and eat. Our strength and power come from the souls we collect and consume at the end of their contracts. Which has been lacking lately, since I've become a lot more preoccupied in the last few months with finding the seven parts of Azrael's harp to open Hell's gate. The famous angel Gabriel has his horn for Heaven, and the demon Azrael has a harp for the underworld. But after discovering the harp existed, God's golden boy destroyed it and scattered its pieces on Earth, where he believed it to be safe. Decades of research, and it's the only way I've found for us to get back home. A backdoor of sorts.

But, of course, the pieces are close to impossible to find. We have scouts everywhere, have paid a fortune to hunt them down, but after all that, we've only managed to find one part. One of the strings. That's all.

Aria is a distraction from what needs to be done—one Dorian thinks I need, but there are times I'm convinced he's given up on the harp and would prefer to stay. But I've indulged him and set up this dinner for the young woman so we can discuss how this… "living arrangement" is going to go.

"We can't keep her locked in her room all day and night," Dorian says from his place at the table. He's picked the spot on my right, and two more settings have been put out for Elias at my left—if he ever arrives—and Aria at the opposite end. One of the servants should be bringing her down any minute now.

A shock of anticipation zips to my groin at the thought of seeing her again. I hate the way my body reacts to her, even when she's not here. It's unnerving.

Grinding my teeth, I tell myself to snap out of it. I'm a prince of Hell, for fuck's sake.

"She's supposed to be our prisoner," I tell him. "Or have you forgotten?"

Dorian's eyes roll to the ceiling like a prepubescent child. "A prisoner or a pet? We already have a rabid dog with Elias. How does treating her more like a guest hurt?"

"I'll let that dog jab go, only because I'm in a good mood." Elias strolls into the dining room dressed in ripped jeans and a plain T-shirt, styled for comfort rather than fashion. If he's not naked, it's his typical go-to. He pulls out his chair, spins it so it's backward, and plops down. "What did I miss?"

Dorian sniffs the air. "Holy shit. You even *showered*?"

"What? I've showered before," he replies.

"Not with soap."

Elias snorts.

Wanting to get back to the task at hand, I turn to Dorian again. "If you think we should be civil with her, what do you suggest?"

"The dinner is a start. The living need to eat actual food, you know," he replies with a wave of his hand.

"And?" I press.

"I don't know. Keep her happy and not wanting to jump out a window? It can't be too hard, can it?"

"All the time on this plane has made you soft, Dorian," Elias adds in. "Why is she even here?"

Dorian leans back in his chair, pushing it back onto two legs. "This is what happens when you leave for days at a time. You miss everything."

"That's the point," Elias says through clenched teeth.

"She's here," I start, bringing their attention back to what's important, "because she has a very specific and rare gift. One we've all seen in action in some way, yes?"

When Dorian nods, I look at Elias. He's grown rigid in his seat.

"Elias?" I begin carefully.

"Yeah, I've seen it," he says suddenly. "Thought she was just a witch using a blur spell or something."

A blur spell? My eyes widen. "What did you see?"

He pauses as if considering his words before he says them. "I found her hiding, cloaked in shadow. But not a natural shadow. One she'd conjured or manipulated. She used it again when trying to make a run for it, but I could still sniff her out."

A shadow…

I thought I'd seen something dark move in her room the first time I'd visited her. Like a spirit or a shadow. It had been so quick, it had been easy to disregard. Especially with Aria standing across the way, tempting me in other ways.

"Did you sense something familiar in her, too?" I ask him.

"She smelled like home to me," Elias says. "Like Hell."

"Maybe your old sniffer isn't as sharp as it used to be,"

Dorian suggests, which wins him a harsh glare from the hellhound.

"I know what I smelled," he snaps. "It's unmistakable."

Dorian is about to push his buttons some more, but I cut him off. "I sensed a familiar darkness in her as well. But controlling the darkness itself… I've never heard of a creature who could do such a thing."

"I think you're both just homesick," Dorian says dismissively.

I clench my fist on the table, my annoyance growing rapidly and my patience wearing thin. "And what about her ability to refuse your commands? Do you think we should ignore that also?"

"Wait. She shot your ass down?" Elias's head snaps back as he barks a laugh. "I'm liking this girl more already."

Dorian's mouth presses into a hard line.

Unlike these two, I am taking this seriously, and the more I think about it, the more I worry that our initial assumption that we could use Aria to somehow get back into hell was wrong. But is her involvement with Lucifer more plausible? What his motives are, I have no idea. Well, besides making sure our torture extends beyond banishment. And if that's true, killing her is our smartest option.

But there are still things that don't quite add up for me. Why try to escape? As my father's minion, wouldn't her goal be to stay and entrap us somehow? Yet she resists. I don't understand it all.

"We need to tread cautiously here," I begin. "We don't know the true magnitude of her power yet. If she hasn't been sent for a nefarious reason, then we may be able to use her to our advantage."

"There's one more thing." When Elias looks at me this time, his expression is deadly serious. "Before I came up here, I found her holding the harp's string."

"What?" I leap to my feet so fast, my chair tips over behind me.

I look at Dorian, who's just as shocked as I am. Maybe a bit disappointed, too.

That proves it. Aria was sent to us because of the harp. "He knows," I say in a rush. "Lucifer must know we're looking for the pieces of the harp to get back home."

"Shit. We're fucked," Dorian says as he runs a hand through his hair.

Why hadn't I thought of it sooner? My father's been one step ahead of us the entire time. Of course he'd send someone to thwart our plans to return to Hell.

"It wasn't like that," Elias mumbles so low I almost miss it in my frantic thinking.

"What do you mean?"

"I watched her for a while without her knowing. It seemed to… call to her, in a way. It hypnotized and scared her at the same time," he says. "I don't think she knew what it was at all. Or why it was there."

"She was acting," I reply.

"No," he snaps back. "She held no fear of being caught in the room, like a thief might. She only asked if I could hear it too."

"Hear what?" Dorian asks before I get the chance.

Elias's eyes meet mine, glowing eerily gold. "The music…"

Not sure what to make of that, I don't respond. We are all quiet for a breath, but there's a shocking pain that shoots through my clenched jaw to my temple in the stillness.

"Masters?"

All of us spin to see one of our servants, a young girl, has walked into the room with Aria at her side. She's wearing new and much more revealing clothing than before, and I suspect that was Dorian's doing. Especially by how low-cut and tight the jeans are. But still, the sight of her chest in the tight tee has me practically salivating. It's a hard thing to ignore.

Aria does everything to avoid our gazes. Especially Elias's, who is watching her intently, stalking her like prey.

"Thank you, Sadie," Dorian says to the servant. I still can't believe he's taken the time to know any of the helps' names. They're here because it's part of their contract—a life of servitude in exchange for sparing their souls. Nothing more. "Help the others bring out dinner, will you?"

When the girl walks into the kitchen and disappears, Dorian gestures toward the spot set for Aria, a smile on his face.

"Sit." He says the command gently, but the word is soaked in his power. I can sense it; it reverberates in his voice as it travels through the air and to her ears. He's testing her again.

At first, she stays put, feet glued to the floor. Maybe just to prove she can and that Dorian's gift of compulsion doesn't sway her. Beside me, he tenses, still unsure what it means. She perplexes me too. But then, after a long, tense moment, she walks down the length of the table and takes her seat.

I pick up my fallen chair and lower myself back into it. Even though there are feet between us, the darkness in her soul calls to me. It's becoming harder to resist. I need to remember that there could be other more underhanded reasons she is here, and if it comes down to it, I may have to kill her.

Just then, the kitchen door opens and four servants enter with covered dishes in hand. They set one down in front of each of us and remove the lids to reveal full plates of roasted duck, steamed potatoes, and mixed vegetables. Elias wastes no time in shoveling the food into his mouth, appearing more like a wild, ravenous animal than a man. Dorian pokes at his plate with a fork as if he's not sure what to do with it. I, on the other hand, barely look at the spread. My attention, my thoughts, my interest lay elsewhere. With the person across the table.

Not touching her food, she peeks up at me, but when she catches me staring, she doesn't drop her gaze like I expect. Instead, hers hardens on me. Challenging.

"You should eat," I say, injecting some hospitality into my tone. I try to keep Dorian's suggestions in mind about making her feel less like a prisoner and more like a guest, but the boldness in her dark eyes has me feeling less than cordial.

I clear my throat and try again. "You've been through quite a lot today. I'm sure you're hungry after everything."

"Everything you three did to me, you mean," she spits back with venom, and her voice climbs. "You took me from my *home.*"

I don't know why she insists on doing this to me, playing this dangerous game of testing my limits. It should infuriate me—and partly, it does—but it also fascinates me. She knows what I am, must know what I'm capable of, yet still she persists. She's aware of the danger all around her, and she's scared—I've seen the fear in her eyes—but neither are enough to stop her from disobeying.

I've never met anyone like her before.

"Eat," I say through clenched teeth. A deadly concoction of desire and anger spins inside me, and it's getting harder to control myself.

"You first," she counters.

Dorian and Elias are watching our exchange intently

now, seeing which one will give in first. They don't dare interrupt.

"Eat," I grind out.

"I'm not hungry."

"This entire meal has been prepared because of you," I add.

"Well, that's a fucking shame, isn't it?"

My fist slams onto the table, rattling the dishes and silverware and tipping over my glass of wine. Startled, Aria flinches. No one moves.

Punishing her is a tempting notion. What I wouldn't do to go over to her, rip her out of that chair, spread her legs wide on the table and make a feast of her instead. Teach her that I'm not someone to cross. And only when she's shaking, spent, and begging me to stop will I *consider* releasing her from my torture.

I shift in my seat, my hardened cock suddenly feeling too restrictive in these pants. Glancing down at my plate, I'm no longer hungry for the food prepared. It pales in comparison to the images in my head. I'm craving something else.

Eyeing me, Dorian's voice drops to a whisper. "Maybe you should tell her what is expected of her while she's here?"

I say nothing as I force the tension in my muscles to unwind. It's not an easy feat. When I'm finally settled enough, I wave the servants to come back and take Aria's plate away. The young one, Sadie, does.

"Hey!" Aria protests.

"You refused it, so now you can starve for the night," I say coolly, ignoring her hateful glare. Before she can combat me again, I add on, "And Dorian is right. It is about time we lay some ground rules, since you'll be staying here for some time. At least until we figure out what to do with you."

Worrying her bottom lip between her teeth, she sinks back in her chair.

Good girl.

"As we discussed before, there will be no more escape attempts. Elias will be able to hunt you down before you reach the nearest town. That is, if the other wild beasts of the forest don't get to you first. Neither will compare to what'll await you when you're brought back."

Elias's grin grows wicked, and Aria's breathing speeds up noticeably.

I go on. "You will come when you're summoned and do as you're told without question—"

"I'd rather die."

I smirk. "We own your soul, my dear Aria," I explain in as calm a manner as I can manage, "which means we own your death as well. You live and die on our terms."

Her eyes widen. "You're monsters."

"Close, but no cigar," Elias adds in.

Blustering with anger, Aria stands and marches out of the room. From my spot at the table, I can see her climbing the steps, more than likely heading for her room. Elias jumps to his feet, about to chase her, but I hold out my hand to stop him.

"Let her go for now," I say to him. "If she's smart, she'll heed my warning."

Shaking his head in disappointment, Dorian continues to pick at his food. "Well, I'd say that went rather well."

Even though he isn't looking up, I know the jab is directed at me.

"She needs to know we're not to be crossed," I tell him firmly. We don't know where her loyalties truly lie. Or has he forgotten that a woman was the cause of our downfall the first time, the very reason we are currently stuck on this plane? "We can't have history repeating itself."

Seeming to be thinking the same thing, Elias's expression darkens. He's never forgiven himself for his part in our banishment, even after all these years. He'd fallen for Serena's lies harder than the two of us. It's a mistake he won't be making again, and neither will I.

Giving up on both dinner and the conversation, Dorian pushes his plate into the middle of the table and stands. "I think we learned a valuable lesson through all this," he says as his lazy gaze roams over us, unimpressed. "You both are absolutely terrible with women."

CHAPTER NINE
ARIA

Time crawls by in this place. There's no clock in my room, no way to keep track of the hours passing by, and autumn's permanently gray skies make it even harder. Maybe three or four days have gone by, if I were to guess, and frankly, that's three or four days too many. The only thing I can rely on is Sadie, who comes into my room and leaves a tray of food for me, never saying much.

Three meals a day and a few seconds of human interaction. That's all I get. The rest of the hours are spent sleeping, rummaging through my room—which is oddly empty—or contemplating my next plan for escape. In all honesty, I'm not sure if I'd rather have the silence or one of the demons bursting in here and shouting demands. Or worse, making me join some staged family dinner and pretend like all this isn't extra fucked up.

Though, they have left me alone for a short while. Maybe I've convinced them there's nothing special about me and they've given up? A girl can dream, right?

As I wait for Sadie's familiar knock on the door for

dinner, I sit on the settee at the foot of the bed and stare absentmindedly at the fire blazing. I can't stop thinking about the three men summoning me like some pet whenever they feel like it, forcing me to do whatever they want on command. Especially Cain. That arrogant, self-entitled asshole. The way he looks at me too… It's like he wants to either kill me or fuck me, and I'm really not sure which. Maybe both.

Some time later, there's a knock on my door. As expected, it's Sadie with another cart of food, some wine, iced tea, and a large slice of raspberry and chocolate cheesecake. I'm being spoiled tonight.

My stomach rumbles, and I all but jump to my feet with excitement. "This all looks great, Sadie. Thank you." I lean close and find that everything is still warm and smells delicious. I expect her to leave then, but she stays put and eyes me.

"Can I… help you with something else?" I ask nervously.

"There's one more thing, Miss." She reaches on the shelf below the food and pulls out a large white box that's tied with a red ribbon. She passes it to me.

I hesitate, my gut twisting with worry. "What's this?"

She doesn't reply, only gestures for me to open it before turning and heading back for the door. When she's gone, I examine the box once more. Presents now? I don't understand. It looks harmless, but that doesn't mean anything. Demons don't give gifts.

There has to be more to it.

Carefully, I tug off the ribbon and open the box. Unfolding the neat red tissue paper, I find a bundle of deep, blood-red fabric.

What the heck?

I pull it out with gentle hands and gape. It's a dress—a

slender, silky number that feels as fine and light as water in my hands. Expensive. Probably costs more money than I could ever dream of owning in my lifetime.

The next thing I notice as I hold it up is the deep plunge in the neckline and equally high slit up the side.

A knot lodges in my throat. I've never worn anything so revealing. Between the choice of material and cutout designs, it leaves very little to the imagination. Might as well walk out in my birthday suit. But I guess that's the point.

Anger prickles. What did they take me for? A stripper?

Yeah, there is no way I'm wearing this.

Shoving the dress back into the box, I toss it onto the bed. A piece of paper falls out and glides onto the floor. I walk over, pick it up, and stare down at the smooth curves of the handwriting. As if my body already knows who it's from, my heart begins to beat rapidly.

You have one hour. -C

That's all it says, but I can hear Cain's accent swirling around every word as I read it, and goosebumps rise.

Goddammit. I hate him. Hate how he can affect me without even being in the room.

I glance back at the dress. Am I really going to listen and put that thing on? I turn to the food platter and lift the cover to reveal a roasted chicken sandwich, which I eagerly pick up and start eating as I stare at the gift from Cain. What an arrogant prick!

The sound of the door opening again has me swinging back around as I finish the sandwich. Expecting to see Cain's black eyes and devilish smirk, a relieved sigh escapes me when I see Sadie has returned.

"Sorry if I startled you, Miss," she says. "I should have knocked again."

I wave the apology away dismissively and command my rapid pulse to slow. "It's okay."

"I've been told to help you get ready." She takes a hesitant step farther into the room.

Of course. Send someone to make sure I obey him. He's probably figured out I'm less likely to fight it because of Sadie, too. The conniving bastard.

Sighing, my shoulders slump in defeat.

"Did you even see what he wants me to wear?" I ask Sadie as I walk over to the bed, snatch the dress, and hold it out in front of me. Eyeballing the gown, it seems like it'll fit me, and the fact that the demons know my body shape and size only irritates me more.

"Any idea what this is all about?" I ask her as she moves into the joining bathroom. She comes out a moment later with a brush, hairspray, a handful of bobby pins, and a small cosmetic bag.

Oh no... She's not going to put makeup on me, is she?

I am not a makeup-wearing kinda girl. Barely wore ChapStick.

She backs me up until my legs hit the settee, forcing me to plop down. I want to protest, but she's already using the brush and hairspray to twirl and pin my hair away from my face. It doesn't take long to get it to her liking, but when she opens the cosmetic bag and pulls out a tube of mascara, I send up a silent prayer.

Sadie gets to work. I close my eyes for most of it, afraid to see what she's doing to my face. Like my hair, it only takes minutes, but it's a torturous time. The poking and prodding finally stops, and Sadie steps back to admire her handiwork. Smiling approvingly, she hands me the dress and slips back into the bathroom so I can get changed.

Pulling off my clothes, I shrug on the dress. The fabric

glides over me, fitting tight around my waist and hips before falling loose to the floor.

Sadie steps back into the room just in time and her smile widens. "It fits perfectly," she muses, but then her lips twist in a frown.

"What?" I ask.

She points to the low neckline where my bra peeks through. I'll have to take it off.

I huff. It takes some finagling with the dress on, but I'm able to slip out of it.

Then she points to my hips. "The panties will have to come off, too."

"What? No way!" I look down. She's right, of course. With the thin material, every line and crease of my underwear is visible.

"Master Cain insists."

Aggravated, I quickly wiggle my way out of my remaining undergarments. Despite the dress, which weighs nothing at all, I feel completely naked before her. And I pretty much am. My nipples poke through the fabric. If I shift the wrong way, the slit on my leg moves too much. One false move and I'll flash the room all my goods.

"I can't do this," I mutter.

Sadie moves closer to the standing mirror beside the dresser and gestures for me to join her. When I don't move fast enough, she grabs my arm and pulls me forward.

"You're stunning," she says. Her smile is a warm one, but it does little to ease my discomfort. She coaxes me to the mirror. "Look."

I glance up, and the moment I catch a glimpse of my reflection, I gasp out loud. The woman standing before me doesn't look like me at all. Hair pinned up in a delicate twist, a few tendrils loose to frame a face painted with sweeping dark lashes, outlined smokey eyes, and bright red lips. The dress is even more stunning on, even with the less-than-modest parts of it, and for the first time in my life, I feel… sexy. Dangerous. Beautiful. They're thoughts I wasn't sure I even had in me. Keeping the smile from my face is hard, because never in million years could I have imagined myself dressed like this, looking like this.

Inside, I feel Sayah swimming around. She's anxious to get out, mirroring my emotions now that I know the next step means meeting with Cain again. But this time, I'm not dreading seeing him. Quite the opposite. I *want* to see him. Want to witness the look on his face when he sees me done up like this after so much time apart. And most importantly, to make him sweat as I tease him.

A knock raps on the door. "The car's out front. We leave in five," Cain states from the other side of the door before his footfalls fade down the hallway.

"You are ready, Miss," Sadie offers as she goes to my bed where the box is and returns with a pair of red strappy stilettos dangling from her hand. They glint in the light as though the lacquer is sprinkled with diamond dust. A level of fright zaps through me at seeing them.

My mouth hangs open. I trip in ballet flats. Joggers, sandals, flat boots—*that* is me. With these heels, I'll break my neck. Sadie places them in front of me, and I lift the fabric of my dress up to step into the shoes. The maid kneels before me and latches the straps at the backs of my ankles.

When she stands, I feel so much taller than her… *How in the world am I meant to walk on these stilts?*

Sadie turns to the box on my bed once again and returns moments later with a long, gold necklace. It's so thin it looks fragile. She moves to stand behind me, and I duck low and lift my hair for her to clasp the chain around my neck. The necklace is long, and a single golden wing sits right between my breasts. I lift the sparkling charm. It's beautiful.

"You better not keep Master Cain waiting." Sadie heads across the room and opens the door.

One last look in the mirror, and the girl staring back at me can't be me. She's way too sexy and confident.

"Miss, hurry up," Sadie whispers, exasperated.

I can do this. Then I swing around and walk out of the room on slow, wobbly steps until I find my stride. By that I mean moving as slow as a snail and keeping close to the walls, then hanging onto the handrail for dear life as I descend the grand staircase. The heels click-clack on the stone floor on my way to the front door of the mansion, which lays open.

Outside in the driveaway waits a black limousine, windows tinted. Standing at the back door, holding it open, is Cain. His head is tilted forward, focused on the phone in his hand. He's dressed in a crisp, black suit, perfectly tailored for him. He wears the jacket open, and the button-up shirt underneath sits gaped open at his throat. Every inch of him is solid muscle beneath the suit.

He waits for me, looking dangerously sexy. This infuriating but gorgeous man's eyes light me on fire as his gaze lifts to meet mine. He's silent, and granted, he may be shocked by my appearance, but I won't deny such a reaction is a huge boost to my confidence.

His lips draw into a genuine smile. It takes me aback. I can't remember seeing him smile, not once, from the moment I arrived at this mansion.

"You're late," he says.

Now that's the Cain I recognize. Taking in a deep breath to calm my nerves into some semblance of normality, I step down the stairs carefully, then I stroll toward him.

My skin pricks from his unabashed gaze roaming all over my body.

I do my best to not flash him from my low neckline, or the ultra high slit up my thigh that the wind keeps trying to push aside to reveal me, all while making the clumsy walk appear effortless. I give a slight swing to my hips; I want him to stare and drool. He's not the only one who can be all dreamy and broody. Two can play at that game. Who would have thought it felt so empowering to dress like this?

He steps aside for me to climb into the back when my ankle suddenly gives way. I feel myself lurching, my heart beating insanely. I'm going to fall feet from the car and look like a fool. I die on the inside while my arms flail wildly.

Strong hands snatch me mid-fall, tight around my waist, and hoist me back to my feet. I gasp for air, my pulse thumping frantically through my veins. Pressed up tight against Cain, he holds me in place as I get my balance. My cheeks flush with embarrassment at being so close to him, at the hardness of his hand at my back. Everything about him drives me crazy— it's just a toss-up from minute to minute whether it's the infuriated kind of crazy or the panty-melting kind.

"Careful. We don't need you breaking an ankle."

Tell me about it.

"I prefer sneakers," I say.

"Ah, yes, but sneakers would do little to emphasize your legs." He pauses and glances away as if he's been caught saying something he shouldn't, and I love the thought of being able to trip him up. Even if it's only momentarily.

"For the dress, you mean. They'd do little for the dress." I look up at him, those gorgeous eyes captivating. Part of me expects to find mirth in them, maybe a mocking response, but he gives none. He is unlike any other man I've ever met, but to be fair, he isn't exactly a man. I have never crossed paths with a demon before.

"Yes, of course. The dress." He clears his throat, but his grip on me never loosens. He continues to hold me close, debating on what to do next.

My ankle still burns from the mishap, but all I can focus on is the lack of space between us, the quickening of his breath. All he's done is catch me from falling, and I'm on fire on the inside. This was my moment to make him squirm, not to tumble into his arms and under his charm.

Dammit, I need to get my shit together.

It takes all my willpower not to fold and keep staring at his lips, wondering if he will kiss me. Here I was, wanting to make him drool over me, yet all I've accomplished is to fall and start daydreaming about kissing the big bad demon. Swallowing hard, I wriggle out of his embrace, my cheeks burning up.

"Thank you," I say and turn to move for the back seat, my grip on the door like iron to avoid another tumble. As ladylike as possible, I get into the car, holding one hand across the fabric on my chest.

Without a word, he shuts the door and strides around to the other side of the limo. The driver up front starts the engine, and now I'm having all kinds of renewed anxiety about how I'm going to balance on these shoes while in this dress. This may end up being the most embarrassing night of my life.

Cain gets into the back and sits across from me. Our eyes lock as we drive away from the mansion. He looks as if he wants to say something, or at least like something is plaguing his thoughts, and my own tongue feels heavy with unsaid words. I want to ask him what this unexpected outing is all about and why we're dressed for the red carpet, but I press my lips together. I'm still burning up with embarrassment from my fall.

I do my best to avoid his stare. My gaze drops to his hands, which are on his lap. He stretches his fingers out and curls them in over and over as he thinks in brooding silence. It's the first time I notice the ring on his right hand. A thick gold band with an onyx gem. Or at least, it appears black at first. When the glow of the passing streetlights momentarily flood the car, it shines red. Blood red. And along the sides, an intricate design is etched. Almost like… a fan of feathers. Or wings?

"You're staring," he says and covers the hand with the other.

My eyes flick to the window instead. Outside, the night is stealing the last signs of day. Trees are all I see, and not even cars pass us on this lonely road. I have no idea where exactly we even are, but now I realize that my escape on foot would have been a treacherous attempt.

"Are you going to tell me where we're going?" I ask.

When Cain doesn't respond, I turn my attention back to him. He sits rigid as a statue in front of me, his muscles wound tight, those spectacular eyes on my chest.

Instinctually, I look down to the deep V neckline that plunges halfway down to my stomach. No bra, boobage everywhere. I've never worn anything that shows so much skin, or even a fancy dress, but this is something else. There's enough on show here to put a streetwalker to shame.

"You look beautiful, Aria." There's a hint of warmth to his otherwise steely tone, and I wonder if he means the compliment genuinely. "Don't be embarrassed of what you have."

I crane my head up to see his lips curled in a heart-stopping smirk. The devilish glint in his eyes sends my heartbeat off to the races, and I realize he's saying these things to get a rise out of me. Not for anything else. He loves seeing me squirm.

And for some reason, even knowing that, his plan works.

"Is everyone else dressing this way where we're going?" I ask him.

He nods once, then his phone rings. Digging into his pocket, he thumbs the screen and puts it to his ear. He doesn't respond at first, just listens. "Perfect. Thirty minutes."

Now my curiosity piques even further on where we're going. I shift to cross my legs when the fabric slides all the way up my thigh. Frantically, I drag it back in place because I have no intention of doing a Britney Spears and flashing Mr. Sin Demon who insists I wear no underwear.

God, please don't let us be going to a swinger's party. I don't have it in me to deal with that sort of stuff. And while I'm on the topic of prayers, please no sacrifices either.

The awkward quiet in the limo is stifling. There's no music, and Cain's stare grows heavy over me.

"You really do look stunning." He breaks the silence.

I relax back in my seat and meet his gaze, his words floating in my mind. "Did you pick the dress?"

He gives one small nod. "As soon as I saw it, I knew it was meant for you."

"I'm not here for your entertainment, you know."

The corner of his mouth quirks up again and he glances out the window. He couldn't be more transparent if he tried.

"Is this a date?" I ask, feeling stupid for the question. But if he isn't telling me where we are headed, I can easily grill him with a thousand questions until he buckles.

"Do you want it to be?" he muses.

"I'm sure you're used to having lots of girls pouring themselves all over you, but that's not going to happen. I don't date monsters."

He laughs, loud and boisterous, and as much as I hate to admit it, the sound he makes is the most delicious thing I've ever heard. It covers me in goosebumps and sends a tingle to the pit of my stomach. Here I imagined it would be awful spending so much time with demons, but my experience so far has been surprising.

Alluring.

Dangerous.

Thrilling.

Maybe I'm in more danger from the lack of control I hold rather than what these men intend for me.

"I didn't think that was possible," I say.

"What's that?"

"You being able to laugh."

"Oh?"

"You seem so… tightly wound all the time."

At that, he frowns, deep creases appearing between his eyes. All the mirth is gone, and I'm staring at the stone version of him again.

Yikes. I probably should have kept that bit to myself.

I attempt to save the conversation by redirecting it. "Uh, what exactly does a demon do in his spare time, anyway?"

"Search for virgins, drain souls, that kind of thing."

I stare at him.

Wait. Was that… a joke?

Another sarcastic smile touches his lips, and I half laugh. Holy shit. The demon does have a sense of humor after all.

But as fast as it appeared, it's gone. Just a flicker of something more about him.

"My foster dad once told me that demons rarely spend time on Earth, and they come here only for feeding or sex. And yet you've got a mansion here."

"Did he, now?" Cain says, and I nod.

He studies me for a long moment. Then his gaze darkens as his tongue glides over his lower lip. "That might have been the case years ago, but you'd be surprised how many evil things live in your town that you're unaware of."

I'm not sure how I feel about that insight. "Are they here to hurt people?"

"They're just trying to survive, like you. Like all of us."

His response stays with me, because something about the word *survive* isn't what I'd ever associate with Cain. Or Dorian or Elias, for that matter.

"Do you think tomorrow I can use a phone to call my friend? She'll be super worried about me."

"Of course. But it doesn't change your situation."

"I know," I murmur. "You have a signed contract and all that, even if it wasn't my choice." Bitterness coats my tone and settles in my chest as my situation comes crashing over me again. I turn to the window, not in the mood to make small talk anymore.

Half an hour later we're in the main part of town. There's a comfort that comes over me to see something familiar, and a desperate urge to escape claws at me, imploring me to open the window and scream for help. As if that's going to work with a sin demon sitting across from me.

So, I watch the life I once knew fly by, watch the people strolling across the street, popping in and out of shops. I've lost track of what day of the week it is in all honesty, but it feels strange to see so many people acting normal when my life has become anything but.

We soon turn down a side street, the streetlights

dimming. Left and right, I can't recall which path we take. Glenside isn't an enormous town compared to a real city, but it's still big enough to have a population of about 150,000, and that's not including the supposed evil things living here that no one knows about.

By the time we stop, we're parked in a back alley with only one flickering light outside on the building across from my window, illuminating the façade. There's a huge, black, metal-studded door and a small silver plaque with the word 'Purgatory' in black with a set of wings off the "P." I snort a laugh. Seems like the perfect name for a place where demons like to hang out.

A flurry of cold wind swishes into the car and chills my skin. I glance over to the other door as Cain climbs out. Seconds later, he's opening my door. I accept his hand while holding my dress together over my thighs and climb out. A wicked wind blows through my hair, while the alley around us seems to crowd in around me. Lofty buildings, darkness… I have no idea where we are. I've never been here before.

Cain steps in front of me, a hand on my cheek, then his fingers slide to cup the back of my neck. "You are mine; remember that tonight."

I know he means because of the contract and nothing more, but a delicious tingle weaves through me anyway. He then guides me to the door, which opens almost instantly at our arrival to a dark room.

Cain takes me inside by my hand.

The anteroom is all black walls, ceiling, and floor, with a bear of a guard by the door, who bows his head at Cain. Must be a regular or pretty high roller to get all this special treatment. A young brunette stands behind a small counter with another small room behind her; it looks like the cloak room.

On wobbly feet, I stick close to Cain's side as a set of double doors open up for us across the room. An explosion of seductive music and laughs and voices burst from inside, stealing the silence in the entry room.

We enter the club where the music flows like a breeze over me, where there are people everywhere. At first, I don't know where to look—at the gorgeous women in designer dresses just as minimalistic as mine, the dancers inside small cages suspended from the ceiling, or the enormous bar that takes up the length of one wall. A mirrored wall, that is. People are sitting at the bar, at numerous tables and leather seatings all over the room. This place is enormous.

A man wearing only leather pants and boots strolls right in front of us. As he passes, the most gorgeous electric-blue wings span out from his back. Two other extremely handsome men hurry to his side and fall to their knees before him. My mouth drops open at those wings.

"Fae lord," Cain whispers in my ear.

That's when I really look around, reminding myself this isn't a club for humans. Everyone here is a supernatural. Most hold their human forms, but I catch the glowing eyes of a girl in the corner, the tail of a gorgeous red-haired woman in a tiny skirt. Shifters, fae, spellcasters—if you can dream up a supernatural type, it's here, including some I don't even recognize.

"Aria," Cain says. "Explore for a moment. I have someone important I must talk to, then I'll bring you a drink."

I nod as he leaves my side, and suddenly I feel naked and vulnerable. This isn't the type of place I normally visit. Most of the girls my age at school sneak into clubs with fake IDs all the time. I never bothered since I had no money and didn't really fit in anyway.

Two girls dressed in white jumpsuits that cling to their perfect bodies like a second skin stroll past me, whispering to one another. They both glance my way, then laugh.

Heat hits my cheeks. I glance down, seeing the dress and my wobbly stance on these heels. I feel like an imposter in this get-up. It's nothing like me. This isn't who I am. Not really.

Inside me, Sayah swirls around, her own way of saying to let their laughter roll off me. She's right, I know. I don't need their approval—or anyone else's, for that matter—but the years of bullying and trauma make it hard to get over old thoughts and habits.

Fuck them. Catty bitches. Besides, I have more important things to worry about right now. Like figuring out how the heck I'm getting out of here. Since I've been left to my own devices, it's time to start making a plan.

CHAPTER TEN
ARIA

My gaze sweeps the dimly lit main floor of the club again. Even though it's newly night, it's super busy with every table and booth occupied and the dance floor in the corner crowded with patrons. They grind against each other and dance to the slow, seductive song.

Sayah buzzes inside me, wanting out like always.

"Too many people," I whisper to her. "Not yet."

She tucks into a ball, not pleased with me. I feel bad for keeping her locked up for so long, but with these demons hounding me to reveal her and my gifts, it's safer if she stays put. First I need to work out what they want with me. For all I know, once they uncover my ability, I'll become demon chow.

But not releasing Sayah has its effects on me, too. I'm crawling under my skin, my anxiety-dial turned up to high. Her darkness weighs heavy on me, seeping into my bones. If I don't release her soon and free myself from her influence, she could change me. Permanently.

It's almost happened once before, when I was younger

and had just discovered our connection. A shadow monster inside me at seven? Talk about nightmare fuel. I was terrified by the power she possessed, so I'd refused to use her. I'd lasted a whole two weeks, discovering that leaving her inside me was worse than letting her out. Her presence began to pull me into the darkness with her; I sank into the raw energy she was made of and lost complete control over myself.

I have no memories of the twenty-four hours that followed. None. Zip. I'd been lucky a police officer had found me passed out on the outskirts of town and brought me back to my foster home. Otherwise, who knows if I would've ever snapped out of it, let alone survived that night.

I can't risk that again. I can't lose myself.

So now, Sayah and I are buddies. We have a symbiotic relationship of sorts. I let her out every once in a while to stir up a little chaos, and she helps me when I need her to. Kind of like… a pet. An evil, shadow-spirit pet.

I scan the club again and note the large, hulking guys stationed around the joint. Especially near the front door. The owners have security all over the place here, so that narrows down my exit routes.

Knowing that there are probably people here who would rat me out to Cain in a heartbeat, I have to be smart about this. I need to get away from any watchful eyes before I make a break for it. I look up at the tall ceilings and find domed cameras spying on the patrons below.

Great. Just great. This escape just got even harder.

As a shirtless male server walks past me, I tap his shoulder and put on my best sweet and innocent expression. "Excuse me, but could you point me to the ladies' room?"

"Sure." He gestures toward a narrow hallway at the rear of the club. "Just down there. Second door on your left."

I nod my thank you as he strides away, then make a beeline on unsteady feet in the direction he pointed. Unlike the rest of the place, this area is quieter, set far enough away from the dance floor and speakers that the music doesn't rattle my eardrums. The hall stretches ahead until it turns abruptly, and red doors line both sides.

There are no windows that I can see. No emergency exit signs or clear routes out. One of these doors may lead to a way out, but searching through them all would be time consuming. Not to mention suspicious. I can't draw attention to myself.

I'll check the bathroom for a window. If I have no luck there and no one else is around, then I'll follow the hall to the end. There has to be another way out of here. Supernaturals have to follow fire codes too, right?

As my mind runs through my plan, I take the second door on my right. Opening it, I realize immediately I've made a mistake, because what I see is far from toilets and sinks. On a black sofa, a man sits spread-legged with a full-figured female on his lap. Wearing nothing but fishnet stockings, she bounces up and down as she rides his cock. The man has both hands on her ass, spreading her cheeks wide, but his face is buried in her chest, sucking and kneading her large breasts greedily.

I freeze in the doorway, my pulse skyrocketing to the moon. I should leave. I *need* to leave, but I can't will my legs to move. It's like my brain short-circuits; I can't look away.

A zap of desire shoots through my belly, and I flush with heat all over. Neither of them see me. They're too lost in their act to notice they have an audience. Their grunts and the sounds of flesh slapping against flesh awaken something in me, and my own breathing picks up. If I were wearing my underwear, it'd be soaked right now.

Then the woman's blonde head turns, and when her eyes meet mine, I'm paralyzed with embarrassment. I've been caught gaping at them like a peeping tom. My heartbeat booms even louder, but instead of stopping or yelling at me, the woman only grins wickedly and keeps up her pace, riding the man's cock rigorously and without mercy. She is unbearably beautiful. Huge blue eyes, dark eye makeup, blonde curls bouncing across her brow. Her pale skin glints with sweat. The man's groans of pleasure shake the room and leave me feeling feverish and unsteady.

Sayah jerks me awake, a warning quivering through our connection. Someone is coming our way.

Stumbling backward, panic crawls up my neck. I flounder with the door's handle but manage to get it closed again. The moment the door clicks shut, the sounds of the couple's sexcapade cut off abruptly. I spin just in time to see Cain standing there, staring at me with a cocked brow.

My heart is in my throat, and I struggle to swallow it back down. How long has he been there watching me? How much has he seen?

"Find what you're looking for?" he asks, glancing briefly at the red door.

My cheeks flame. He knows what I found. I'm sure of it.

"Uh, n-no." My voice hitches, and I barely make it through the two-word sentence. I don't move. My insides are still a quivering mess from what I've just witnessed, and I can't control myself.

His piercing blue eyes never leave me, pinning me in place as they study me.

I attempt to speak again. "I-I was just trying to find the bathroom."

He points to the doors on the other side of us clearly

labeled 'Men' and 'Women,' the very ones I had missed in my wanderings.

In an effort to evade him, I sidestep toward them. "Oh, right… I'll just—"

He moves quickly to block me again. "Funny… Because it appeared to me like you were enjoying the show."

Shit.

My stomach somersaults. I've lost my words.

"You found the Red Rooms," he says, his voice growing huskier. He takes one step closer to me, and I backpedal.

My mouth dries, and I lick my bottom lip. The simple gesture isn't lost on him as his gaze darkens.

I take another quick step back. "People can pay to…"

"Indulge in their darkest fantasies. Yes."

That means Purgatory isn't just a social kind of nightclub. It's a sex club.

My backside smacks against the wall, and I gasp in surprise. I hadn't even realized I was still moving at all. Like our very first meeting, he's backed me into a corner without doing much at all.

Cain's in front of me suddenly, his body only mere inches away from mine. He slaps his hands against the wall on either side of my head, and I jump at the sudden loud sound.

He's caged me in.

His breath smells like whiskey, and I wonder if he'll taste like it, too. Strong, intoxicating, and addictive if I'm not too careful.

"What are you doing?" I ask as he leans in.

His gaze flicks from my eyes to my mouth, and I hold my breath. He's going to kiss me. I should push him away, yet I feel myself getting swept away in the moment. He presses closer to me, the heat pouring from his body scorching, the erection in his pants nestled against my stomach. He knows exactly what he's doing—*I* know exactly what he's doing—and yet I sense myself slipping under his spell.

The desire to taste him, to finally give into this gorgeous man who drives me insane, is wearing me down. One kiss with this original sin demon… would it be so bad?

My mind and body don't quite seem to agree on the decision, but the way my pussy pulses each time I clench my thighs intensifies the arousal rising through me. It's all animalistic, raw attraction claiming me.

I make the decision for him and close the distance, my eyes slipping shut. But before our lips touch, his hand clasps around my throat, stopping me right before we make contact. My eyes snap open. He applies enough pressure to stun me, but not enough to cut off my air supply.

"That was very bold of you," Cain says, his face still hovering inches away. For a death-defying second, I wonder if he'll kill me here in the middle of the club with so many people nearby. But the tingle of fear is drowned out by an even greater swell of desire. I can't help it. Whenever I'm near him, my body isn't my own. "I think we should test it, hmm?"

"Test?" I rasp against his hold.

As he stares down at me, I could swear his crystal blue eyes darken a shade. "Let's see just how bold you can be."

Is he challenging me?

Before I can ask what he means, his free hand falls onto my thigh. Electricity buzzes through my body from that single touch. With a quick flick, he exposes more skin through the dress's high slit. I suck in a breath.

I don't know what he's planning on doing, but I'm already so turned on. The image of the couple fucking in the Red Room flashes in my mind, and I know that if Cain wanted to bring me into one right now, I wouldn't fight him. Which is so wrong. So, so wrong.

But instead of dragging me away into a private place, his fingers continue to glide up my leg. The chill of his ring contrasts the heat of his touch as his hand sneaks under the silky dress, toward the place where I burn hot for him.

Oh my God.

Sayah vibrates under my skin. She doesn't trust him, and I don't blame her—neither do I. But still, I don't stop him. The need humming through my body is too great, my craving unimaginable.

"I hope you followed my instructions and aren't wearing any—" Instead of finishing the sentence, his fingertips brush my sex, and I flinch. He grins wickedly. "Ah, perfect."

Does that mean he's had this planned from the beginning? He'd been looking for his chance to corner me?

His finger dips further along my slick heat, and when I shudder at the touch, a growl rumbles in his throat—an actual growl, like some untamed beast. "You're already wet for me."

His voice has changed, too, his accent growing thicker as the tone turns deeper. He goes rigid before me as if he's struggling to keep control of himself; meanwhile I can't breathe as arousal runs amok inside me.

The sound of people's whispering snatches my attention toward the bathroom doors behind him. A group of scantily dressed women watch, talking and pointing as they pass. Suddenly aware of how visible we are in the middle of the hallway, embarrassment crawls over me. I wiggle against his hold, trying to move away, but his hand tightens around my neck, his finger continuing to slide over the seam of my slit. I sputter and cough as I try to suck in more air.

I shove my hands against his chest, but he's a stone wall.

He only cranes my chin up with a thumb to meet his gaze again. "This is what you wanted. What I've craved since laying eyes on you in this dress."

I'm torn between melting and needing to push him away, the struggle inside me ferocious. But the more he strokes my fire, the deeper I fall, the stronger the allure to let myself go grows. To discover what it would be like to be taken by a demon. By this dangerous asshole I can't seem to get out of my mind.

"But-but everyone can see us." I choke out the words. More guests walk by, gaping our way.

"Let them watch."

Cain's aggressive words strike a match in me, and I'm burning up from the inside out. The possibility of being watched is both terrifying and exhilarating at the same time. Especially with him. The pad of his finger finds my clit and begins to stroke me. I'm already trembling with need and so soaking wet that his finger glides over me with ease.

With his other hand still firmly around my throat, a small squeaking sound escapes my mouth without my permission. Delicious tingles spread from his touch through my belly.

One finger pushes into my tightness, making me yelp in surprise. His hand squeezes a little tighter on my neck to quiet me. More people pass us to walk into the bathrooms, all taking their time to gawk at us, and I'm hit again with unease.

"Cain…" His name comes out more like a plea than anything else. "Maybe we should go somewhere else—ah..."

Another finger slips inside me, pushing in deep, and I lose the rest of my words to the spiral of pain and pleasure wrapping around me. It's becoming quite obvious to me that he's the one in control right now, and there's nothing I can do to stop him. *If* I wanted to.

Faster than ever before, I feel the familiar pressure of my orgasm begin to build. My entire body tightens as the mounting sensation grows. Cain must sense it too, because he starts to pump his fingers while his thumb circles my sensitive nub at the same time.

"Oh, God." My voice shakes.

He smirks at that. "Quite the opposite, actually."

My eyes start to flutter closed, but he squeezes my neck again and they fly open.

"Look at me," he demands.

I do, and for some reason, staring into his eyes as they are swallowed up by blackness isn't scary anymore. It's incredibly sexy and hypnotizing.

I've forgotten all about the onlookers. Okay, not forgotten. But I don't care anymore. My hips move on their own, grinding against his leg and his harder-than-steel erection. Even his breathing speeds up. Just the thought of him enjoying this as much as me has me hurtling toward pure bliss.

Then, everything stops. His hand falls away from my neck and his fingers withdraw from me to grip my thigh instead.

"What? No," I whimper as all the pleasure is lost. I'm plunging fast from the high. "Don't stop."

I hate that it sounds like I'm begging, but I was *so* close. *Soooo* close. Pulling away now is a form of torture.

"Summon your shadow."

His command is so unexpected, it strikes me dumb. Did I hear him right?

"Shield us from view and I'll give you the release you crave." He makes sure to press himself against me, so I can feel *all* of him to make his point clear. "I'll wrap those long legs around my waist and fuck you right here in the middle of the hall. Right now."

I gasp.

"Show me that darkness lurking inside you, Aria," he growls.

I blink rapidly, still unable to believe what he's saying. My shadow…?

So he *had* seen Sayah our first day together. Or, at least, Elias had seen me use her during my escape. And that meant that this—*all* of this—had been a set-up to get me to release her and prove him right.

I can't believe it.

Or maybe I can. He is a demon, after all. I should've known better than to let it get this far. He was just using me.

Anger whips within me. At myself for being so fucking stupid, and at him for trying to manipulate me this way.

"You bastard." I hear the slap before I see it. He's holding his jaw and my palm stings when I finally realize the mistake I've made. Striking a Hell-dwelling sin demon? That's about as dumb as it gets. But at least it's gotten him to put some distance between us.

He stares at me for a long moment, saying nothing, only rubbing his jaw and staring at me with those evil, all-black eyes. Sayah shuffles inside me. She's afraid he'll retaliate and kill us. And he just might.

A thread of fear weaves through me, but it's not enough to overcome the fury I feel.

Even as he glares at me in shocked and angry silence, I wish I'd hit him harder.

I wait for the outburst, but it never comes. Instead, he straightens, and the demonic color drains from his eyes. His stone wall, tight-lipped facade returns, and I'm unsure if he's livid or impressed, possibly even disappointed that things didn't end the way he'd wanted. All those emotions seem to pass over his face as he stands there, but I know that as mild as his reaction seems to be, I am going to regret this later.

"It's time to leave," is all he says as he gestures for me to step back into the main part of the club. Knowing I've already pushed my luck for tonight, I walk ahead of him toward the entrance.

My attention trained on my feet and trying not to topple over in these heels, I do my best to weave through the crowd. One man steps in front of me, and when I move to go around him, he steps with me, blocking my path. I look up to see a frighteningly familiar face. White hair chopped flat, thick sideburns, a pale goatee, a wrinkled face... It's Sir Surchion, the collector from the antique store. He wears the most outrageous oversized fur coat. It only enhances his over-the-top aesthetic, and he stares down at me through circle-rimmed glasses.

Fear tumbles over me, and I freeze on the spot. His giant crow sits on his shoulder, eyeing me.

"What a striking little beauty we have here," he says. His tone is sweet, but there is no sign of warmth on his face. "I'm sorry if I startled you, my dear, but it seems Mordecai thinks he knows you."

It takes me a second to realize he means the bird who's glaring at me, like he's about to peck my eyes out.

Could a bird recognize a person? From the way it's glaring at me, I'd say so.

"I-I-don't see how that's possible," I stammer.

"My dear Mordecai never forgets a face. Especially one as pretty as yours," he replies. A chill runs through me. He suspects me of something. Possibly of stealing the orb, if he doesn't already know for sure, but I can't give him anything to pin it on me.

So I paste on a stiff smile and glance at the crow. "I'm more of a cat person myself."

As if he understands me, Mordecai squawks loudly and bats his wings. Sir Surchion shushes him gently to calm him down. Then he glances down at my leg. I have a good guess what he's looking for—bite marks—and I'm lucky the leg exposed by the dress's high slit isn't the one his dogs had chomped on.

"If you'll excuse me, I have to go." I try to maneuver around him again, but he shifts.

"Sir Surchion." Cain appears at my side and his arm snakes around my middle. Every muscle in my body stiffens at the contact. He nods his head at the old man in greeting. "I thought we discussed bringing your animal in here before."

Sir Surchion's beady eyes flick to Cain and back to me. His scowl deepens. Cain's presence has spoiled his fun.

"Yes, we have, but aren't we all just animals really? I mean, look around." He makes a grand sweeping gesture with his arm toward the crowd of supernaturals with tails and pointed ears and wings.

"The crow is not allowed in here." Cain's tone deepens with authority. I wonder why he cares about the bird being in here at all. What does it matter to him?

The defiant old man lifts his chin. "Mordecai is family. Where he goes, I go."

"Then you both must leave."

Sir Surchion stiffens, taken aback by Cain's command. I personally can't keep the smile from my face.

Cain waves a hand, and in seconds two buff bouncers shoulder their way through the crowd toward us. "Escort this gentleman off the premises," Cain tells them. I'm starting to think he works here. Unless he's a frequent visitor of the Red Rooms or something.

As the guards guide Sir Surchion away, Cain turns toward me. "Let's go," he says. Ahead of us, Sir Surchion glances over his shoulder one last time. His crow does the same, and my stomach drops with worry. They know it's me who broke into their store; I can feel it. If it wasn't for me being with Cain tonight, things could have ended very differently.

Cain takes my elbow and tugs me a different way, cutting through the busy club toward the bar. As we get closer, I see the hidden door among the mirrored wall. Another exit.

I wrench my arm out of his grasp. "You know, you don't need to manhandle me. I'm capable of walking on my own."

He says nothing, only pulls open the door. As I step through, I misjudge the step and stumble forward onto the sidewalk like a fool. Cain doesn't reach for me this time. I catch myself, straighten, and push hair out of my face. "See?" I gasp as my pulse struggles to settle down. "I'm fine on my own."

He cocks a brow, amused, but doesn't say anything. The limo is there already, and I raise my chin and head straight for it. The wind howls, billowing into my hair and tugging on my skirt.

This time, Cain doesn't hold the door for me, and I'm left to climb in myself.

The leather seat is cold through my dress, but I don't care. As long as this thing gets me out of here. I can't tell what's burning worse... my cheeks from being fingered in public or my pussy because the ass never finished what he started. I'm no fool; I know he's playing his control games. Even so, he has this way of captivating me when we're close, where I fall so deep into his gaze that I'm completely lost.

Well, that was clear tonight. I must've lost my mind to let him do that to me.

To make matters worse, I bumped into Sir Surchion, of all people. Of course that old fart would visit a sex club. Gross.

My knees bounce the more I think about him. What was he going to do, anyway? Demand I return the orb? Over my dead body. That's my escape ticket when I finally shake off the demons. Until then, I make a mental note to find a better hiding spot for the orb, just in case shit flies sideways and comes right for me.

Cain climbs into the back, sitting across from me again. He has taken his jacket off and now lays it on the seat next to him. The dark shirt he wears perfectly follows the contours of his biceps, round muscular shoulders, his chest… he is incredibly stunning. Sitting wide-legged, he makes no attempt to conceal his discontent with me.

I look up at him, and the earlier fire of him tricking me in the club still burns me. "You used me," I say.

"And?" he answers in a deep voice.

"And it's wrong."

His marveled expression says it all.

"Yeah, I get it, you're a demon, but I don't appreciate being played."

"And I won't accept secrets."

For a second, we just stare at each other, and I can just imagine that if I were someone else, he might have torn me to shreds by now.

I don't back down though. "What difference does it make if I am or am not an ordinary? Will that make it easier for you to decide if you will kill me or use me?"

Lines at the corners of his eyes deepen as he tilts his head slightly forward. "People like you create drama out of nothing. It's the reason humanity is falling apart."

I glare at him. "People like me? It must be awful to be with such a low-life *like me*." The words sting, reopening old wounds of worthlessness and rejection. Even if he hasn't said them, exactly.

His wide shoulders lift in the subtlest of shrugs. "There's no need for such an overreaction. I pleasured you in public. You seemed to enjoy it."

"You had an ulterior *motive*," I snap. His blasé expression only angers me more. "Besides, I didn't seem to be the only one enjoying it. You were pitching quite a tent there, buddy."

He blinks rapidly, stunned by my reply. It's the first time I've ever seen him frazzled. It's as if I've found him with his hand in the cookie jar, and he doesn't want to admit he's been caught red handed.

His confusion quickly turns to that controlled rage and stoic mask he wears so well. I can't help but feel like he's a ticking time bomb, about to go off at any moment if I don't tread lightly.

After a long, tense moment, he says, "I assumed we could both get what we wanted out of it."

I feel used, and that makes me feel disgusting, too. I'm angry at myself for playing right into his hand, but I'm furious at him for putting me into that situation in the first place. It was a dirty trick, and we both know it.

Leaning back into the seat, I cross my arms over my chest. "Is this all just some demented game to you? A way to get your rocks off? Dress me up, take me out, parade me around like I'm arm candy, make me think—" I stop myself, realizing my feelings had been completely my own. That had been my mistake.

"Make you think what?" he presses.

I shake my head and sigh. "If you're going to kill me, I

wish you'd just hurry up and do it already. I'm tired of the bullshit."

"You really think so little of yourself?" he asks.

Fuck! That's when reality hits me. He's done it again, hasn't he? He's gotten under my skin.

"Touché." I slump lower in my seat and glance out the window at the bright city lights and people we pass on the sidewalks. "You got me, happy?"

"Not even close. I've lived a long time. I've seen worlds rise and fall. Watched suns burn out, races go extinct. Not much amuses me anymore."

"Monsters like you will always exist in the darkness and prey on the weak, right?" I say it to be biting and mean, but he appears unbothered.

He only studies me. "One cannot exist without the other. There must be dark to balance out the light."

Oh great. Like Murray, this guy's chock-full of random bits of knowledge. I can't escape it.

I roll my eyes at him. "Did you steal that from Confucius?"

He leans forward, coming so close he's practically in my lap. "You are angry tonight. It's obvious. I'll remember that depriving you of an orgasm is your trigger."

I throw him a glare.

When he pulls back from me, that dirty, challenging smirk is back, and worry starts to cling to my spine.

"Humans have a saying. 'Never go to sleep angry.' So let's fix this, shall we?" he says.

I'm not sure I like where this is going.

"Finish yourself here, now," he states. "Bring yourself to orgasm."

Is he joking? By the way his eyes gleam with excitement, I doubt it. "Are you insane? Hell no!" My heart races, while an excited tingle erupts at the base of my gut. The same one I felt back in the corridor in Purgatory.

Shit, what is wrong with me? Have some control, girl.

To my surprise, Sayah rolls around inside me, liking the idea.

You're out of your flipping mind, too, I tell her.

She wants me to take on Cain's dare and use it against him. Tease him to the point where he loses control, where I then hold the power over him. It's a fun notion, to beat him at his own game, but the idea of touching myself in front of him terrifies me.

He's toying with me again, always pushing and pushing until I crack. Wouldn't it be nice to hit him where it hurts? Right in the blue balls?

"Well?" He prods me with his question, the challenge hanging between us. Of course I'm of two minds here, but the more I stare at his cocky grin and remember what he did to me in the club, the more I want him to suffer. To pay. To be left needing something he can't have.

It's so wrong. My stomach is churning at the idea, yet my mind is screaming to do it. Best case scenario, I satisfy the emptiness he left me with and he ends up in a position of sexual starvation. Worst case scenario, I satisfy myself but my show has no impact on him. Still feels like a win to me.

I've never done anything like this before.

My skin pricks with goosebumps at the thought of touching myself in front of him. There's no way I can just spread myself open. Nope, I'll do this as lady-like as possible.

"I need music," I request, my voice shaky, and it doesn't go unnoticed by Cain. He watches me for a long pause as though he can't believe I've given in so easily. Yep, he had every intention to hold this over me, didn't he?

He turns in his seat and raps his knuckles on the black glass divider behind him, signaling for the driver. The panel slides down and Cain asks for music.

Moments later, an upbeat song sweeps out from the speakers. It stops moments later, then a slower, more seductive one begins.

"Perfect," Cain calls out over his shoulder, and the window to the driver pulls back up.

We're alone again.

Cain reaches over and taps the opposite door. A click sounds, and a small black compartment with two shelves slides out. On the top tray are two whiskey glasses and a bowl of ice. He collects a bottle of honey-colored elixir from the bottom shelf. Dropping a couple of cubes into both glasses, he pours whiskey into them, two fingers worth, then tucks the bottle away.

He hands me one and nods. "For some courage. Something tells me you're going to need it."

I want to shove it in his face, but in reality, I need to drink the whole bottle. I accept his offer, and without thinking, I press the glass to my lips and swallow the liquor in two mouthfuls.

Heat swallows me in seconds. "Oh, that's intense." I shake my head as the fire runs down my throat, leaving in its wake a smoky sweetness. I expected it to burn more than it did, though I suspect Cain only drinks top-shelf whiskey.

His laughter fills the limousine cabin. "Good girl." He takes my empty glass, then sits back, one hand on his thighs, the other swirling his glass of whiskey. The small clinking sound of ice hitting glass suits the velvety song.

A familiar intoxicating expression sweeps over his face, one filled with mischief and danger, like the one he'd given me at the club.

Licking my lips, tasting the faint traces of smoky liquor, I close my eyes to ground myself, to calm my racing heart, while the drink heats me up fast.

Sayah is close to the surface, curious how I will pull this off, so I turn my focus on the song, refusing to let doubt enter my mind.

"Tell me what you will do," he says, telling me he's a dirty talker in the bedroom.

I open my eyes, and I feel a crackling energy pour over me. "Have patience," I tease.

The way he watches me is unlike anything I'd expected. He's engrossed, addicted, as though he's forgotten about the rest of the world.

He's the predator.

And me... the prey he studies. He doesn't stop checking me out. My nipples respond instantly, pebbling and pressing against the fabric of my dress, catching his attention.

Desire comes over me in waves without me even trying, without even touching myself. It's the effect he has on me. Here I thought Dorian-the-sex-craving-incubus would be the dangerous one. Cain is a whole different level of monster, isn't he?

Taking a deep inhale, I lift my gaze and let myself be swept away by the music before my bravery fades. Images of Cain pinning me to the wall, his fingers on my heat sizzle through me.

Slowly, I raise my hands and run them over my breasts. The stroke of my nipples awakens the arousal Cain had ignited back at the club. A single wicked touch and I'll come undone.

I let my hands feather down my stomach as I lower my gaze to Cain's. His eyes lock onto my hands, following their every move. He's frozen in time, not breathing for those few seconds as my fingers reach the apex between my thighs.

Fingers curl over the dark fabric of my dress, pulling it back in slow motion, the material collecting in my hand, revealing more and more of my legs.

I don't rush.

Cain's nostrils flare as he takes a sudden raspy breath. His reaction is all I need to keep going. It heightens my confidence and makes me bolder.

Finally, my fingers brush the small mound of hair, and I slide my hand down my slick core, parting my legs only marginally. Enough to gain access but not show him too much, if I can help it.

I don't need him to say anything. I see the eagerness in his gaze. Something tells me he's going to wish he hadn't dared me.

My middle finger slips between my slit, finding my fire, my drenched core. The sweet scent of sex fills the car. A small touch, and an involuntary moan rubs over my throat.

I feel dirty.

Aroused.

So fucking horny I want to cry out.

Maybe it's selfish of me, but I take my time, my finger gliding over my clit, the silkiness of my wetness making it so deliciously easy.

The faster my strokes work, the quicker I get lost in the excitement building within me. My pussy pulses and I slide lower in my seat, my head tilting back as I grope a breast with my other hand, pinching my nipple through the fabric. Our knees touch, and the simple contact has him tensing, his fists clenching tight.

The intensity hits me fast, and now that I've jumped onto this rollercoaster of unstoppable desire, there's only one way off. And I'm climbing that steep hill.

Breaths race. I continue to rub myself, letting out more whimpers and moans. Stopping myself now is out of the question. An impossibility. My lust needs satisfying before it drives me crazy.

I lower my gaze to Cain. He's captivated, unsure where to look. One swipe of his tongue over his lips, and that's all I can think about. His head buried between my thighs, that devilish tongue lapping up my desire, tugging on my swollen lips, his mouth claiming all of me. He'll press his finger inside me, then another, and when he forces a third in, he'll take my pussy into his mouth and suck me hard while looking at me. Always holding my stare.

Pressure escalates in my core, coming so fast it takes me by surprise.

I shudder with the orgasm; the purest form of pleasure whips me away from this world. The whole limousine goes white as I clasp my eyes shut.

I scream, quivering, clenching my thighs together. I never stop rubbing my clit, elongating the most incredible climax. My body stiffens and I'm miles away, floating on waves of ecstasy. My toes curl, and I arch my back. Satisfaction radiates from every inch of my body, and I gasp loudly at how amazing it feels, to make sure Cain knows exactly what he's missing out on.

Breathing heavily, I lay there for a few moments, eyes shut, my body buzzing. I let myself believe I'm anywhere but in the back of a limousine, drowning in the bliss washing over me.

When I open my eyes, I steel myself at the sight of Cain watching me. Something about him has changed. His eyes are completely black, his chest rising and falling rapidly, and he's inched forward in his seat.

That's when I notice his clenched hand is bleeding.

Dark stains color his pants, there are ice cubes on the floor, and glass shards are scattered everywhere.

He broke his whiskey glass. There's no pain on his face, only hunger and flickers of his own internal battle... Not touching me right now is torture for him.

I grin.

I ease my fingers from my slick heat, readjusting the dress to cover myself back up. During the orgasm, my breast must have popped out, because my nipple is on full display and intensely erect. Shyly, I quickly tuck her back in. I don't know why I'm blushing when I just played myself like a fiddle in front of a demon. Apparently, I'm capable of a lot more seduction than I ever thought possible.

The high I'm still floating down from is unbelievable. I'm loving how the orgasm still tingles through me.

Sitting upright, I collect myself and smile at him. He hasn't said a word, so I break the silence. "You're right about what you said earlier. I'm going to sleep like a baby now."

Then I glance down to the erection straining in his pants and smirk at his discomfort.

But for him... It looks like he's in for a restless night.

CHAPTER ELEVEN
CAIN

I stand outside Aria's bedroom in the mansion, shrouded in shadows. The guard standing feet away doesn't make a sound. Yet here I remain after escorting her back.

She's more devil than me tonight, having played me when I least expected it. She called my bluff and won. I can't take that from her, but it seems I can't resist her either. She's that fucking incredible.

My mind floods with images of her writhing in arousal, stroking that tight little pussy. When her breast slipped free from her dress, tipped with the rosiest of nipples, my cock punched in my pants. I lost myself—something that *never* happens. Not to me.

It took every ounce of restraint I had to not claim her then and there. To force those sexy legs apart and fuck her into Hell and back. Coupled with her sweet scent of sex, I don't know how I resisted, but fuck—now she's imprinted on my mind, filling my senses. Back at Purgatory, she was a lamb, vulnerable and under my control. I loved that. But in the limousine...

Damn! There she became someone else, and now I crave that side of her with every fiber of my being.

My cock twitches with desperation to unleash the build-up within me that she stirred. That, coupled with the new cuts on my palm from the busted glass, has me facing two annoyances. This temptation is not what I want to deal with, and neither is getting so fucking hard that my balls turn blue.

I walked into that trap. I see it now.

But that's fine. She can keep this win. Never again, though. Next time I'll have her stripped and screaming before she knows what's good for her.

If she is working for my father, then I need to toe this dangerous line between us cautiously. Don't let her know I'm on to her and Lucifer's trick while figuring her out. If she's not part of his loyalist legion, then there could be a chance her unique gifts can help us. Especially if what Elias says is true and the harp's string reacted to her in some way.

It all has to mean something. But what, I don't know.

I turn abruptly and march down the hall, seething that she'd bested me. No matter how much I tell myself it doesn't bother me, it's a fucking lie. It stings like a bitch.

ARIA

One moment I'm sleeping, the next my eyes snap open to the morning sun drenching my room through the window. I lay there for the longest moment, trying to remember where I am. Half my mind still lags in sleep, and when it finally catches up, so does last night with Cain.

I should cringe at what happened, but instead I smirk,

and a delicious tingle starts at the base of my spine. Who would have thought I'd be an exhibitionist? I surprise myself every day. Though it did feel incredible to beat him at his own game.

The moment Cain walked me to my room and shut me in, I stripped and fell onto the bed. Then I was out like a light, and that had to be one of the best sleeps I've had in too long.

I shift onto my back and roll right into someone lying next me. They moan like a bear.

Heart catapulting against my ribcage and back, I throw the blanket off me and scramble out of bed quick smart. I whip around to find Elias snoring away, flopping onto his back, taking up the whole bed. He's dressed in normal clothes, like he somehow stumbled in here while drunk and just crashed into the first bed he found. Except my room is locked. Or it's supposed to be. Maybe Cain had forgotten to lock it? In all honesty, I don't remember what happened once I hit the bed.

I snatch a pillow and whack it across Elias's head. "Why are you in my bed?"

He moans, moving as slow as a snail, scrunching up his face before sliding open one eye to look at me. Sleep clings to his eyes, and his dark hair messy.

"You're naked," he groans out and collapses back into sleep, snoring like a beast.

"What the fuck!" I whack him in the face a few more times for good measure, then storm into the bathroom to drag on the only clothes I have in there. Day-worn skinny jeans and a white tee that hangs off one shoulder, plus my bra. No underwear. I'll live. I'm not used to waking up next to a man, let alone finding a demon in my bed.

When I step out of the bathroom, I find Elias sitting on

the edge, leaning forward, elbows on his thighs, head hanging low like he's been drinking.

"Hard night?" I throw at him, brimming with sarcasm.

He twists his head to look at me, shadows dancing under his dark eyes. "Weren't you just naked? Should have stayed like that. Suits you better."

I roll my eyes at him. "So how'd you end up in here? Had a long night of furry debauchery during a full moon, then lost your way to your own bedroom?"

"You got something against fur?" He pushes up his shoulders and straightens his back, stretching. I hear bones crack.

"Not at all. I'm not going to hold it against you if you're into furries. That's your gig, dude. I just want to know why you ended up in my bed."

A smirk tugs on his full lips, and he looks at me so sexily, my knees soften. There's mischief swimming behind his gaze—not what I expected from Mr. Hellhound.

"Don't worry, baby cheeks, if I wanted to fuck you, I'd wake you first. I'm not into somnophilia."

I should be shocked, but I'm getting used to them not holding their tongues around me. He pushes himself to his feet and shoves a hand through his messy hair.

"You coming for breakfast or going to stand there trying to work out what somnophilia means?"

I stiffen and march out of the room after him, thrilled to be let out for something as normal as breakfast.

"You're a rude bastard in the morning, aren't you? And of course I know what it means." I don't have a clue, but from the context, I assume it has something to do with making a move on someone sleeping… or is that the word for creepy jerks who have sex with the dead? I cringe and my stomach turns. Why did I even think that? Surely that's not what he meant.

"You going to tell me what you did last night? Drink too much?" I ask, catching up to him as we weave down the grand staircase. The waft of bacon finds me, and my stomach growls with ravishing hunger.

"It takes a lot to get us even a little tipsy," he says.

"That wasn't an outright 'no' to my question, so…"

"Do you always sleep naked?" he interrupts me, clearly avoiding the subject.

I cut him a hard stare. "That's none of your business."

"Oh really?"

His long strides have me struggling to keep up. "You can't just pop into my bedroom in the middle of the night and decide to have a sleepover. It's not right."

Elias doesn't answer but laughs to himself.

He marches up ahead of me now and right into the dining room, while I look around for something to throw at him. All I find is a vase on a wooden table. As much as I'd enjoy seeing it break over his head, I resist.

Instead, I storm in after him, clenching my teeth. But then the spread of food on the long dining table captures my attention, and I forget everything else.

The anger.

Him perving on me naked.

How much of an ass he's being this morning.

Bacon is now my focus. A plate piled high with it calls my name. Along with pancakes and eggs, and all of it smothered in maple syrup.

Shut up and hand me the fork. I'm sitting across from Elias in seconds, helping myself to food. One of the female maids, the one with mousey hair and kind eyes, fills my cup with the elixir of the gods.

"Cream with the coffee?" she asks.

"Please." I reach for the bottle of syrup and drench my

meal. I'm salivating at the sight and the sugary smell in the air.

"Want some food with that diabetes?" Elias states, but I don't have time for his annoyance.

I'm so freaking hungry, I dig in and cherish every damn bite. Salt and sweet mingling on my tongue is heaven. Those freaks who don't let this syrup ambrosia touch their eggs are just that… freaks.

"You sound like you're about to climax at the table. Wouldn't surprise me, seeing you did so in the limousine last night."

I freeze, fork halfway to my mouth. "W-what did you just say?" Inside, I'm shriveling up into a husk of myself from embarrassment.

He takes a big bite of bacon and chews it, staring at me with mirth in his expression. When he finally swallows, he reaches for another long strip. "There are no secrets within these walls. Cain told me the moment he walked into the mansion last night about your little *show*."

"That bastard," I scoff. "And for your information, he dared me to do it." My cheeks are suddenly burning.

"Glad to see you're not chickenshit," he answers, sounding impressed.

I frown at him. "Whatever, you weren't there so you don't get to comment."

I return to eating, but my stomach sours. I shift through the rest of the meal without looking at him, but I sense him watching me the entire time. Is that why he ended up in my room? Expecting me to somehow put out or something, because I was some horny girl? He's in for a rude awakening then. Sure, we kissed once and it was insanely good, but it had been a lapse in judgement.

When I decide I can't take it anymore, I lift my gaze to Elias. He's on his fourth plate and still going strong. "I'd like a phone to call my friend. Maybe you have a charger for my cell, and I can use that?"

He stares at me as he shovels more food into his mouth, then he shakes his head.

"Cain said I can call my friend."

He thinks about that for a long pause, wipes his mouth with a napkin, then pushes away from the table. "Come with me."

I all but leap out of my chair. Just the thought of talking to someone outside these walls makes excitement buzz inside me. I follow Elias out of the dining room, across the foyer, and into a more crowded space at the front of the house. Not quite a living room—there's too many antiques and expensive-looking pieces of furniture for it to be considered something that normal—but it does have walls of built-in bookshelves and couches.

It doesn't matter what they call it, really. My gaze finds what I'm looking for instantly: a phone perched on a side table. To fit the old, Victorian motif that seems to run through this place, it's one of those black standing kinds, with a turn dial and separate earpiece.

I laugh.

"What's so funny?" Elias asks, hovering close.

"This is a joke, right?" I ask. When he doesn't reply, another chuckle escapes. "How in the world am I supposed to use that?"

"Would you prefer smoke signals? It'll be slower."

"Where do you live? The stone age? Have none of you heard of a cell phone?"

His one brow with the scar arches. "Of course I have. Own one, too. That doesn't mean I'm going to let you use it."

I huff and turn back to the antique phone. Guess this will have to do.

Sitting on the couch, I pluck the receiver out of the holder and fiddle with the rotator dial, turning in Joseline's number. God, imagine having to dial someone in an emergency using this phone.

Elias watches my every move with extreme curiosity.

"Do you mind?" I ask him. "Some privacy, please."

He snorts. "Really?"

I glare at him as crackling sounds in the speaker by my ear.

"Fine." He walks out of the room, but with his super animal hearing, there's no doubt in my mind he can listen in if he wants to.

"Hello?" The moment the jingle of Joseline's sweet voice sounds through the static, my heart beats faster.

"Joseline? It's me," I start, moving closer to the cone-shaped receiver, but she's quick to cut me off.

"Aria? Oh my God. Where are you? Are you okay? I've been calling your phone like mad! It goes right to voicemail every time! What's going on?" Her questions come rapid-fire. Only when she takes a breath am I able to slip in a reply.

"I know. I know. It's a lot to explain right now, but I'm okay. My cell is dead—"

"When are you coming back? We didn't even get to celebrate your birthday. I spotted a rent sign downtown, next to the library."

There she goes again, talking a mile a minute in a single breath. I smile at the familiarity of it, even in my fucked-up situation.

"Joseline, listen to me," I say over her endless chatter. "I'm okay, but I'm stuck. Murray—the fucker—traded me to demons to pay his gambling debts and who knows what else. I've been here since my birthday."

"Wait, demons?" she squeaks.

"Yeah, and that's not a figure of speech or anything. Real, Hell-made demons of the underworld."

For the first time in... well, *ever,* Joseline is quiet. Rendered speechless isn't something she's capable of. At least before now.

I glance out the doorway, where I'm sure Elias is eaves-dropping somewhere out of sight, and lower my voice. "Don't worry about me. I'm going to get out of here."

There's another few seconds of stiff silence, but then she responds. "Murray, what a slimeball."

Understatement of the century there.

"Can I see you, at least? Do they have you locked in a cage or something?"

"No cage. I'm mostly just bored out of my mind," I say. "And it's not safe for you to come here. One of them is a freaking hellhound, and I think he may be into furries."

A light shuffle sounds outside the room.

"And where's 'here' exactly?" Her voice trembles. "I don't like this, Aria. Not at all. How long do you have to be there, anyw—"

A sharp click sounds, abruptly cutting off Joseline's voice. I look up to find Elias standing there with his finger on the lever. He's hung up on her in the middle of our conversation, and I didn't even hear him sneak up on me.

"What did you do that for?" I reach over to dial her number again, but he snatches the phone and yanks the line out of the wall. He takes the receiver from my hand too.

"That's long enough," is all he says.

While I wonder if it's because of the furries comment, the seriousness plastered to his face hints at something else entirely.

"You cannot disclose the location of this house to anyone," he says through a clenched jaw.

"Joseline's my friend—"

"*Anyone.*" He snarls the word, eyes glowing yellow. I jump back. He's taller and bigger than me in every way. On size alone, he's intimidating as fuck. Add in all those scars, tattoos, and the fact that he can turn into a bloodthirsty animal at will, and I know I need to be careful with this demon. Maybe a little more so than the other two.

"Come," he says. His voice has changed to something less refined, something more guttural and animalistic. "It's time for you to return to your room."

DORIAN

Of course he'd make me wait. The arrogant bastard.

I check my watch for about the fifth time. It's approaching thirty minutes past the time Maverick wrote on the note, and my annoyance is quickly turning to anger. In the early hours of the morning, a thick fog clings to the earth, the autumn mist dense enough to soak through my jacket and chill me to the bone.

He's making me wait on purpose. I know it. The moment I strode into my room and smelled the distinct sulfur scent, I knew Maverick's note was soon to arrive. Surprise surprise, a second later, there was a flash of flame on my side table as the folded piece of parchment popped into this plane.

Ignoring it was always an option—and a tempting one—but the last time Cain's asshole brother sent a note to me through the veil, he'd offered me a way back to Hell. But just me, and that in itself had made me refuse.

Why only me? I have no idea. Maverick may be the demon of Greed, or Avarice if you wanted to be fancy about it, but he's sneaky as fuck. I didn't trust him as far as I could throw him. But I might be able to garner some information on Hell—*home*—from whatever he has to say.

So here I am. Standing on the wrong side of the veil in front of Hell's sealed gate, waiting for Maverick to show up and waste my time some more.

I'm smacked in the face with the immense heat and sulfur scent of home. A familiar red-orange glow appears in the rock of the mountainside, temporarily turning molten as Maverick approaches. His demonic form is silhouetted against the light, his curved horns and elongated limbs shrinking to more human-like proportions the closer to Earth he gets, and soon he stands before me in a polished white-on-white suit. It matches his platinum blond, almost silver, hair. His eyes, though, are as dark as his soul.

The gate seals behind him, cutting off the heat, and I feel the biting cold of the morning again. Maverick adjusts his lapels and sleeve cuffs, unrushed and unbothered that he's kept me waiting so long.

"You're late." My annoyance bites as much as the cold. "Again."

He shrugs his shoulders. "I wasn't sure you'd show."

That's bullshit and he knows it. It's clear by the smile splitting his lips. He knew I'd come; he has all the leverage, after all. And he enjoys making me wait on him.

"What is this about, Mav? Need to borrow more money?"

His grin quickly transforms into a scowl. Want to piss off Greed incarnate? Mention money and how bad he is at keeping it. Gets him every time.

"Fuck off," he snaps. "I've come on behalf of my father."

That stuns me for a moment, and I stand there in silence. Lucifer sent him? The very asshole we tried to dethrone, the one who banished us to Earth? This is going to be fun.

"What in the underworld does he want?" I growl.

Another frigid breeze rustles through the trees. Maverick lifts his head and glances around the dark sky, his expression full of disgust. When we were first dropped on Earth, we hated everything about it, too. It's so different from Hell, which breeds such a deep-seated stigma of the living that his reaction doesn't come as a surprise.

When his gaze falls onto me again, he says, "Do you remember the proposition I'd given you before? About returning home?"

"And leaving my friends behind? Yeah, I remember your shitty excuse for a deal."

"Well, Lucifer has sweetened the pot. The dog is welcome to come back as well," he replies.

"Elias?" Sure, I make animal jokes about him all the time, but for some reason, hearing Maverick do it makes my anger prick. "And what about Cain? I'm not leaving him behind, and I know Elias would agree."

That mischievous twinkle sparks in his eyes again. The one I fucking hate. "Ah, you see, that's the beauty of it. You won't have to worry about my brother at all."

I cock my head and wait for him to go on.

"He must be disposed of."

My next inhale chokes me. I can't have heard him right. He really didn't have the balls to suggest such a thing to me… did he? "Ex-Excuse me?"

"You heard me," he insists. "Kill Cain and the two of you can return to Hell."

I stay like that for a long moment, my anger bubbling inside me the more I wait and let his words dig their claws in. Family doesn't mean jack to demons, but I can't help but wonder why Lucifer wants us to do this. Why us, and why just Cain? We'd all defied him by plotting the uprising and mutiny.

To torture us is the only reason I can come up with. Have us betray Cain like Lucifer feels his son tried to do to him. Kill his son. It is cruel. It is devious. It has Lucifer written *all* over it.

"You're both out of your fucking minds." The words explode from my mouth as my fury continues to build and rise. I'd never backstab Cain. Never. Even if offered all seven levels of Hell with every virgin soul as the cherry on top. My friendship with Cain went further back than Elias's, but I know he wouldn't hesitate to reject the offer either. We all made a pact before the takeover attempt that we'd stick together in this, no matter the consequences.

"My brother has become a nuisance. Even on this plane, Father doesn't like the power you all have managed to get ahold of, and I don't blame him." He eyes my Ralph Lauren clothing and scoffs. "Doesn't seem like a punishment at all."

We had to scrape and scrounge for decades for what we have now, but I'm not going to tell him that.

"I don't understand why Father doesn't just kill you all, but Cain seems to be his main focus. So, before he takes care of him himself, he wants to offer this opportunity to you and the hellhound. To… please the masses." A twisted grin spreads his thin lips.

There it is. The real reason for this. Lucifer doesn't want to kill us—any of us—because he knows we're popular among the other demons. Our plans created unrest, and he's afraid of a revolution. He's unstable. Picking a war with Heaven is suicide, but Lucifer doesn't care about any of that. He never did. His hunger for vengeance stems back to when God struck him down and ripped off his wings. And us trying to stop him from retaliating got us evicted.

With Hell supporting us, he can't touch us right now. But if we take each other out, it looks like our alliance, as well as our cause, was never sturdy to begin with.

It's very clever on his part, but not unpredictable. Will Lucifer eventually get fed up enough to come after us himself? I have no doubt. But until then, I'm not in any rush to get back to Hell. Especially if that path is paved in my closest friend's blood.

"You can go ahead and tell Lucifer to go fuck himself. I'm not interested," I snap and turn away. I'm about to start my long walk through the thick woods, back toward the clearing where a car waits, when Maverick calls out to me once more.

"He's your king! The ruler of the underworld and the damned."

I clench my teeth, remembering what we went through and the things Lucifer did that make him a fucking monster, even to demons.

"Not anymore." I don't even hesitate or spare him one more look. Just keep trudging on through the thick brush of the woods, following the car's dimmed headlights as a guide.

The next time another Hell note poofs into my room, it's getting tossed into the fireplace, right onto the flames. Right back where it belongs.

CHAPTER TWELVE

ARIA

Three days of utter boredom.

The demons are rarely home during the day, and at night after dinner, I'm locked in my room. This isn't living, now is it? At this stage, I might willingly throw myself into Hell for sheer entertainment. Things are becoming predictable too. Every morning, I wake up with Elias in my bed. He's on his side, never touching me, but he refuses to tell me why he's there. Part of me is starting to suspect that he doesn't know either.

Another routine I've noticed seems to be that once it hits eleven p.m., the guard outside my door slips away and doesn't return. He thinks I don't hear him, but I'm sitting with my back to the door listening. Every night without fail.

None of the demons will tell me anything else, but I'm starting to piece together the threads. Picking up small whispers here and there. Several times I've heard them mention strings right after they talk about a relic. It has to be the one I found down in the lower grounds of the mansion. It's important to them, which has me moving over to the wardrobe where I hid my own relic. I pull open the door and dive into the back corner under the blankets where I stash my satchel. With it in hand, I flop on my bed and switch on the lamp. The small chandelier in my room isn't bright enough once night falls.

Digging around in my bag, I pull out the orb. It's round and so beautiful, the dark mercury inside swaying back and forth. The object buzzes under my touch.

"Clossssse," it hisses over my thoughts, and a shiver runs down my back.

"What do you mean?" I study the object, running my fingers over its cold, smooth surface.

"Clossssse," the word comes again. I remember the demons' conversations, then an idea pops into my mind. What would happen if the orb and the golden cord were brought together?

I can almost hear dramatic movie music in my head, a sure sign I'm going mad from being alone too long. Maybe it's a need to do something, or maybe it's curiosity that has me pushing the orb into the front pocket of my hooded jersey and putting on my boots. The clock on the wall states it's ten past eleven, so the guard is long gone. In haste, I pick the lock to the door and am out in no time.

The corridor I found the first time isn't hard to forget… especially not with my twitching toe leading the way. I march down the grand stairs and then follow the maze of corridors. In reality, the passage only goes one way with smaller corridors shooting outward, but they are all dead ends. I see that now. Personally, I don't understand how there can be so many rooms down here compared to the size of the house, but I'm underground, so anything is possible, I guess.

The number of doors I pass intrigues me, yet instinct tells me to steer clear. Elias mentioned Pandora's box last time he caught me down me down here… what if all these rooms hold dark secrets I don't want to know about? Murdered figures from those they sucked souls from? Not that it smells like rotting bodies or anything, but I let it go for now.

Quickly, I rush onward, checking over my shoulder at every turn. My skin pricks with goosebumps and my stomach churns at being down here again, considering how pissed Elias was last time. But no one seems to be in the mansion, and I'll be fast. No one will suspect a thing.

Silent steps bring me through the dimly lit passages, which now smell like freshly dug earth for some reason. Up ahead there are hessian sacks of soil slumped up against the wall, at least a dozen of them. I guess that explains the smell. What are they doing with all of these sacks? There are no markings on them to work out where they came from.

I pause and look around, fear collecting in my chest. Did I take a wrong turn somewhere? I don't remember there being any sacks of soil last time.

It's dead silence down here.

With no time to waste, I keep going forward, turning left and right as the passage takes me, scanning every small corridor I pass. They are all the same—dark and empty—but it isn't long before the beautiful luring song I heard last time finds me again.

The soft, sorrowful melody floats on the air like a breeze, curling around me, calling me. And the orb seems to respond, vibrating in my pocket.

"Closerrrrr," it buzzes in my skull, and I flinch at the sudden voice.

I won't deny it, it's unsettling to be down in the demons' underground lair trying not to be found while having an eerie voice whisper *'closer'* over my thoughts.

This is how horror movies start, and like those idiotic girls, I'm going to go toward the danger instead of away from it.

Breathing faster now, I clench my teeth and keep going. I'm determined to find out what is going on with the demons and these objects and me.

The next corner has the orb humming frantically in my pocket and the string's song growing louder, and I know this is the right place. I swing down toward the same black door and grab the handle. It resists, and I curse under my breath.

Damn Elias. He locked it, I bet.

Lucky for me, I've become quite a wiz with a hair pin, so I crouch and pull one out of my pocket. When the door unlocks, I push to go inside slowly. Part of me can't help but think Elias put a booby trap or something in here in case of my return.

The door swings open with a squeal that leaves me cringing as the sounds echo all around me. Light from the hallway at my back steals the darkness in the room, revealing just the single table and box like last time.

"Closerrrrr. Closerrrrr. Closerrrrr."

"Hold your horses," I murmur and step into the room in slow motion. No attack or trap. Several more steps, and I'm standing in front of the engraved box. I flip it open, and before me lies the thin, golden cord on a bed of black silk, curled around itself like a serpent.

I retrieve the orb from my pocket, and in that same heartbeat, it stops vibrating and the music in my head flatlines.

My stomach flip-flops with anticipation, but my instinct tells me this is right. I stretch my hand, holding the orb toward the other relic.

The magnetic pull between the two objects is instant. It

wrenches the orb from my grasp with unimaginable strength.

I flinch backward, unsure what to expect. My eyes remain glued to the objects, which seem to move together in a strange dance, swirling around one another. My breath catches in my throat as I watch with intrigue.

There's a sharp metallic and electric tang in the air. It's so strong, I taste it on my tongue. It's the sudden snap of dark magic flaring around me. At the same time, the cord coils itself around the orb, the tail end fusing right into it. They're merging, and now the orb now has a thin, golden tail.

Then it collapses on the black silk and sits there. Gingerly, I reach over and prod the orb with my finger. A prickling of energy races up my hand from the touch, just as it had before. But when I wrap my hand around it, there's now a warmth to the surface.

"Careful." This time, when the voice emerges in my mind, it's different. No longer an ear-splitting tune, it's melodic, morphed with the cord's sweetly sad song. It's so much more beautiful now. My orb has become a singsong siren, it seems. I don't know what to make of the merging or what these objects even are in the first place.

But I know they are important. They have to be—why else would the demons keep their relic down here and be so touchy when I found it?

"Danger!"

My heart somersaults in my chest. Frantically, I shove the orb with the tail into my pocket, thankful it's no bigger than my fist, and swing around. I expect someone in the doorway, except it's empty.

I expel a sigh of relief and hurry the hell out of there, locking the door behind me. Had the orb miscalculated the danger? I don't risk it and break into a run, one hand pressed to my pocket to keep the relics from jiggling about.

Careening around every corner, my heart beats faster when footfalls sound behind me.

Fuck! Someone was down there with me this whole time? What the hell? Fear spikes and I dart faster than I thought possible, looking over my shoulder constantly.

As I burst out from the last passage, rushing toward the stairs that lay farther ahead to my left, I look back.

A dark, long shadow stretches outward from around the corridor I left seconds earlier.

My skin crawls.

I sprint forward and swing up the stairs, taking them two at a time. I barely feel the ache in my thighs from how fast I spring up to the next floor. Without looking back, I jolt down the hall and burst into my room. With the door shut behind me, I shove a chair under the handle and step back.

Heart beating too fast, I charge toward the wardrobe and quickly push the two magical relics into my satchel and back into my hiding spot.

A thunderous knock pounds on the door.

I jump in my skin, frantically covering everything with the blankets and shut the wardrobe.

The door handle rattles. "Open the door, Aria!" Elias bellows out in the hallway.

Fuckity fuck fuck. Of course it's him. Thanks, universe.

With my best soft voice, I reply, "Why? What's going on?"

"Open it now or I'll smash it down," he growls.

Fear strangles me, but I won't back down. "Give me a freaking second to put some clothes on, geez." I mess up my hair and kick off my sneakers, shoving them under the bed. Sayah is just below the surface, pushing to come out, but that will only raise suspicion.

I pad across the floorboards and pull the chair aside, then open the door, forcing a fake yawn. "Where's the fire?" I rub my eyes for effect. "Why are you banging on my door like a lunatic?"

Elias is heaving for breath in the hallway. He shoves a hand to the door, causing it to slam open and hit the inside of the wall.

"I warned you what happens when you break the rules. You get punished." His nose wrinkles while his lips twist into a scowl. His hair is wild and dark, his hands dusty with soil. So he's the one bringing all that earth into the mansion's basement.

I recoil, my breaths like tar, sticking to my insides and not coming out fast enough. "I don't know what you're talking about. I've been here—"

"Why were you near the entrance to the tunnels again? The basement? Your scent is all over the place down there."

Damn. He sniffed me out.

Still, I stare at him with forced confusion, continuing my act. "I just woke up."

Not buying it, he marches right up to me. His massive form towers over my five-foot-five height, and instinctually, I back away until my legs smack into the bed.

He lashes out, grabs me by the shoulders and swings me around to face away from him. He steps up behind me, pressing his hard chest to my back. His breath is in my ear, and all I can smell is his musky, spicy, earthy scent. Hell, it smells divine.

"I'm beginning to think you want to be punished," he scolds, his cheek so close I feel the stubble on his jaw against my neck.

I stiffen. He releases me fast, and I'm sucking in air as

his large hands slide around my waist and pop open the button of my jeans, pulling at the zipper next.

Fear collides into me, because clearly the kind of punishment he is talking about is not okay in my books. No matter how delicious he smells.

I shove my elbow into his ribs, but he doesn't budge.

"The more you fight, the more it'll hurt."

"Don't you touch me." I stomp down on his foot, and he winces. A slight ease of his grasp over my arm and I throw myself away from him, my eyes glued on the open door.

Sayah hovers on the edge, about to hop out the second I give her the okay. It's been so long since I've let her out, her dark presence feels more powerful. I know she wants to help me—help us—but I tell her to stay put. She pushes against my control. If she really tries, I might not be able to hold her back this time, and that scares me.

Elias snatches me by the back of my shirt and wrenches me backward. I scream, and my feet stumble before my back crashes right into his rock-solid chest.

"Actions have consequences," he tells me.

I yell out, writhing against him while the bastard laughs.

His fingers drop into the top of my jeans fast, and he hauls them down my legs, exposing my butt to him before I can react.

Heart thumping, I swing around with my fist leading the way, but he has me off my feet, the other arm sweeping under the front of my legs.

In seconds, he's sitting on the edge of my bed and I'm laying across his lap, my ass bare and in the air. I feel so exposed.

A large hand pats my right ass cheek almost intimately. Then he lifts his palm and brings it back down hard, connecting with the middle of my bottom, almost evenly across both cheeks, the sound loud and sting terrible.

I draw in a shocked breath and go deathly still, my whole body tensing. *He's spanking me?*

I hiss from the sting and try to roll off his lap, but he clamps an arm over my lower back, holding me firmly in place. Bent over his lap and vulnerable.

"What the hell?" When I crane my head around to look at him, there's a quirk to his lips, a gleam in his eyes. He's fucking enjoying himself at my expense. "Let me go!" I roar.

"You think this is a joke?" His gaze shifts to my rear and his hand comes down fast and hard. There it is again, the threat of more to come carefully wrapped in a flirtatious manner.

My scream is accompanied by a warm, melting sensation in the pit of my gut, a buzz traveling over the slick of my heat. What is wrong with me? Him slapping me shouldn't come with stimulation, but with each loud smack, my clit pulses. My breath hitches with each hit. I squirm to get away, but he's holding on strongly.

He awakens something within me, a deep-seated craving I never knew existed.

"Stay still." There's a tinge of arousal to his voice.

Instinctively, my hips rise to meet his large palm, waiting, longing for another delicious strike, my pussy clenching with unbearable need.

I hear him suck in a rapid breath. He knows the reaction he's created in me. There's no hiding the fact that not only am I an exhibitionist, but I love being spanked. Who in the world am I? I don't know myself anymore.

With each strike, a whimpering moan slips past my lips while adrenaline soars through my veins. But I refuse to give in to him so easily. I shove against him, punch his legs, anything to escape. Which only leads to him slapping me faster.

His cock hardens beneath my stomach. Is this meant to be punishment, or fulfillment of his dirty fetish?

When he finally stops, his hand slides over my ass cheeks tenderly, rubbing over my burning, bare skin. His fingers skillfully trace along my crack and dip just enough between my legs to leave me gasping.

"I like the look of this pink color on your ass."

I don't move—*can't* move—as my pulse thumps over my clit. I'm soaking wet, and my emotions make no sense to me. Elias is something else… I can barely breathe. I can't believe he just did that to me.

"You'll think twice before disobeying me again, won't you?" he says. "Though I rather like the way you look right now, so I encourage you to break the rules at every chance you get."

I don't even know how to respond. He lifts me off him and onto my feet. I scramble to lift my pants back up and cover myself, zipping my jeans. My ass is raw and hurts, but I don't even care because I'm seriously on the brink of an orgasm. I struggle to look at him at first, flames crawling over my face from embarrassment that he treated me like a child, yet I got turned on by it.

Elias gets to his feet, so tall and fucking handsome that it takes every thread of strength I have to not drag him over to me, to keep myself from spearing my fingers through his wild hair and kissing him.

"Goodnight, Aria." He strolls past me.

My mouth drops open. "Really?" I turn to watch him step into the hallway, then he looks over his shoulder at me.

"Would it really be punishment if you didn't feel pain?"

That filthy smirk returns before he laughs at me and shuts the door, vanishing from sight.

With my heart clenching, I groan loudly, unable to believe what he just did. Unable to believe myself. What the hell is with these demons and teasing me relentlessly, then walking away?

Quickly, I push the chair up against the door, then rip off my jeans. If I don't finish myself off, I might very well die of a stroke with how fast my heart is racing.

And I hate that his stupid punishment has worked after all.

My eyes flip open to the morning sunshine drenching my room, my mind still consumed with what happened last night. I mean, I should be consumed by what the two relics joining implies, except I can't stop thinking about Elias spanking me.

Something is wrong with me to have enjoyed his punishment.

A loud snore erupts from someone in the bed next to me.

I grit my teeth and twist my head to find Elias sleeping. The fuck!?

I'm up on my feet in seconds, still in my pajamas, glaring at a fully-dressed Elias. At my door, the chair I'd propped up to keep him out lays smashed into pieces.

The bastard smashed his way in here and I didn't hear a sound? How deep had I been asleep? After finishing myself off, I fell asleep moments afterward.

I cross the room, stepping over the debris, and wrench open the door with a busted doorknob.

A guard stands there, but what use is he?

He raises an eyebrow at me. “Something wrong?”

I glance back to my bed, then back at him. He’s smirking.

“Get your head out of the gutter. Can you get him out of here?”

He shakes his head. He doesn't answer to me, after all. One of his bosses is in my bed.

So, I swing around and march back into my room. I lay my hands on Elias’s arm and shake the hell out of him.

“Get up!”

He snaps awake and jolts upright so fast that I back away, a sliver of dread curling in my gut. For those few seconds after he wakes he’s lost, looking around and trying to remember where he is.

Breathing heavily, he pushes his hair out of his face, then stands as his gaze finally lands on me. “Morning,” he groans. Then he struts out of my room.

What in the world? He seriously has something wrong with him. He’s like Dr. Jekyll and Mr. Hyde. Two sides on the same demon coin.

I then turn to the guard and ask, “Was this room once Elias’s bedroom?” Figure it might explain why he keeps ending up sleeping in my bed.

He shakes his head. “It’s always been for guests.”

So much for that theory. I shut the door, that no longer locks, and head into the bathroom to shower and get ready. The whole time, I keep going over the relics merging. Then Elias's strange behavior with his sleeping, the sacks of soil in the corridors under the house. What exactly are these demons doing?

I eat breakfast alone. It seems that I’m now permitted to

eat in the dining room by myself—under the watchful eye of a guard, of course. There's no sign of any of the demons. Afterward, I wander into the front parlor room and flop onto the couch in front of the fire, the guard watching over me from the doorway. He isn't dragging me back to my room, which is a huge bonus, so I enjoy the moment, taking the time to study the books on the shelves. Most look like ancient encyclopedias. Others are an eclectic collection of gardening, city architecture, cooking, and fashion. Then I spot a few classics and grab *Wuthering Heights.* I have no idea why the demons own this, but it's better than reading about how to raise goats. These demons are strange; so much about them doesn't make sense.

Hours pass as I curl up on the couch, keeping warm and reading, the pile of books near me growing. Finally, I get up and stretch, my spine clicking from being cramped up too long.

My guard hasn't moved and looks like he has fallen asleep on his feet. The familiar sound of the front door shutting echoes through the room, and I hurry to check out who it is out of pure boredom. Seriously, I can't live like this, with my life wasting away.

Cain emerges from the foyer, his head lifting, eyes meeting mine as I step out of the room.

My heart skips a beat at his presence, and my feet freeze, stuck to the floor. Something about him affects me so deeply, it's hard to comprehend his influence over me.

"Why aren't you in your room?" he asks as he peels off his black leather gloves, then shrugs off his long coat. A maid comes out of the shadows and collects them from him. Underneath he wears all black, like he always seems to do. A fitted button-up shirt follows the curves of his built arms and strong chest, tapering in at his waist. His tailored pants look freshly pressed, the belt buckle depicts a silver flame, and his shoes shine. Despite having just come in from outside, his hair remains immaculate—brushed off his face, short at the sides, and those eyes... Oh, those captivating eyes draw me to him. If I had to picture the devil on Earth, seductive and wickedly dangerous, this is how I'd picture him. Exactly as Cain.

He steps forward, and I mentally slap myself for letting these demons get into my head so easily.

"I'm bored to death," I say, ignoring his question about why I'm not in my room. "And I need more, Cain. I am not cut out for a life of sitting around and reading books. Pretty soon I will become dusty bones."

He studies me up and down, then strides past me and right into the room I'd been in for most of the day. I'm on his heels, both of us ending up in front of the enormous stone hearth.

"Is there a way to void a demon deal?" I ask, glancing up at him. "Something I can do to cancel it out?" With me wearing no shoes, I feel so much shorter than Cain, and it reminds me of my place in the relationship and how much of a disadvantage I am at in comparison.

"The only way out is by killing the demon, or in your case, *demons,* who own the contract." He cuts me a narrowing gaze, challenging me again.

"Could be fun." I laugh nervously, but I know it's an impossible feat. Kill all three demons? Yeah, that's out of the question.

To my surprise, a slow, calculated smile twists his lips. "I'd like to see you try."

I swallow past the knot in my throat. Even when talking about death, he finds a way to make my knees weak and my chest ungodly tight. I'm literally flirting with a devil here.

I am starting to think I have a death wish or something.

"Okay, another option then. If I'm here for the rest of my life, what am I supposed to do *for life?* I always thought when a demon owned your soul, they only came to collect when a person died. Maybe you can release me, and I'll see you again when I'm on my deathbed. Deal?"

Unlike me, he doesn't find my recommendation funny in the slightest. "It's more than your soul we own, Aria. It's body *and* soul. Remember that."

Body and soul.

An excited shiver races up my back.

"I'm dropping a lot of hints here, but you don't seem to be listening," I insist. "Let me spell it out for you. I. Am. Bored."

His face flashes with an emotion too quick to catch… maybe pity or frustration. Could be either with him. He doesn't respond right away, and I give him the chance to think things through as I turn to the fire and stick my hands out, warming them. For some reason, this mansion is constantly cold, even when the sun shines brightly outside.

"You will work for me," he finally announces.

I twist around to face him as he gracefully sits down on the sofa and crosses his leg, an ankle propped onto his knee. He seems damn proud of himself suddenly, and that only worries me.

"Work for you? How?"

"At Purgatory," he muses. "As a bar hand."

My mouth opens, then it closes again as I process his words. "Wait, you own Purgatory?"

"Wasn't it obvious?"

I blink at him. Looking back, yeah, maybe it was obvious, but our first visit was fast, then after I found the Red Room, well… the whole night took a different turn, now didn't it? But the more I think about his offer, the more it warms my insides for one simple reason. It gives me lots of chances to escape.

"I don't have a bartender's license, but I'll learn fast." Words rush past my lips.

"There's no need. You'll just be delivering drinks and whatever else to tables."

So, a waitress, sorta.

Well, I don't care. The potential of getting out of this place is too alluring. Excitement bubbles up inside me.

"So, that's a yes then?" he asks, and I nod frantically. "Good. I'll arrange it and you will be trained on the job."

I'm practically jumping up and down on my feet, my mind swirling with a dozen scenarios where I can make this work in my favor and how I can make a quick getaway.

"There will be rules," he begins, snuffing away my happiness. "You try to escape once, and you will be locked up in your room and no longer working at the club. Anyone hurts or touches you inappropriately, I need to know immediately. And lastly, you belong to us."

I just stare at him, still not convinced with the whole 'they own me' thing. They keep reminding me, but that doesn't mean I have to accept it.

"Okay, so I can start tonight, then?" I ask eagerly.

He laughs, that impenetrable face finally cracking. I narrow my gaze at him, even if my insides melt at the sound and fill me with something dangerously addictive. All these demons impact me in ways I never expected.

I bite on my lower lip, waiting for him to finish his little show.

"You will start when I say you're ready."

CHAPTER THIRTEEN
DORIAN

The living are fascinating creatures. Their drive to adapt and survive is admirable and a bit impressive. No matter what bad luck befalls them, they adjust and move on. Something even we as demons struggled to do when we were cast out over a hundred years ago. Sure, we had our fun and took advantage of the livings' naivete in the beginning, but truly adapting? No, we are just getting by. Surviving.

Cain and Elias are too wrapped in the betrayal and loss to move forward. I, on the other hand, want to take what we've been given and learn from it. Embrace it. Grow stronger for it.

Take Aria, for example. As I stand in front of the shithole of an apartment where she lived for years in deep poverty, I ask myself, how can a person who has nothing and came from nothing be the feisty powerhouse she is? Even when faced with two monstrous creatures—and one sexy-as-fuck incubus demon—she can somehow sleep soundly at night. It amazes me.

She amazes me.

I look up at Ramos, our dhampir debt collector and sometimes mercenary, depending on the client's ability to pay. He waits for me at the door partially hidden in a back alley between a twenty-four-hour Chinese restaurant and a boarded-up storefront. I hold my expensive coat's collar closer around my neck as the wind bustles, taking note of how out of place I must look wearing it in this part of the city. But I won't be long. I just need to meet Murray Whitman, the old warlock and Aria's foster father, and get the information I need. Should be twenty minutes, tops. Ramos is more here for directions. And because he'd been the one to accept Aria's soul in exchange for Murray's. If he'd made a mistake, well... he'd have to pay for it.

Ramos knocks on the faded paint of the door, and to our astonishment, it creaks open as if it's been left unlatched. Not very smart in this neighborhood, but I'm not going to judge.

Ramos seems more uneasy about it than I, and he makes his way inside and up the uneven staircase ahead of me. The air smells heavily of dust, mold, and cigarette smoke. There's also a distant odor of decay lingering in the background that only becomes stronger the higher we climb.

When we get to the topmost floor, the scent of rotting meat is so strong I almost gag. *Vile.* Even more strange is that like the main door, the apartment's door is open, too, wide enough for anyone to stroll in whenever they please.

It doesn't take a rocket scientist to know what's happened here, and as we step inside and see a body slumped over a kitchen table, the smell of putrefaction confirms the death.

Stepping over an array of papers scattered across the carpet, Ramos walks over and touches the man's neck to check for a pulse. It's a useless gesture really, since he'd be able to hear his heart beating as a dhampir, but he does it anyway. Then he nods at me, his silent way of telling me he's dead.

Taking a short step back, he kicks the chair. Stiff with rigor mortis, the man's head jerks only slightly, but it's enough to see the purple bruises around his neck and the bloody holes that were once his eyes. Strangled and mutilated. Hopefully, for his sake, in that order.

"Is this him?" I ask Ramos, wondering if this man was in fact Aria's foster father. Murray.

Again, Ramos nods. He's always been a creature of very little words. Facing a grizzly murder like this is no exception.

I sigh, aggravated. There went our answers. Right down the tubes.

I mean, a man who collected more debts than Donald Trump and then sold out his barely-legal foster daughter's soul probably deserved a death worse than this, but still, how were we going to find out more about Aria's birth parents and origin now?

Pacing across the room, the random mess of papers crunch under my shoes. I pause and pick one up. Scanning it over quickly, I realize it's an old report titled, 'the child', from a social worker who was concerned about Aria in a previous foster home. Words like 'potential abuse,' 'clear makings,' and 'neglect' pop out to me. I frown and pick up another paper. This one is a copy of a police report where an officer found Aria unconscious at the edge of town with no recollection of why she was there in the first place.

How strange.

All these papers are about Aria. About her past and present.

"We need a birth certificate. Or something to tell us

about her parents. A last name. A city of birth. Something," I tell Ramos.

He shifts through the wreckage, but the more I scan the mess at our feet, the more I'm sure it's unlikely we'll find what we need. Whoever killed the warlock must have found what they were searching for.

That means we aren't the only ones interested in learning more about the mysterious Aria No-Last-Name. Not anymore.

What is she hiding?

Looks like our little hellcat has caught the eye of someone else—someone who's willing to do whatever it takes to get what they want. Even kill.

Back home, I make my way to the mansion's library where I know Elias and Cain will be waiting for me. I've texted them both to meet me there but have left the details about the warlock's death out of the message. Some things are just better left said in person, and discussing our next move with Aria wasn't something I wanted to type out. Especially when Elias was known for rarely ever carrying his phone. The man spends most of his days running naked through the woods, after all.

Once Cain saw the text, there was no doubt he'd find Elias and bring him along. This was important. For us all.

I still haven't told anyone about Maverick's note or Lucifer's ridiculous kill request, and part of me feels guilty for keeping it from them, but the other part feels like they don't need to know. I'm not taking the deal, so what does it matter? Cain never wants to hear anything damning about his siblings anyway, even from me, and I'd rather not deal with his wrath or excuses. It just isn't worth it.

Now my focus is on Aria, and what I've found—well, didn't find—while at her apartment. Without the warlock to question or any of Aria's birth paperwork left behind, we're on our own to figure out what the next step is going to be.

I find Cain and Elias right where I need them.

Cain looks anxious already, and for him, that means short-tempered. He stands in the center of the library, arms crossed and lips pressed in a tight line. "What is it? What did you find?"

Elias is more bored than anything else. He's in one of the reading chairs, legs spread wide and picking twigs out of his hair. "This better be good."

"The warlock is dead," I reply bluntly. "Ramos and I found him strangled with his eyes gouged out."

As expected, neither Cain nor Elias are moved by the man's death. They wait for me to continue to the more important parts.

"The place was ransacked. Papers all over the floor, all of them pertaining to Aria in some way, shape, or fashion. But the ones we needed were gone."

"What do you mean, gone?" Cain asks. "No birth certificate? Nothing with a mention of her parents or a last name?"

I shake my head. "Not a damn thing. We'll have to find another way. Maybe we can contact a previous foster family?" I reach into my jacket and pull out all the papers I collected at the apartment, just in case something could be of use. Passing them over to Cain, I say, "There's a police report in there, too. Maybe we can call in some favors at Glenside's precinct and pull some strings there."

Cain quickly flips through the stack. "We may have to."

"So wait. Someone killed the warlock to get information on Aria?" Elias sits up, suddenly interested.

"I would assume they got the information *before* they killed him, but yes. It seems to be that way."

Elias snorts in annoyance.

As usual, Cain's deep in his thoughts. I can almost see the smoke coming out of his ears.

After a long, tense moment, he says, "Someone is looking for her. Why?"

I shrug. "The same reasons we are, I assume."

A low rumble climbs up Elias's throat. "She's caught someone else's eye."

He's always been a possessive one, Elias.

"Did you find any clues as to whom it may be?" Cain asks me.

"Besides a cold corpse? Not really," I reply. "Whoever killed the warlock knew what he was doing."

"Wha—What?" A frail woman's voice sounds behind me, and my heart plummets. I whip around to find Aria standing in the archway, brows pinched with a combination of sorrow, anger, and disbelief. "Murray... is dead?"

Cain steps forward but says nothing. Human emotions are still a bit foreign to him, and he's unsure how to proceed. Elias is no better. He stares on like a fool, eyes flickering to the two of us for guidance.

Hopeless. They're both utterly hopeless.

"Aria," I offer gently. It's going to be up to me to ease her into the news. I'm not sure how long she's been listening in, but she's heard enough. It's clear by the anguish on her beautifully tormented face. Tears glisten in her eyes now, and her chest heaves as the pain takes over. "Let me explain—"

She doesn't let me, though. She spins and hurries away, her footsteps echoing through the hallway as she leaves.

Only a moment later, the creak of the front door sounds as she opens it and then it slams shut.

She's left the mansion.

My chest clenches with sympathy for her, surprising me a bit. But I can't help the heaviness I feel knowing we'd —*I'd*—been the one to ultimately upset her. I thought she'd hate the man who'd sold her out for his debts, but apparently, some other feelings for him still lingered in her.

Elias pushes past me to chase her down, but I whip out my arm to stop him. "No, don't," I tell him. Being roughed up and dragged back is probably the last thing she needs right now. And why do I care? Well, I'm not really sure.

Peering down at me with confusion, Elias says, "She's trying to escape again."

I might be wrong, but I don't think she is.

"I'll get her this time," I assure him. When I glance at Cain, he gives me a subtle nod. Elias backs off, and I waste no time running out of the library and chasing her tail.

CHAPTER FOURTEEN
ARIA

I don't stop running. I won't.

The woods blur past me, tears pricking my eyes. My foster dad wasn't the best father figure—he rarely had food in the house, never paid for my schoolbooks or clothes—but Murray's home was the longest one I'd ever had. I'd been safe there. And unlike so many of the others, I never had to worry about being touched or groped. There was never any kind of abuse.

Looking back, it's easier to see what I did have. It's always that way, isn't it? Murray gave me a roof over my head, my own room and privacy. And that was more than the others were willing to give.

Sure, we lived in a shithole, but it was our shithole. Sure, the idiot had a gambling problem and sold me to demons. And don't get me wrong, I fucking hate him for doing that, but I never wished him dead.

Maybe it's the shock that makes me cry like a baby. Maybe it's the feeling of not being able to do anything while stuck here, but I recall fond memories too. Movie nights when he had four foster kids under his roof, the bonding, the almost unrecognizable feeling of family. Even a broken, lopsided one like ours was better than nothing.

Pausing, I press my back to a tree to catch my breath as I let the truth sink through me. I never had much to begin with, so losing even my asshole foster dad hurts so hard. I sob into my hands; it somehow feels like someone broke into my home and stole everything while I wasn't there, and there's nothing that can make things right again.

My emotions tug me in two directions, swinging violently between anger for his betrayal and grief of losing one of the only stable things in my life.

I squeeze my eyes shut, hugging myself. He's gone. I thought I might have had a place to go to if I ever escaped the demons, even temporarily, but that's now no longer an option.

A snapping branch has me opening my eyes and twisting around. Dorian is leaning a shoulder into a tree several feet away, his hands deep in the pockets of his jeans, one leg crossed over the other at his ankle. The expression on his face isn't one of frustration, but something calm, which takes me aback.

It doesn't surprise me that it's him who's followed me. Out of the three demons, he seems the most in tune with his emotions.

"Are you here to drag me back inside?" I murmur.

He shrugs. "There's no rush."

In truth, I expect further explanation from him, but he just lowers his head, giving me space in his own way. "I don't want to go back," I say.

"You know that's not possible." He pushes off the tree, striding toward me, all shoulders. Powerful, strong shoulders, walking with so much confidence. For a short while, I forget why I'm out here and lose myself in the way he carries himself. I can see now that his power as an incubus works far beyond just when he tries to lure people to him. The power exudes from his very being even when he isn't trying. Unless he is trying now and I'm just utterly blind to it. He is the epitome of sex, after all, from the smoldering expression that captivates me, down to the large package bulging in his pants. Heck, he doesn't even need to use his ability, I bet. Women will fall at his feet regardless.

"Why wasn't I told right away about my foster father getting killed?" I hold myself strong, furious that they left me out.

"We just found out ourselves. Here, come with me. I want to show you something." He strolls right past me and continues deeper into the woods.

I glance back to the house amid the dense trees, and then turn toward Dorian who slides into the shadowy forest. A demon calls me into the woods with him… is it a smart decision to obey?

Of course it's not, but these aren't ordinary circumstances, and going back to the house means dealing with Cain and Elias. So I choose the lesser of the two evils and trail behind Dorian, quickening my steps.

The land slopes downward, and each step I take is cautious to avoid falling onto my ass. Dorian takes long strides as if nothing can touch him. Once the land levels out, we emerge from the forest to stand before a gloriously huge lake. It stretches outward and curves around the mountain to our right. Blues and oranges gleam over its mirrored surface.

"Wow!" My mouth falls open.

Trees brimming with deep russet colored leaves clustering closely to the edges, and farther on my left a small deer appears and takes its fill from the lake. The perfectly still water ripples gently outward.

A deep sense of serenity flares over me as I stare out at the beauty as Dorian walks behind me.

"Elias may be a bullish idiot sometimes, but he knows where all the best views are around here. He showed me this one, but I suspect he keeps the best ones for himself," Dorian explains.

I turn and find him lounging on a wooden log, arms by his sides, legs stretched out, chin high as though his favorite pastime is sunbathing.

"Do you come here often?" I ask him.

"Probably not as much as I should. It's nice to be able to get away from those four walls sometimes. Especially with those other two sulking up the place."

Boy, is he right about that. "What else does a demon need time out from?"

"You'd be shocked at the shit that washes up from Hell." He pats the spot on the log next to him, offering me a seat. I walk over and take it.

"Do you even have the sun in Hell?" I ask.

"Sometimes, though it's rare."

"I'm surprised the sun doesn't have you smoking up or something."

He peeks sideways at me. "Are you confusing me with a vampire?"

I frown at him. "I'm not that stupid."

"You don't know much about our kind," he answers for me.

I nod. "There are stories, of course, but I've never met any demons besides you three."

"That's good then. Most people don't want to meet us. Not unless they're doing something they shouldn't be or need to make a deal."

I look out across the twinkling water, my shoulders

heavy with sorrow. "Yeah, well, that's not always the case, now is it? Just look at me."

"You… You are a special case." He chooses his words carefully but smiles through them. Warmth spreads through my chest.

Then, tilting his chin up and closing his eyes, he adds, "But when I burn up, I'll be sure to let you know."

"You know what's strange?" I say, mostly because the silence just resurrects my grief, and I don't want to drown in it.

"What's that?" he asks.

"That you three chose to live out here in this beautiful place rather than in the city where it's chaotic and filled with sinful people."

"Aria, I'm shocked you'd stereotype like that."

I swivel around to face him, straddling the log. I study him for a long moment, wondering why he really followed me out here in the first place. If not to bring me back, then why? To show me the landscape? I'm not sure I believe that.

"Are you doing it again?" I ask him.

One eye opens. "Doing what?"

"Trying to compel me."

He shifts back until he's sitting upright again before fully turning to me. "Are you currently on your knees sucking my cock?"

I blanche, completely dumbstruck by his words and the image they create in my head. "Uh, no."

He chuckles at my obvious discomfort. "Then no. I'm not."

A thick stretch of silence passes over us, but instead of being awkward or tense, it's refreshing. We continue to admire the scenery and the sound of the beautiful autumn day. It's a bit cold for just a sweater and jeans, but I don't want to leave just yet. It's nice to be sharing this moment with Dorian, as weird as that may be.

The breeze tosses his hair away from his face. He's spectacular, not a single flaw, his features god-like. Swinging back around, I stare at the way the sunlight sparkles over the water like a treasure chest. It's peaceful out here, and my thoughts drift back to my foster father.

He's dead.

Gone from this world, taken from me.

Joseline always told me to not get close to him, that he wasn't a good man. Once she even wished him dead, but she wouldn't tell me why. I believed her and pulled away from him. And now the sadness crowding my chest has more to do with a sense of loneliness that I have fewer people left in the world I can turn to. I sound selfish, but isn't grieving about those of us left behind and what we've lost, and not so much about those who have moved on to the next stage of their lives and what they've lost?

A tear rolls down my cheek.

Dorian reaches over and catches the tear as it falls over the edge of my jaw. "Did you know some people believe tears carry power?"

I wipe my eyes and glance over to him. "Like who?"

"Witches and warlocks mostly." He shrugs and wipes his hand down his jeans.

"When I think back, Murray almost never practiced magic at home. He was pretty bad at spellcasting."

"It takes a great deal to create something out of nothing. If witches or warlocks don't use their gift often, it becomes harder to perform, too." He smiles. "It's the 'use it or lose it' mantra."

"That's true. I never really thought about it that way."

We fall silent again, and the damn tears won't stop. It's like talking about him draws on my emotions.

Dorian straddles the log like me, both of us facing one another. He draws me closer and I let myself lean against his chest, my stomach bursting with butterflies as he embraces me. With my cheek pressed against his hard chest, the waterworks continue. My insides ache for the loss, for me being more alone than I thought, and all while my stomach flip-flops at having an incubus demon like Dorian holding me so close.

My reaction to him was instant the first time I met him… To be truthful, it had been the same with all three demons. But when I'm close to them, I lock up and my body tightens like I've lost the inability to think straight.

I'm all over the place, but I have so many questions too. "Who killed him?"

"Hmm?" He rubs a hand at my back in small circles, and I won't deny there is a calming effect to his touch.

"Murray. Who killed him?"

"We don't know yet."

Does that mean they're going to try and find out?

"I want to visit my foster home." I crane my head back and our gazes lock. The deepest green eyes look into mine intensely, like he might be trying to read my thoughts.

My heart stops for a moment, and all I can do is hope he'll kiss me.

I know I shouldn't be thinking such things for a multitude of reasons, but the compulsion to taste his full lips grips me in a vise so forceful it's all I can think about.

There is only one explanation. Dorian's using his damn power to make himself irresistible to me.

DORIAN

As Aria's stare bores into me, something passes behind her eyes. Something strange, dark, and unrecognizable, but as quick as it comes, it's gone, and I wonder if I've imagined it.

She leans into me again, pressing those perfect little breasts against my chest, her breath quickening. She is fucking gorgeous and sexy as hell, causing all kinds of reactions in me. I'm letting arousal lead me though. Usually I encourage it, but I came after Aria to console her and bring her back to the mansion, not get an erection that leaves my balls so tight they fucking ache.

But I won't mess with her emotions, not when she's so vulnerable.

We stay that way for a long while, and I stroke her hair and back, which she seems to enjoy. When she shuffles closer to me, my cock twitches. She's bespelling me, beautiful and so damn sexy all I can think about is tasting her.

She quiets down and remains attached to me, her arms curled against her chest. If there's one thing I've learned about human females, it's that they love being held and stroked. I've mastered the ability, so we sit silently in this pristine location.

The longer I hold her in my arms, the more my body starts to respond to hers, my heart racing, my blood diving south. She shifts and pushes her breasts more against me. I look down at her.

"What do you want, little girl?" I ask. I know I should resist this need growing inside me, but I'm weaker against her charms than I thought. For the first time in my entire existence, there's no need to release my power onto another to get what I want. There's no need for manipulation of any kind. It's all... real. Natural. And more powerful than anything I could conjure on my own.

It takes her several moments to find her voice and glance up at me. "To forget everything," she murmurs, batting her eyes. "To escape."

Oh, she's good. I open my mouth to tell her the contract is binding and leaving us isn't an option when I realize that is not the escape she's craving. I recognize that desperate look in her eyes where she'd do anything to avoid feeling the ache in her heart. The loss. The sorrow. And *I'm* her escape.

All the things I want to do to her, to awaken pleasure in that tiny body of hers… Oh, I know exactly how to help her escape. My hands skate down her arms and fall to her hips. In a heartbeat, I draw her toward me, lifting her onto my lap, her legs automatically curling around my hips.

She gasps her surprise, but she's not fooling anyone. Her sweet pussy burns with heat as it presses against my thick cock.

I lean in closer, whispering in her ear, "Tell me what you desire."

She pulls back, her teeth pressing into the full flesh of her lower lip, pulling it into her mouth.

The black thing in my chest thumps like a drum, counting down faster and faster.

I think of nothing but her stripped and riding my cock, of her tits bouncing while she screams for more.

Fuck me, I crave to fill her completely, to flood her with my seed.

"Have you lost your voice?" I prod her.

Instead of responding, she pushes herself toward me, her hands fisting my collar.

Our mouths clash, and she kisses me hungrily. Her lips taste like the sweetest nectar, the flavor of innocence. Even though she's not a virgin, she's inexperienced, and I can't wait to be the one to show her pleasures beyond her wildest dreams.

She presses her tongue into my mouth, and I greedily take her as I cup her ass.

Oh, little girl… she has no idea what she's opened up by starting this. Backing down now just isn't possible. Not when she's the one pushing me, pulling open the buttons on my shirt.

And if she needs to escape, fuck. I'll give her that and so much more.

CHAPTER FIFTEEN
DORIAN

"Is this what you want?" I growl the words, the arousal inside me hitting hard as I lift us both up and off the log. The little minx is latched around me, her gorgeous, toned body holding on, sexy legs gripping my hips.

My cock is so fucking hard nestled between her legs, and she's rubbing herself against me. Her eyes gleam wickedly when she looks at me. I barely even recognize her, but I'm loving it, this new, wild part of her.

She makes quick work of unbuttoning my shirt with one hand, the other locked around my neck. Then she slides her palm across my bare chest, her touch on fire.

I pause for a moment because this isn't the Aria I know. She always pushes back, looks scared most days. She has that shy girl-next-door look on her face that drives me insane because I want to be the one to corrupt her. But now she's morphed into a goddess exactly to my liking. Which is too good to be true.

Her fingers pinch my nipple as she pushes closer and

claims my mouth. I shudder with desire. *Well dammit.* It's like she knows exactly what she's doing after all.

I walk her to the closest tree and pin her between me and the trunk. And speaking of trunks, I grind mine between her legs, while she makes tiny moaning sounds in my mouth.

If there's ever a time when I should back away, it's now... except this is something I've craved from the moment I laid eyes on Aria. Usually, I'm the one who has power over others, except my little girl has affected me in a way no other female has. Talk about conundrums.

Fuck it.

I return the kiss, our tongues wrestling, my hand groping her ass, the other pushing under the fabric of her top to find scorching-hot flesh.

"You're all mine now," I growl as a sense of possessiveness takes over me.

Aria's mouth is on my neck, licking the curve of my throat. "Please, Dorian."

The vulnerability in her voice drives me insane. I can't get enough of her moaning sounds, of her body burning up, her clinging onto me. Her sex scent engulfs me.

"Are you sure this is what you want?" I ask. The question takes me by surprise, and I'm not sure why I ask it. I'm barely holding back as it is.

We look into each other's eyes. Once I claim her, there will be a connection between us that she may not be able to break. It's the most potent facet of my power, why so many women cannot resist my calls. They become tethered to me, unable to resist. It's never bothered me before to ask the women I bed, but with Aria...

Since she can avoid my compulsions, it's possible she won't be affected like the others, but is that a risk I'm willing to take?

The more I stare into her glassy eyes, the more I know it's her drive to escape that makes her behave this way.

She groans and kisses me harder, tilting her pelvis toward me, pressing her heat against my cock.

"I can't promise you anything sweet," I say, nestling my face at the curve of her neck, leaving a trail of kisses toward her mouth. Then I lick her lips.

"Never said I wanted sweet," she answers breathily.

My cock is rock hard, punching in my pants. Her fingers creep down my stomach, but I've had enough of this game.

I lower my hellcat to her feet and pull her top up and over her head, needing to be skin-to-skin. A deep rose-colored nipple pokes through the lace bra, and I peel the bra straps down her arms, releasing those delicious globes.

She chews on her lower lip, hesitation crawling over her expression. I make my way down her neck, over her collarbone and to her breasts, taking one into my mouth. So soft and delicious. Fuck me, I need her.

Her hands are in my hair, fisting it, nudging me to go lower.

Praise the devil, but now she's speaking my language. I drop to my knees before her.

"I need more," she moans.

"Oh, you need me?" I tease, and when I glance up at her, her darkened gaze is anything but humorous. It's dark, hungry, wild, and incredibly sexy.

I reach for her pants and unbutton her jeans before sliding down her zipper.

"Yes…" Her voice trembles with need.

Looking straight into her eyes, I wait for her response as my fingers curl under the elastic of her underwear. I slide deeper over the small mound of hair to where she's drenching wet.

She gasps as I press a finger between her lush lips.

"You were saying?" I persist.

She leans back into the tree, her chest rising and falling rapidly with each breath.

"Are you thinking about my big cock in your tight little pussy? Is this what you really want?"

A blush curls over her cheeks, and now I see where the real Aria is. She's hiding behind this bravado. I promised myself I wouldn't take advantage of her vulnerability unless I was certain she was in the right state of mind.

She moans and keeps looking away from me.

Pushing deeper over her slickness, I glide a finger into her.

Her eyes widen as her pussy walls clench around my finger, and she closes her eyes, lost in her own world. This is the escape she wants… to be tempted to the point of forgetting herself, but is this the way I want her the first time? Is this how I want her to remember us?

"I'm waiting, baby," I ask. I'll burn up alive if I don't get a chance to put out her flames with my body, but doubt now threads in my mind about this being a smart decision. "Talk to me."

"I…" she whispers and swallows loudly. Then she shakes her head, changing her mind. "Let's skip the talking. It's too distracting." She reaches for me, fisting my shirt, pulling me to her, but her voice trembles.

Her words make me hesitate. As I feared, she's not fully engaged in this. She's distracted, wanting a way out of her emotions and thoughts. And as much as I want to be her escape, I can't be the one to give her that if she will regret this and hate me later.

Making up my mind, I pull away from her. As always, the temptation is there to take her. All I can picture is being buried deep inside her, fucking her raw, reminding her who she's with. But in the back of my mind, a damn voice keeps reminding me it's a mistake.

The voice is supposed to be the devil on my shoulder, not a son-of-a-bitch angel telling me to do the right thing.

When I look at Aria, all I see are the tears, the sorrow, the need to forget the world at any expense.

So I do the craziest thing I've ever done and whisper, "Not today, sweetheart."

My balls might as well be shriveled peanuts now. What the fuck is wrong with me? But the longer I stare into her glistening eyes, the more I know this is the right decision.

"I won't take advantage of you, little one." Grabbing her sweater from the ground, I dust it clean of dried leaves and hand it over to her. She snatches it and pulls it back on, tucking those gorgeous tits away. Then she zips up her pants.

"You're a real jerk, you know that?" Her cheeks are bright red.

I know how it must look. Like I'm denying her for whatever reason. I also know I'm an asshole who normally takes what he wants, so this whole 'pulling back and listening to my conscience' thing is new. I fucking hate it. But there's something about Aria that has my instincts demanding I keep her protected, even from myself.

My power may be able to control and manipulate others, but everyone I sleep with goes into it willingly. I make sure of that. I just heighten their own underlying desires. If I don't stick to my own rules, then I might as well go join those mindless, wretched Hell-leeches who scavenge Earth in the shadows. Parasites.

Aria huffs and storms back into the woods the way we came, obviously furious with me.

I crack my neck and sneer under my breath. What the

fuck is wrong with me? Since when do I let a prize like that walk away?

I want to fuck her so badly; I'm fuming at myself.

A second later, she's vanished from sight. I run after her before she disappears in these dangerous woods.

CHAPTER SIXTEEN
ARIA

The next day drags. After the encounter in the woods with Dorian and finding out Murray was killed, I'm relishing my time alone in my room. It still bites sharply that Dorian pushed me away… God, if an incubus demon rejects me, what hope do I have? My stomach turns every time I think about it, so I've been burying my nose in a book to forget.

Sayah has been free and lurking in my room for hours, gliding over the walls and ceiling, going slightly bat crazy with boredom. *Aren't we all.*

She keeps skimming along the gap at the base of the door that the guards fixed after Elias broke it, waiting for me to give her permission to go out and explore. Except I don't want to bring any attention to us from the demons. Plus, there's a guard out there. I hear him pacing about.

An abrupt knocking bangs on the door, and I flinch, the book in my hand slipping out of my grasp and falling onto the bed. Sayah zips back into me like a rapid yoyo just as the door pushes open.

I meet Dorian's green eyes as he trudges into my room

like a storm, gaze wild and breathing rapidly. He's dressed in faded Levis and a white tee that's tucked roughly in the front, drawing taut across his chest. No shoes either, and his deep golden hair sits messily off his face like he's run his hands through it a few too many times.

What's he doing here? My cheeks flush instantly because when I look at him now, all I can think about is me throwing myself at him like a lunatic and him pushing me away.

"What's up?" I push my legs over the edge of the bed and remain seated as Dorian closes the door behind him.

"I wanted to check on you," he admits. He steps closer but makes sure to stop with some distance still between us. He looks unsure, not like his confident self, and it's a bit unnerving to see him this way. "After yesterday in the woods, I—"

"I'm perfectly fine." I cut him off, not needing him to come and tell me 'it's him not me' or whatever other bullshit guys give.

He studies me for a long moment, not even blinking, and as curious as I am to work out what he's thinking, I remain silent.

Suddenly, he offers me his hand and waits for me to take it.

I stare up at him. "What do you really want, Dorian?"

"To show you that you're wrong."

I arch my brows and half-laugh. "Wow, that's a great way to try to patch things up. Does it work for you often?"

"Yes, actually," he answers with a genuine tone.

"Well, good for you." I pick up my book and attempt to read it, though no words are registering as sparks are going off in my brain with Dorian in my room. He is the worst kind of distraction.

When he gives no sign of leaving, I sigh and drop my

book back on the bed, then get up. "Look, I get it. You feel guilty or something about yesterday, but no need to. I was delusional with grief. It won't happen again."

His brow arches. "Would you say you're delusional with grief now?"

Annoyance bubbles inside me. I really don't want to talk about yesterday. His rejection still stings. I swing around him to the door and wrench it open. "Can you just leave me alone?"

He spins and closes the distance in two strides. His hand shoots out and he shoves the door shut. Then he's on me. Hands on my arms, he drags me toward him, holding me with an iron grip.

"You want to know the truth, little girl." He tells me rather than asks and doesn't wait for me to respond. "I've spent many years seducing women into my bed as a pastime. I had to fill my days somehow, and it's a hobby I'm rather fond of. Most women drop to their knees before me, eager to suck my cock, to do as I order. And I was perfectly fine with that until you came along."

I roll my eyes at him. "Was I not submissive enough for you? Is that it?"

"Fuck, Aria," he growls, his hold tightening. "You know what I can't get out of my mind? That I should have taken advantage of you yesterday when you were at your lowest point because from the beginning, I've wanted to fuck you. If it were anyone else, I would have, but with you… I couldn't do that to you. I couldn't."

I'm barely breathing at hearing his confession. He had wanted to take that next step with me yesterday but didn't because he wanted the choice to be my own. He didn't want me influenced in any way.

An incubus, a sex demon with the power to force his

will on anyone, didn't want to take advantage of *me?* As if he had a conscience?

A demon with morals… I'm not sure I believe that one.

He clasps me tighter, his face inches from mine. "I didn't mean to hurt your feelings because of it. That wasn't my intention."

I lean back to create more distance, but it's close to impossible. "Okay, fine. You feel better now?"

Darkness washes over his face, and he smiles wickedly. "What am I going to do with you?"

Is this some kind of trick? I don't understand why he's telling me this at all. Or why he cares. "Leaving my room is a good start."

His laughter catches me off guard, and he spins me around in a flash, then pushes me up against a wall, face first. His hand rakes through my hair and fists it behind my head. He tilts my head back as he pins me with his legs between my thighs.

"The fault is mine. I've let myself become too complacent, too soft with you, haven't I?" He presses his body to mine, and the erection in his pants nestles against my ass.

My brain screams at me to fight him, while my body sways under him like it has a mind of its own. There's a glimmering enticement skimming over my mind, awakening my arousal with ferocity. All I can think about is begging him to take me. Use me. Fuck me. Oh god, the burning heat climbing through me is so intense I can barely think straight.

"Stop using your power on me," I snap. "Or are you afraid that maybe all women don't want you?"

His grip constricts and his breath is on my ear. "That's where you're wrong. The burning between your legs, the ache that renders you weak in my presence is all you, Aria.

I'm not influencing you in any way, and I haven't tried in a long time."

I bark a fake laugh as he slides a hand around my waist, finding flesh. My body sizzles, and all I can concentrate on is that point of contact. The bastard knows it and teases me. When he slides higher along my stomach and brushes a thumb feather soft just below my breasts, I gasp.

I shouldn't be allowing him to touch me like this. I know I shouldn't. Conflict battles inside me, and the desperate urge to give in to him burns through me. His mouth is on my neck, licking me from my nape to my earlobe. He inhales my scent.

I shudder with an unbearable need. There is no way this can be just me. No man has made me feel the way these demons do.

He draws his fingers under my breasts once again, barely touching them, and I'm trembling with need.

"Do you enjoy this?"

My throat feels raw, and I swallow past it, searching for my voice. "What do you want from me?"

"I want to make sure there's never again a moment where you think I don't want you."

His words surprise me, but they also make goosebumps rise.

"Don't ever doubt me," he whispers in my ear as his hand cups a breast, squeezing, his fingers pinching my nipple.

A moan spills past my lips, and I'm lost for words, my heart hammering.

"I *want* to give you the greatest pleasure you've ever known." His voice drops to a husky whisper against my hair. "I *want* to fuck you until you're gasping for breath and too weak to stand on your own two feet." Then, he lowers his hands to my hips.

His filthy talk only excites me more, and in that moment I realize that he's right. The arousal building inside me for this demon is all me and the thrill of the dangerous unknown. It has nothing to do with his power at all.

I reach down to take his hand and place it back on my breast. He squeezes it hard in response.

"Yes, baby," he says behind me, and the energy suddenly changes in the room. Gone is the tension, replaced with hunger. I suck in each breath, knowing what I need.

"Dorian," I murmur.

"I'm right here." He tugs my shirt and removes it with my bra in one swift tug up and over my head.

I try to turn around, but he places his hand quickly on my back to keep me facing the wall.

"Never said you could move."

He yanks down my pants and underwear, which I step out of. The sound of his zipper sounds next, and my pulse gallops with anticipation. Then his hands are on my body, running from my back, down my waist, and over the curves of my hips. The need to look over my shoulder and watch him is overwhelming, but when I attempt to turn again, he barks, "The wall," and I snap my face forward again.

I may not be able to see him, but I know he's grinning. I can feel it somehow.

"You are spectacular." His velvety voice sends shivers of excitement through me.

He loops an arm around my waist, drawing me backward and against him, flesh to flesh, his huge cock caged between us.

His hand drops to my ass and slides down the middle to between my legs. "Spread for me." His voice grows dark and dangerous.

Is it stupid of me to give in to him, to sate my own desires? Trying to look past my sex-induced thoughts leaves me further conflicted. It's useless because I want him just as much as I did yesterday. He hasn't even touched my fire, but I'm soaked.

His hand slides up my back and he forces me to bend forward. My nerves are so taut, my body feels like it's trembling. When I glance over my shoulder, Dorian drops to his knees behind me.

"I can't wait to discover how sweet you taste. I've been dreaming about this." He runs a finger down my ass and pries the cheeks open, opening me up before him. My muscles tense automatically. I'm fully exposed to him, but he only growls with admiration.

I've never had generous lovers in the past, so to have a man devote so much attention to me is exhilarating and terrifying.

"I'll have this beautiful little ass soon enough," he says. "But first…" The warm air of his breath on my sex sends a buzz down to the pit of my stomach. His mouth is on me in seconds, and I gasp. I prop my hands up on the wall to hold myself because my knees soften with the intensity of him devouring me.

His tongue lashes over my clit, and every stroke shoots pleasure through me.

"Oh fuck!"

His pleased hum vibrates through my core.

The notion of getting away hits me now, along with a strong case of imposter syndrome. I don't belong with a man like Dorian. I'm just someone he feels pity for.

When he pushes a finger into me, then two, I forget everything. I cry out, my hips rocking back and forth, urging him to pump into me faster.

He kisses my ass cheeks, then takes small bites, and he isn't gentle either. The pain and pleasure drive me insane.

"I want to hear you, Aria. Scream for me," he commands.

I lose control of myself and a loud moan spills past my lips, the build-up like a hurricane ripping through my body.

Just as fast as he started, he pulls out and stands.

Gasping for air, my body is floating, and I can't even form words as I glance at him behind me. He's palming his cock, his eyes locked on my backside, but like each time before, he forces me to face away from him with a rough hand. "Nah-ah-ah. Not yet."

He uses his grip on the back of my neck to push my cheek against the cold wall and holds me there.

"Are you ready?" he asks, like we're about to take off on a ride.

"Hell yeah," I respond, and he breaks into a delicious laugh.

Grabbing my hips, he positions himself behind me, his cock easily finding my heat, and he inches into me.

I brace myself, my hands flat against the wall, my fingers curling the deeper he pushes into me. I suck in rapid breaths because… "Oh, God!"

"He has nothing to do with this," he snarls and thrusts into me.

This time I scream, my body tightening. He fills me, stretches me, and his aggressiveness is surprising. There's no pause, just him fucking me, claiming me. The friction flares to life inside me, swallowing me whole. There's something intoxicating, unbearably captivating to have a strong man take me with such passion and arousal. What we have is raw and primal. My body hums… I'm floating and moaning so loud, I completely forget where I end and Dorian begins.

Each slapping sound he makes is accompanied by his devilish groan, and it does things to me to hear his enjoyment. His thumb strokes over the crack of my ass, circling my rear end. Now *that* is complete virgin territory.

His finger encircles my hole, and I stiffen under him. I'm not sure I'm ready for that yet. "Ahh."

"Just relax, baby." He glides back and forth into me, both his cock and thumb working me back into an arousal. "If you want to and trust me, we'll get there eventually, but right now, your pussy is mine."

We're rocking back and forth, my hands on the wall to avoid hitting my head, and somehow this sex god fucks me faster, harder.

My knees weaken beneath me, but he holds me in place.

"Call my name," he commands, but there is none of his compulsion magic attached to it. It's just me and him.

"Damn, Dorian! I'm so clos—" I cry out, the orgasm shooting through, stealing everything but the pleasure coiling around me. My clit pulses as he keeps plunging into me, fucking me, growling his own release.

I convulse, drowning in the most incredible feeling. Dorian pulses inside me, fueling my own desire, fingers digging into me. We both cry out. My orgasm keeps coming at me, crashing into me like waves, one after the other. Dorian remains buried inside me.

"Fuck, squeeze me harder." His sounds flood the room while I shudder under him. He loops an arm around my waist and helps me stay upright as my muscles weaken, while he's still embedded in me.

I gasp for each breath, my nipples tight, and I'm dripping wet between my legs. I never knew sex like this was even possible.

"What the hell have you done to me?" My voice is nothing more than a scratchy gasp.

"Being fucked by an incubus comes with lots of benefits. One being that I'm ready to go again."

I'm swaying between intoxicating need and fear that the depth of which I crave to be satisfied might end up killing me. "Remember when I said I wasn't looking for sweet? Maybe I changed my mind a bit," I say.

He laughs and swings me toward the bed. "I want you to ride me and show me how those tits bounce."

Drawing out of me, I'm finally able to get a good look at the size of him, and I choke on my next breath. He's huge, bigger than any guy I've ever been with before. I can't believe he fucked me with that!

He breaks out into a grin and says, "We need to make up for lost time, and I'm not done with you yet." He grabs my arms and draws me against him, kissing me with a possessiveness that shakes me to the core. I've never been with anyone who kisses me like he owns me.

Then he breaks free. "Before I forget," he says. "I did come to tell you that you start your first day at Purgatory tonight. If you can walk straight after this, that is."

My mouth drops open, but before I can blast him with questions, he kisses me again. Harder.

I let myself fall under his spell and kiss him back, needing Dorian more than I ever thought possible.

CHAPTER SEVENTEEN
ARIA

The ride to Purgatory has me shifting in my seat. The road is rough, and each bump reminds me of the delicious ache between my legs, of the three times Dorian fucked me. I collapsed on the bed afterward, my heartbeat and lungs struggling to return back to normal. The demon was insatiable. Even now as he sits across from me in the back of the limo in his black pants and grungy leather jacket and transparent net top underneath, he eyes me like he's still fucking me in his mind, and my pulse gallops.

Elias has joined us in the back as well, his large frame taking up most of the seat next to me. Gold eyes shining with anger, he glares at Dorian, while Cain chose shotgun up front. The window between us is lowered.

Yep, the whole happy little team is off to see me on my first night at work. It's a family affair. This should be fun.

I tug down on my tiny shorts that are seriously riding up my ass and the crop top I wished covered more skin. Another outfit Cain had insisted I wear. I was a little disappointed it wasn't another dress, but according to him, working and visiting for pleasure warrant two very different attires.

Unfortunately, the heels had to stay. These aren't five-inch stilettos, but I'm just as uncoordinated on them.

"Is there anything I ought to know about working at the club?" I ask the demons. "Who to look out for, the troublesome customers, that kind of thing?"

Besides Sir Surchion and his stupid bird...

God, I hope he's not there tonight. My stomach is a jumble of nerves as it is.

"Just follow the rules and you'll blend in," Cain answers from the front without even glancing back at us.

"As long as the hellhound here doesn't try to mark his territory like last time, it should be a quiet night," Dorian muses, cutting Elias a side look.

"Fuck you. I wouldn't have had to take down that lion shifter if you didn't lure two of his wives out the back. That's all on you," Elias barks. "I saved your ass."

Dorian scoffs and turns to the window, not biting back.

The air suddenly feels thicker, heavier. The aggression is tangible between these two.

"The problem is that you can't keep it in your pants, can you?" Elias continues, not backing down.

"And what's your problem? Can't keep it up?" Dorian says. His calmness only seems to aggravate Elias more. He huffs and snorts like a wild beast beside me.

I catch Elias's gaze sweeping over to me then back at Dorian. And suddenly heat crawls across my cheeks because he must know what we did.

Shit, how could they not with all the screaming? How could it've never occurred to me until now? I curl in on myself in the corner, wanting to vanish.

"Enough," Cain shouts from the front.

But Dorian isn't listening and edges forward in his seat.

"All you fucking do is hunt in the woods. Run around with the wildlife. Maybe that's where you unleash your cock."

Elias's fist lashes out and collides into Dorian's face.

I yelp and thrust myself backward as Dorian jumps onto Elias and they start brawling, all fists and snarls. And fuck, I'm right there.

The limo comes to an abrupt stop, sending us all into a forward lurch. I grip the door handle while the two of them slam to the ground between the seats. It doesn't stop them though. Elias is on top of Dorian, punching him repeatedly, while Dorian laughs and laughs.

Seconds later, my door wrenches open and Cain snatches my arm, dragging me out of the limo. I stumble before standing to find we are in the middle of Glenside, pulled aside on a side street. I recognize it. We're not too far from the secret entrance to the magical underground, to Storm.

"Let's go," Cain snarls as he whistles and hails down a cab.

"What about them?" I glance back at the limousine rocking from side to side, a large thump sounding from the inside, but I can't see anything beyond the tinted windows.

A cab pulls up in front of us. I notice the small painted umbrella on the side, indicating this driver is of the supernatural variety.

"They're fucking idiots." He seizes my elbow and nudges me into the back of the car. I shuffle in and he climbs in after me, then we take off.

I look out the back as Cain gives the driver instructions on where to go. "Do they often fight like this?"

"All the fucking time. I'm close to taking them both down." Cain slouches in his seat, arms by his side, his jaw clenched tight.

"It's because of me," I whisper, unable to stop myself. "Isn't it?"

"Yes," he says, exasperated.

I sit back into the seat and stare out of the opposite window, too terrified to ask the question on my mind because I don't want to hear the answer. If Elias is pissed at Dorian for sleeping with me, how does Cain feel about it? There's no doubt he knows, too.

When we pull up in front of Purgatory, I get out as Cain pays the driver. As I wait for him by the door, I take note of where we are in Glenside. Surprisingly, we're still on the human side of the town, but close by Storm's secret entrance under the highway overpass. Right on the verge of the two worlds. Cain's choice of location must have been strategic for some reason—everything with Cain is—but I wonder why here instead of inside Storm's limits. I'd have to remember to ask him another time.

When he's through with the driver, he marches toward me like he's on a mission, his eyes darkening. He lashes out and grabs my jaw, forcing my head back.

"We have rules in the house, and you belong to me first," he growls, his hold squeezing slightly.

And there it is, his jealousy, his possessiveness, just like the other two. I glower at him, irritated that he thinks he can control who I sleep with, but at the same time, my stomach flip flops at the idea of him wanting me. Even in his own fucked up way.

Hell, I shouldn't even be entertaining the idea of being with any of these demons. Being drawn to all three is lunacy. Something is very wrong with me.

When the door to the club opens, he releases me, and I recoil, rubbing my jaw. Asshole. This is why I need to get away from the whole lot of them.

He reaches into his suit pocket and pulls out a thin gold

chain. When he drapes it around my neck, I realize it's the same necklace he'd given me before, during our first night out. The single gold wing.

"Keep this on at all times," he says.

I want to ask him why—what's the significance—but before I can utter a word, he slides a hand to my lower back and pushes me inside, straight into the club.

"After you," he insists, his tone still lacking warmth of any kind.

The place is crowded, maybe even more so than the last time we were here. People are everywhere, the bar is crammed, and the music thumps with an upbeat song tonight.

With his hand still on me, Cain guides me to the end of the bar where it's quieter and darker. He waves at someone, and in seconds, a gorgeous young woman waltzes over to us. With a tiny black studded skirt, long curvy legs, tiny waist, and a black leather corset that pushes up her ample breasts, she's the epitome of a pinup model. Absolutely stunning. The leading lady in most men's fantasies.

When I meet her gaze, I gasp and my heart pounds in my chest. I know her from my last visit to the club. After all, I'd accidentally walked in on her having sex in the Red Room. Blonde hair with soft curls tumbling over her shoulders, crystal blue eyes lined in heavy eyeliner, and a confident stare that said "*Jealous?*" And boy was I. I wished I had even a quarter of her self-esteem.

"Hey sexy." She winks at me, recognizing me, too. And now I just want the world to open up and swallow me whole.

"Aria, I want you to meet Charlotte." Cain introduces us stiffly. "She runs the floor and will be your trainer. Follow her instructions and you'll be fine."

Charlotte smiles beautifully, and suddenly a sense of

insecurity washes over me. "She's good with me, boss." She salutes Cain with a hand to her brow.

Cain groans, unamused, then turns away and marches toward the staircase to the second floor, where I assume his office is.

"Okay, he gave me the heads up you were starting tonight," she says, and I blink up at her, staring at her long lashes, at the sparkling eyeshadow and rosy lips.

Next time, I need to pay a bit more attention to appearance for sure. I had run a brush through my hair a few times.

"I'm not that scary, am I?" she asks, offering me a wonky smile, and I already like her.

Shaking my head, I say, "Everything is so... different."

She laughs and curls her arms over my shoulders. "Rule number one. Everyone here has sex in one of the two dozen rooms at some point. So, there's no need to blush up like the sun. You saw me, and I caught an eyeful of what your master was doing to you out in the hallway."

"You did?" I squeak. *Oh God. How embarrassing.* I clear my throat, feeling *so* out of my comfort zone. "He's not my master."

Her laughter is hypnotic, and she draws me deeper into the club. "Rule number two. Always make sure the patrons have a drink in their hand. That's what pays the bills and keeps this establishment in business. All you need to do is take orders to Antonio behind the bar."

"And rule number three?"

"Chill out and smile," she says as she reaches for something behind the bar and comes back with a small notepad and pen. "Write down all orders and the customer's full name on the pad. Everyone here has a tab."

I nod, staring out at the large room with close to a hundred people squeezed in here. In the far corner, a petite blonde sits on a man's lap holding an empty martini glass. "I've got this."

"Can I offer you one more tidbit of advice?"

"Of course."

She points to my feet. "Wear comfortable shoes. Your dogs are going to be barking in those."

"Comfortable to me are sneakers," I say. "Is there even such a thing as comfortable high heels?"

She chuckles and leans closer to me to whisper her next words. "Here's my secret. I bring my own pair of fuzzy slippers. Wear them in before my shift, then stash them under the bar for my breaks or any lulls in the night. A quick switch when needed, on and off real fast, and no one knows. It'll save you big time."

My toes were feeling cramped already, and I'm pretty sure I had a gnarly blister brewing on the back of my ankle. "That's a really good idea, actually."

"You'll thank me for that one. Believe me. But remember, drinks, tabs, smile."

I pull my shoulders back to show her I'm ready. "Okay. Seems easy enough."

"Oh, and don't let anyone bully you. Sure, customers flirt, and tips are always better the more skin you show, but if someone tries anything funny or makes you feel uncomfortable in any way, you let me know. Or call for security. Even though you're working at a sex club, no still means means no."

The jitters are back. I really hope this isn't a common problem here. I get enough rough-handling from Cain, Dorian, and Elias. I don't want it at work, too.

She slaps my ass. "Off you go."

I flinch, hurrying off. When I look back at her, she gives me an encouraging thumbs up.

Squaring my shoulders, I grip the notepad and make

my way across the club and find a couple on the leather couch with empty hands. Rule number two. Everyone needs drinks.

"What can I get you?" I ask the blonde.

She narrows her gaze at me, scowling like I accidentally stepped on her tail or something. The man she's sitting on sports a green mohawk. He swings his attention to me. "Are you blind?" he snaps at me.

My stomach churns while the couple across from him laugh at me.

"I'm not sure what you mean?"

"You come and insult my girl, then act like a bimbo. We'll have four Blue Havanas on the house, bitch."

My nerves bristle, every muscle tensing. "Excuse me?"

Charlotte slides in next to me in seconds. "Of course, they will be on the house." She hooks her a hand under my elbow and draws me away quickly. "That is a Hungarian pixie. They're mute."

"They are?" I glance back to where the pixie and mohawk man are now making out. I've never encountered pixies before… and why are the Hungarian ones mute?

"I recommend you brush up on their kind. The supes who come here have a lot of money, and egos to match. Think of them as the movie stars of the supernatural world. Only the rich and powerful come to Purgatory."

"Thanks for that." I bet I can find something about them in a book from the manor's library or parlor.

"Antonio, meet the new girl, Aria," Charlotte calls out, leaning over the bar.

I look up at the bartender in a black button-up shirt, collar high, sleeves rolled up to his elbows. He's a young man with glowing tan skin, short black hair, and a black eye patch. I don't ask what happened, and I am guessing he won't appreciate pirate jokes, so I smile. "Hey, great to meet you."

He arches a thick brow.

Charlotte's fingers find my necklace's pendant between my breasts, and she holds it up for Antonio to see. "She's Cain's."

I'm not sure how I feel about that introduction, but he seems to understand what it means. He nods firmly. "You know the drill? Hand me the form with drinks and names."

"Yep, all over it."

"Sweet. Then we'll get along famously." He swings back around to collect two bottles off the back wall and prepares our drinks.

I glance around just as Dorian and Elias march into the club and instantly go in opposite directions. Elias heads straight for the far end of the bar, while Dorian moves to the sofas near the stage where dancers swing around poles. Their puffy lips and black eyes don't look too bad, and I assume demons heal quickly, but damn, they were fast to attack each other in the limo.

Moments later, Antonio sets a tray with four blue drinks in tall glass tumblers in front of me. White smoke pours out of the drinks, spilling onto the tray. The theatrics are incredible.

"Nice touch with the dry ice," I say.

He leans in closer, resting a bent arm on the bar counter. "Darling, that's not dry ice. It's troll hair. Burned it over the drinks; it's meant to be a great aphrodisiac."

Bile hits the back of my throat at the image. I might be sick.

I quickly pick up the tray and carefully make my way around the tables and other patrons to the table at the back of the room. There's a sense of pride that I'll pick this up in no time, and part of me even toys with the idea of asking Cain for a salary.

Maybe it's because I've been cooped up in the mansion for so long or how busy the night is, but the hours at Purgatory fly by. The next time I glance at the clock behind the bar, it's close to one a.m. Four hours have already passed.

I can hardly believe it, but my aching feet can. They're covered in blisters, and every step brings tears to my eyes. I'll definitely be taking Charlotte's advice and bring a pair of slippers next time.

Even though it's already one in the morning, the club is still in full swing. The music thumps so loud it rattles the heart in my chest, and there are so many people crowded on the dance floor, I have to squeeze between the rubbing and grinding bodies just to get to my tables. Dressed in this ridiculous get-up, I'm uncomfortable as it is.

After coming back from making my rounds, I look forward to just standing still for a few seconds to nurse my feet, but the moment I set my tray on the bar, Antonio fills it back up with a new array of drinks. Since I haven't given him another order, I peer up at him, confused. "Who's this for?"

He nods to a new group of dangerous-looking men entering the club and heading straight for the first table. It's occupied by another couple, but the moment they see them coming, they scramble to vacate. Tattoos, leather jackets, a load of muscles and yellow eyes, they look like the type of group you don't want to mess with. Plus, I'm not completely sure what exactly they are and prefer to avoid pissing them off.

"The Full Mooners," Antonio says. "Ever heard of 'em?"

I sputter a laugh. "Mooners? You're kidding me. Whoever came up with that name should be shot."

"They probably were." Charlotte appears next to me, reaches over the counter, and takes one of the seltzer hoses to refill her tray's glasses.

"You've really never heard of them?" Antonio asks.

"Poor Aria here lived under a rock. Didn't you know?" Charlotte replies with a chuckle.

Pretty much. Well, besides the nights Murray would call me or Joseline to pick his drunk ass up at some rando bar in town. Even my school had been with other humans, since all supernatural academies were privately funded and had tuition, which I couldn't afford.

"They're a werewolf biker gang, one of our regulars," she continues, not appearing nearly as nervous as Antonio. "Rude fuckers. And terrible tippers."

Glancing around nervously, he shushes her and lowers his own voice. "Do you want to end up in the bottom of a river somewhere with cement shoes?"

Charlotte rolls her eyes. "Oh please. Viktor would slaughter them all if they so much as sniffed my way." Turning back to me, she winks. "The pros of having a master vampire boyfriend. I highly recommend it."

That man I caught her with in the Red Room is a master vampire? I'm not sure what to say. I've heard stories of their ruthlessness, and from what I remember, Viktor controls most of the northeast. He's incredibly powerful and known for his jealous tendencies. So, why is his girlfriend working here?

She takes my tray and switches it with hers. I'm now holding the seltzers. "For table four," she says, nodding across the room. "I'll take the big bad wolves' table for you."

I smile. "Thanks."

She waves my gratitude away. "We probably shouldn't offer you up as fresh meat on your first day. We'll give you some time at least." She strolls away, swinging her hips in her miniskirt to give onlookers a peek of her round ass with every step.

Antonio leans over the counter, watching her go. "She is something else," he murmurs more to himself than anyone else.

"I'd be careful. That vampire boyfriend might come for you if he catches you staring," I say.

To my surprise, he bursts out laughing. It takes him a moment to settle down again, and when he does, he says sweetly, "Oh, honey. I don't bat for that team."

It takes me a second to get his reference, and when it finally hits me, I laugh at my own stupidity.

"Although I wouldn't mind stealing Viktor for myself. The man is scrumptious." He mimics licking sauce off his fingers before turning back to me. "But in all seriousness, Aria, the clientele here are some of the more powerful and dangerous people on the east coast. Maybe even in the country. You need to watch your back working here. Purgatory isn't for the weak-hearted."

"I live with three demons," I say. "I can handle it."

He eyes me skeptically. "We'll see."

I try not to let his ominous words get to me, but they crawl over my skin. I try to shake it off as I make my way on throbbing feet to table four with the tray of innocent seltzers. I make it okay, only spilling minimal, and when I put the drinks on the table, one of the men hands me a twenty-dollar bill. My biggest tip tonight.

Sticking the money in my daisy dukes pocket, I shuffle my way through the dance floor again, bumping into everyone. Fingers slip into my belt loops and tug me back, making my knees give out and my ankles roll. Whoever has hold of me yanks me harder, giving me a major wedgie, and when I look up, I'm staring into the pox-scarred face of one of the Full Mooner werewolves. I can tell by his yellow eyes and the moon insignia patch on his jacket.

"Aren't you a pretty young thing," he says, his rancid cigarette-smoke breath washing over me. A southern accent clings heavily to his words.

I glare at him. "Let go of me. Please." I make sure to add on the pleasantries, just for the sake of keeping my job.

"How about I pay you a little extra, and you and I spend some time in one of the Red Rooms in the back?" he says, wiggling his eyebrows at me.

What does he think I am? A prostitute? "No thanks." I jerk my hips, and he finally lets go of my pants. I'm about to walk away, but the werewolf grabs me by the waist and spins me around. I smack into his chest with a loud *oomph,* the tray the only thing separating us.

He grins down at me. "I'm not sure you heard me right. You're comin' with me."

My pulse races with familiarity. I know that look. I've seen it so many times before in the eyes of my abusers. And unfortunately, my past is full of them—disgusting, piggish men who claimed to be a friend only to sneak an inappropriate grab here and there or wait until we were alone to force themselves on me.

This asshole is no different.

I shove the tray against him to separate us, but his nails dig into my bare flesh, hurting.

"You didn't hear *me* right. I said let go," I bite out.

"Woah, this bitch got a bark." Laughing, he waves at his Full Mooner friends who are watching his show from their table. They all join in on his joke. Then, he inhales deeply, his nostrils stretching wide as he takes in my scent. "Ah, and she's in heat, boys!"

They all hoot with laughter.

I push him with all my strength and try to knee him in

the balls, but he shifts to avoid it, all the while never letting go of my waist. The more I squirm, the more delusional joy contorts his face.

"I think I'm gonna tame this one. Anyone want sloppy seconds?" he calls.

The gang lift their chins and howl—literally *howl*—at that.

Growing more desperate, I glance over my shoulder at the bar. Antonio is busy helping customers, and Elias is gone from his spot in the corner. Charlotte's off talking to the guests at one of her tables, so I look for Dorian. He's missing from his spot on the sofas.

Fuck!

The wolf's fingers snake in my belt loops again, and he uses them to pull me hard against him. The fabric rips, the terrible sound loud, even with the heavy bass of the club's music. "Keep fighting and I'll bend you over right here and fuck you raw like the dog I am."

He leans in super fast and licks the side of my face.

I tug as far from him as possible as my veins turn to ice and my stomach roils with sickness. "Fuck you." I use my tray to push against him, but when that doesn't work, I swing it at him instead. "Get the hell off me."

He remains unfazed.

Sayah vibrates under my skin in warning. At first, I think she means the werewolf, but she's urging me to turn around. I do just as something whirls past my face. There's a blur of black and gray, and suddenly I'm being thrown backwards. I collide with someone else hard and land on my ass, all the wind knocked out of me.

When I look up, Cain's now standing in the place I'd just been. Only he doesn't look much like himself. His skin is gray, like marble, his eyes two eternal black abysses. The demonic ink of them seems to snake through his veins, lining his face like spiderwebs. Even though the werewolf must be around two hundred and fifty pounds, he has him suspended in the air by his throat as if he weighs nothing at all.

I gasp. He barely looks like the Cain I know. No longer refined, polished, and in control. He's terrifying and immensely powerful. It's the first time I see the original sin demon that he is.

The club's music cuts off abruptly, and dancers jump out of the way. Panicked screams rake against my eardrums, but some other brave souls form a circle around us.

The werewolf claws at Cain's arm, taloned nails tearing into his flesh, and tar-like blood seeps from the wounds. But he's unfazed.

The other Mooners shuffle forward, hesitating to come to their friend's aid. Cain's head whips their way, his demonic glare enough to make his threat clear, and the black lines travel farther down his face and neck until they disappear down his collared shirt. The wolves step back.

I freeze on the spot.

Slowly, his gaze drops to me. His head tilts as he regards me for a second, but he looks so different, so terrifying. For those few seconds, I can't tell if he intends to lunge at me or turn away.

"C-Cain?" His name squeaks past my lips.

He says nothing. Only turns back to the struggling man in his grasp.

My entire body trembles. I don't know much about Hell, but I'm starting to think he's more than a demon. There has to be more to him than that. What I'm seeing... it's like the devil himself stands before me.

I want to look away, but I can't. Sayah perks up inside

me, watching with newfound adoration. She likes seeing him this way, and honestly, so do I.

The werewolf's face is the brightest shade of red, but it quickly turns more purple, and he chokes and sputters for a breath he can't get ahold of. Then there's an audible squishing sound and something sickly-warm splatters across my face and chest. I blink, unsure what's even happened, but when the werewolf's body hits the floor with a loud thud, I know it's something terrible.

I look down. I'm covered in blood. The Mooner's blood. It's all over me—in my hair, down my shirt, across my stomach. And more of it is pooling under the werewolf's limp body. His throat has been ripped out.

He's dead.

Body vibrating, Cain holds a chunk of blood, skin, and muscle in his hand. He looks at it, his lip curling in disgust, before throwing it on the floor next to the corpse. His chin lifts, and the crowd of onlookers step back in unison.

"Get. Out." He pronounces each word through a clenched jaw, but that's all it takes. Everyone scrambles for the exits.

Hands are suddenly under my arms, and I'm being hauled to my feet. I look up to see Dorian on my left and Elias on my right, holding me and guiding me farther back, away from Cain and the stampede of customers rushing for the doors.

"What's going on? Is he okay?" I ask them.

"Just a mild temper tantrum," Dorian says, but despite his joking tone, his expression is deadly serious. It's disturbing seeing him that way.

"We should get her out of here," Elias tells Dorian, who nods in agreement.

I glance over at the bar where Charlotte, Antonio, and

some of the other employees are watching in horror. Worry worms up my back. "But, what about work?"

"Looks like we're closing early tonight," Dorian says. He starts to tug me toward the secret exit by the bar. "Come. We'll get you home and cleaned up."

One more look at Cain, and he hasn't moved. It's hard to tell if he's even breathing. The bloody puddle now surrounds him, soaking into his expensive shoes, but still, he does nothing but stare blankly with those haunting, inky black eyes.

Not sure what I can even do to help him, I let Elias and Dorian drag me out of Purgatory and into the waiting limo, leaving him behind.

CHAPTER EIGHTEEN
CAIN

"Where is she?" I demand as I storm through the front door to the mansion, catching Dorian about to head upstairs.

He turns on his heels to face me and leans a bent arm on the staircase banister. "Tell you what—you leave her alone for tonight. She's been through enough today."

His patronizing words infuriate me, my fists curling into balls, but it's not a fight I'm after unless he pushes me. "Just tell me where she fucking is."

He stills, well aware that when fury takes me, it's hard to reel me down. And the incident with the werewolf in Purgatory still has my demon hovering on a thin edge of control. Just thinking about that creature's hands on her makes my blood boil. He didn't deserve the quick death I gave him, but my rage took over and made it merciless.

He'd been lucky.

"I think you should give her some time, man," Dorian huffs. "She's trying to relax by having a bath."

I shove past him, my footsteps thudding up the stairs.

"Just don't be a dick and scare her any further," he calls up after me.

Scare her? I glance over my shoulder for a heartbeat. "Have you forgotten who we are?"

"You know that's not what I mean."

I don't have time for this crap. I turn and take two steps at a time.

On the next floor, I swing left as Elias saunters down the corridor in my direction. He eyes me with that same cautionary look in his eyes that Dorian had. Like I have no fucking control of my dark side.

His mouth twists and parts.

"Don't waste your breath." I march right past him and toward the main bathroom. There's no tub in Aria's chamber, and I don't see Dorian taking her anywhere else besides the best.

Thinking about how the bastard had claimed her first, fucked her first, jabs at my self-control again. I don't know why I'm as furious as I am—all three of us have claimed her soul—but knowing that he got to her before me makes me enraged. I know my anger is misdirected. I know the fault lies with me for not taking her body in the beginning, but that only adds fuel to my fire.

Pausing outside the bathroom door, I suck in a ragged breath before rapping my knuckles on the door. Not waiting for her to respond, I open it and step inside the white marbled room.

"Occupied," she snaps, while hurrying to sit upright in the free-standing porcelain tub and press herself against the side. Water gushes out and over the edges. The heat of the room is suffocating; steam fogs the wall of mirrors and leaves the air heavy and damp.

I'd come in here in a rush, but now that I'm standing

before her, knowing that she's completely naked and wet… all my bravado drains from me.

"I wanted to come check on you." For some reason, my voice doesn't sound like my own when it reaches my ears. It's too weak and fragile to be mine.

Her huge, deep brown eyes are what I focus on first, dark hair flat around her round face, her lips curled downward. Her shoulders are curved forward as she huddles against the side of the tub, her blushing cheeks revealing her embarrassment. There are still smears of blood in her hair and streaking her shoulders.

The girl intrigues me more with each passing day. I can't get her out of my damn mind, and tonight I shut down Purgatory because of her.

What is it about her that affects me to this extent? I don't understand it. The moment Ramos brought her into this house, I lost myself. And it infuriates me that a woman could affect me so. I need to know why so I can end it.

She watches my every move like a mouse caught in the corner by a feral cat.

"I'm not going to hurt you," I assure her. My feet have moved on their own, and I stand before the tub, in the middle of a puddle of water. My gaze roams over her body, which is carefully concealed by the sudsy water and bubbles. My fingers tingle as I think about running them over her soft, pale skin.

"I know, Cain," she finally responds, drawing my attention to the apprehension clouding her gaze. "But tonight at Purgatory..." Her words flatline.

"Tonight was a lesson. Now everyone will know you belong to me."

"Belong to you," she repeats. Her hand finds the necklace, and she fingers the wing pendant. "What does that mean, exactly?"

I hesitate. I know what I *want* it to mean, but that's not what I'll say. "That your soul is mine, and therefore, you will not be touched by anyone else." I realize too late what that sounds like, and quietly add, "You'll be protected."

Her head tilts to the side, curious. She's caught my mistake. "But I thought Dorian and Elias own my soul, too. The three of you."

"Yes. This is true." I clear my throat to cover my blunder. "But I came to make sure you weren't scared of what you saw tonight."

She holds my gaze. "You killed that werewolf."

"And? He touched you."

Aria glances at the floor, unsure. "I probably should hate what you did, but I don't. The asshole deserved it."

Indecisiveness weaves through her words, and I smile at the battle she's facing with herself. But there's something else coiling in my chest, a wave of warmth shooting through me at hearing she approves. It elicits a strange sensation of pride, and heat rushes up my neck.

"I'll destroy anyone who hurts you."

I reach over a hand and slide a finger under her chin, guiding her to look at me. Seeing the necklace on her may have calmed the anger in me, but it awakens my possessiveness over her even more. After the shitshow at Purgatory, everyone will now know who she really belongs to, and we won't run into any more problems like tonight with the loose-handed werewolf.

No one would dare touch her again, if they valued their lives.

"Something is wrong with me," she whispers, like saying it out loud makes her words real. "I shouldn't love that you killed him to protect me." Her chin trembles.

"But you do, don't you?"

She doesn't respond right away, except the answer is

written right there on her gorgeous face. "I've been… abused before. In some of the past foster homes." Anger flashes in her eyes suddenly. "It's not a secret. I was young and vulnerable then. And they took advantage of me. That werewolf reminded me of those scumbags."

"Sometimes, seeking out vengeance is the right decision. Especially with what those bastards did to you." Just knowing she's been hurt before leaves me tense, and I grind my back teeth, furious.

"But I don't want to be like that," she murmurs.

"Tell me." I lift her chin higher to look me in the eyes. "Would you not want to punish those who have wronged you?"

For a moment, I believe she won't respond, then she gives me a slight nod.

"Some assholes will never change with mere words. There's no such thing as fairness or mercy," I say, remembering my father and how his selfish, power-driven ambitions led to our takeover attempt and then banishment. "There's only one way to strip them of their power. Destroy them."

My gaze drops to her mouth, and I find myself leaning closer to her. The urge to taste her lips wraps me in a dangerous grip, and I force myself to shake my head clear. I pull away and exhale heavily. The more time I spend with her, the more human I feel. And that's just not fucking acceptable.

ARIA

Evidently, I'm siding with the devil on the matter of revenge. Maybe it's because I haven't released Sayah as much as I should have these last few days and her darkness is influencing me. Or maybe it's the lingering anger and trauma from my past, but my insides twist with satisfaction at the memory of Cain holding the werewolf's throat in his hand. Still, my brain tells me it's wrong.

I meet Cain's icy blue eyes, so different now from the black demon ones I'd seen before, but somehow just as hypnotizing. "My foster father used to say that if you wear a mask long enough, you start to forget who you really are. I don't want to forget who I am. I don't want to think it's okay to hurt people."

Cain removes his dark jacket and places it on the counter against the wall. On his way back, he loosens his cufflinks and places them into his pocket, then rolls up the sleeves of his shirt. The fabric curves around his muscles, the top buttons sitting open at his throat.

I stiffen instantly. He's so dangerously sexy, it's suddenly hard to breathe.

He grabs two folded towels and drops them near the tub before he lowers himself onto his knees.

Only the porcelain bath wall lies between us, me naked and him staring at me like he might climb into the water with me. My heart skips a beat at his close proximity. He cups my face with one hand, leaning in closer. All I can look at are his full lips, while my emotions are a tangled mess of desire and fear.

"That's why you have me," he affirms. "I fear no evil. I am the monster lurking in the dark. And I am the punisher for those who cross you."

I swallow, hating to admit that he somehow sounds even sexier when he speaks this way. Apparently there are many things about myself I'm starting to discover around these demons.

Cain lets go of me and dips his hand into the bath, then pours water in his cupped hand over my hair.

Threads of blood spiral down my shoulders from my hair, and that's when I realize I must still have splatter of the werewolf on me.

I strangely enjoy having Cain care for me, which is the opposite of how he normally behaves. He studies me, probably expecting me to push him away, but I only stare up at him.

Gingerly, he splashes the blood out of my hair before reaching over for the bottle of shampoo. I gather more bubbles floating on the water to cover my breasts as he lathers my hair, his fingers gentle across my scalp. I won't deny, a girl can get used to this kind of treatment.

Last time I felt this laid back was when Dorian took me to the lake, which reminds me of something he said to me when we first met. "Dorian told me you are an original sin demon. That you are Pride. Is that true?"

His nostrils flare as if I've annoyed him with my question. Or maybe it's the mention of Dorian. I'm not sure. "Lay down so I can wash your hair."

I want to push for an answer, but his stoic expression tells me he isn't changing his mind, so I cross my arms over my chest and gracefully slide under the bubbly surface.

Reaching down, he slowly splashes water over my hair to wash the shampoo out. He isn't looking at me anymore.

I ask him, "Did I say something wrong?"

He sweeps suds from my brow. "Dorian is right. I am Pride." He pauses. "Did he also tell you about my father?"

I study the tightness around his mouth, the darkening of his voice. His dad is a touchy topic, and I can't tell if this is a trick question. "No."

He doesn't respond right away as he debates how much to tell me.

"Lucifer," he says finally. He sits back on his heels as he grabs a towel and dries his hands. He watches me like he's waiting for my surprised reaction. "Lucifer is my father."

It doesn't hit me right away, but when it does, I'm left breathless. I sit up abruptly. Water sloshes everywhere, splashing him too, and he narrows his eyes at me. "Wait a minute. Lucifer is your father? *Lucifer,* Lucifer? As in *Satan?* The Devil? The angel who fell from Heaven?"

"One and all." His expression is unchanging. As if carved from stone.

"You're Lucifer's son." It's a hard concept to wrap my head around.

His gaze darkens. "The oldest of seven and a prince of Hell, yes."

A prince... of Hell...

I swallow roughly. Suddenly his presence feels different. He's much more deadly than I originally thought.

"Or at least I was," he says. His gaze dips to my chest, and I look down to see my breasts are out of the water and all on show. Quickly dipping back under, I press my chest back to the side of the tub and face him.

"What does that mean, 'was?'" I ask, trying to get the attention off me and back on him. "If you're his son, then why are you here?"

"We were banished," is all he says to that.

"Wait, what?" *We?* As in all three of them? My head spins with the overload of information he's just dumped. "But why? What in the world did you do? Start dating an angel?"

He doesn't respond and climbs to his feet, his upper lip curling into a silent sneer. "You're clean from blood. I'll arrange for the maids to bring you fresh clothes."

Pivoting on his heels, he turns abruptly and marches toward the door. Just as he opens it, he glances over his shoulder at me and says, "Elias will take you tomorrow to visit Murray's home to say your farewell."

Then he walks out and shuts the door behind him with a thud.

I don't move at first, stunned by what I've just learned. Even being allowed to go home is overshadowed by Cain's reveal.

His father is the devil himself. Lucifer. Cain is a prince of Hell, the oldest of the sin demons. He's been banished with Elias and Dorian for some reason, so whatever they did had to have been bad. Really, really bad.

And lastly, Cain has major father issues.

I slide down into the water, the bubbles floating around my chin. In truth, learning about his messed-up family and problems makes him more human than he realizes. At first, he came across as this perfect, untouchable demon. But he's really just as broken as the rest of us, isn't he?

Misery loves company after all, which is absolutely true. Even if it's sadistic.

CHAPTER NINETEEN
ELIAS

Being in the city always makes me itch. I'm not used to the hum of so many bodies, the dense noise, the congestion, how out of place I feel. Exposed. Vulnerable.

I fucking hate it.

But I'm here because of Aria. I'm not sure how I got dragged into this chore. The sensitive stuff is more Dorian's thing, but I guess there was worry about her making a run for it. And, let's face it, my hunting abilities far surpass Cain and Dorian's combined.

So far, she shows no signs of escaping. She's been standing on the sidewalk, staring at the apartment's door for ten minutes, saying nothing. I know Ramos is upstairs waiting on us, but even though her actions are strange, I don't want to push her. After finding out about the warlock's death and who Cain's real father is, along with our banishment from Purgatory, she seems a bit shaken up.

Though I've noticed changes in her these past few days. In the mornings, when I wake up beside her, she barely even reacts to me anymore. I'm not sure how I feel about her accepting me so much easier now.

I need to find a way to stop the dreams. Maybe then I'll stop sleepwalking into her room in the dead of night.

I can't control it. Barricading myself in my room, tying myself down—hell, even when Aria had furniture in front of her door—somehow, I get through it all. I don't know why I do it or even how, but my dreams are always about the same person. Serena.

Just thinking her name hits me with a tidal wave of fury. A growl builds in my throat. Her betrayal goes beyond me. I'd loved her fiercely, blindly, and that'd been my mistake. But what she did affected us all. It's the reason we're banished to this plane in the first place.

I'll never forgive myself for trusting her and for not listening to Cain or Dorian's warnings. I was a fool then. But I'll never make that mistake again.

"Are you okay?" Aria's sweet voice carries me back from that dark place, and I find her staring at me now with concern wrinkling her brow. "You're purring like a cat."

I snort. *Purring? I don't purr.*

Talk about an insult.

It's a good thing Dorian isn't here to have heard that one. I'd never live it down.

A biting remark hovers on my tongue, but I try to be civil to her, so my jaw clenches instead. "Are you ready to go inside yet?"

Frowning, she glances at the door. "Can I go alone?"

"You already know the answer to that."

She sighs heavily, and once again I'm reminded of how small and petite she is next to me.

She pushes open the front door and steps inside, heading to the staircase just ahead. Paint peels from the walls, and an immediate stench of something decaying floods me. All windows have been sealed shut, making the air stale and putrid, which says a lot considering how revolting parts of Hell smell.

I follow close behind her as she takes two steps at a time, eager to reach Murray's apartment. When we finally reach the top floor, she turns right and shoves open her door, which easily swings open.

Dorian explained he'd gotten the kitchen professionally cleaned right after the forensics team from the local precinct declared they no longer needed the scene taped for investigation. They collected all the evidence they needed, apparently, which has led to no arrests. So naturally, that means they have zilch.

Fuck all the investigation bullshit. We had it right back in Hell. Send out demons like me to track down the culprit and rip them from limb to limb. That is justice.

I tilt my head back and take a deep inhale, hoping to catch any hint of an intruder's scent, but with so much putrefaction and harsh cleaner burning the air, it's a waste of time. Not to mention the dozens of people who have traipsed through here from the police investigation. All that combined makes detecting the person responsible impossible. In hindsight, I should have come here the moment Murray's body was found, but my skill isn't foresight. It's hunting.

Aria stares at a spot by the kitchen where I notice a fist-sized hole through the plaster. I wonder what that's from, but Aria quickly vanishes down a corridor and into a room just as Ramos emerges from another across the hall. Then he swings his attention my way and strolls over.

"Find anything new?" I ask, lowering my voice.

"Nothing. Whoever came here before was thorough."

I stare out to the living room, to the sliding glass doors that lead to a balcony overlooking the busy street. I try to picture Aria living here, watching TV and doing what normal humans do. Except, she's not quite human, not with whatever shadow ability she has.

Ramos is staring at me. Right, he's waiting for something to do.

"Let's do another sweep," I say. "Even the smallest thing can be a clue, so bring anything you find back to the mansion."

Ramos nods. "Of course." He turns and heads into the living room, where he pulls open the drawers on a long table against the wall.

Not sure how I can be useful here, I walk toward the room Aria disappeared into and step into the open doorway.

She's kneeling near her bed with the bedside table drawer open. Next to her is a black duffle bag half filled with her belongings.

Sensing me, she looks over her shoulder as she wipes her teary eyes. "Guessing the bank is going to foreclose on the apartment now, so I want to take back as many of my things as possible."

"What can I help with?"

She shakes her head and turns back to whatever she's holding in her hand, her head tilting forward. She sniffles, and I retreat, giving her space and time alone to grieve. This will be her only chance to be close to anything representing Murray for her farewell since warlocks perform secretive burials for one another. And families are forbidden.

ARIA

As much as Murray pissed me off, being back home, I find myself missing the stupidest things about him. His twist on cheap boxed mac and cheese with corn kernels. I scrunched up my nose at first, but it was decent. And the time he took me to the zoo for my birthday. Sure, he had a secretive meeting with someone near the lion exhibition, but I had the best time with Joseline.

Dumb things to miss about someone, but maybe I wasn't as ready to leave home as I had thought.

I stare at the photo of us three at the zoo, at the monkeys in the background. Joseline posed while giving a peace sign, while Murray rolled his eyes. He detested photos, and it's the only thing I have left of him.

Sucking in a shaky breath, I shove the photo into my bag and get to my feet, realizing everything I own fits in a duffel bag. Kind of sad when you think about it.

I drag myself out into the hallway, and from the living room, Elias and Ramos's voices reach me. Only words I catch are 'Aria' and 'birth certificate.'

Frozen on the spot, I try to decipher why in the world they would want that? My mind sweeps to the demons constantly asking me about my shadow, which might mean they want to find out about my past. Well, good luck to them. I've never had luck in getting any information from Murray or the foster care system. And I've searched this apartment upside down. Well, as much as I could in Murray's room, since he kept it locked when he wasn't home.

I lift my gaze to the door across the hall from mine, sitting ajar. A quick look to ensure Elias or Ramos don't see me and I dart into Murray's bedroom. The pillows and mattress are tossed across the room, clothes from the cupboard strewn everywhere, as are the books from his bookshelf. My heart clenches, knowing he would hate seeing his belongings discarded this way.

Reaching down, I collect a book on magic from nature, then another, and two more, then replace them on the empty bookshelf. I collect another armful and stack them next to each other, feeling like it's the least I can do to create some semblance of normality. Which is ridiculous, I know, but it makes me feel better.

I turn around when the wooden floorboard under my feet creaks. I glance down and look more carefully at the wider-than-normal crack between the wooden panels. Down on my knees, curiosity gets the better of me, and I'm pawing at the narrow gap, well aware Murray loved hiding things. I once found a credit card in my cereal box. When I asked him about it, he just joked it was the gift, but he was quick to snatch it from me.

Tracing my fingers along the crack, the wooden panel lifts slightly, and I quickly pull a piece the length of my arm away from the floor.

There's a shallow hole inside. It looks empty, and it's not dusty, which tells me someone was in here not long ago. Maybe Murray suspected someone wanted him dead, so he rushed to get what he was hiding here? Couldn't have been the killer, because with the state of the room, why bother concealing this secret compartment?

I lean forward for a better look in the corners when something white grabs my attention. Quickly, I stick my hand in and grab an envelope. Inside are all kinds of papers, and I unfold them, scanning them to work out what they are.

Bank certificates for various apartment addresses all over the country, from Detroit to Chicago and even one in New Orleans. Are these places he owns? That bastard was so tight-assed and never gave me a dollar, yet he owned.... I shuffle through the papers to count them, when one catches my attention.

The header didn't read RBD Bank, but Saint Charity General Hospital in Centreville, Illinois.

It's a payment receipt for the sum of $18,590.

Then I lose my breath when I see my name in line with the amount paid.

Aria Cross.

I can't move or make any sense what this means, but the payment was for me. Scanning the note, I set my sights on the date of issue.

Exactly eighteen years and two weeks ago. And next to my name is the time, 11:30 p.m.

That's the time of my birth, which ironically is the only thing Murray had told me. I sit back on my heels, my stomach hurting because what I'm looking at is the hospital I was born in. A clue to my past.

What exactly was the receipt for? Hospital costs of my mother giving birth to me? Or had I been sick? Maybe my mother died after I was born. But why would Murray hold onto this receipt? What is the significance?

My stomach rolls over on itself and bile hits the back of my throat. Thumping footfalls approach the room. I frantically replace the wooden panel over the hole in the floor and stuff the papers into the envelope before shoving it down the front of my pants. I cover my stomach with my top just as Elias steps into the room.

"What are you doing in this room?" His voice deepens.

I shrug and get to my feet. "Saying my farewell." Lowering my head, I pass him and walk into my room, grab my duffle bag, and join Ramos in the living room. "Are we done?" I call out, itching to get out of here, *now.*

Elias is on my heels, and his gaze scrutinizes me like he's trying to pry into my thoughts. But my head isn't in a place to share this with anyone until I can make sense of exactly who I am. And how in the world Murray ended up with me.

"You can talk to me," Elias assures me, standing over me like a mountain. The guy clearly doesn't understand sensitivity.

I'll admit that the urge to give in and turn to him with all my problems pushes at my mind. But I remember him talking to Ramos about my birth certificate, so he isn't telling me everything, is he? And I'm not going to be the first to reveal, either, because I still haven't worked out the demons' agenda.

Drawing away from the duo who don't seem to be moving, I walk straight out of the apartment and downstairs, needing fresh air. Suddenly, I'm feeling claustrophobic and can't breathe as reality strangles me.

Footfalls rush behind me, but I don't stop until I shove past the front door to the apartment and pause halfway down the front steps. Cars rush past, people stroll down the sidewalk, a couple of young girls across the street giggle at something. I miss these small things that remind me of growing up here, of being part of humanity.

Except, Murray kept a secret from me all this time. He knew where I was born and maybe even knew who my parents were, and now he's dead and I can't ask him anything.

The door behind me creaks open just as someone calls my name from down the street.

"Aria!" The familiar female voice comes again, and I twist in the direction to find Joseline, wide-eyed and shocked, rushing toward me. She's got her backpack flung over her shoulder, and she's wearing black slacks and a white button-up shirt from the department store she works at. Mousey blonde hair is drawn back into a tight ponytail, and she's wearing her favorite fire-engine-red lipstick.

My heart hits the back of my throat at seeing her, eyes pricking with tears, and I rush down to meet her, both of us clashing together. She hugs me hard and doesn't let go. A sense of calm flares over me, and I hold onto her like somehow she can pull me out of the hole I've fallen into.

"Please tell me you're back," she mumbles quickly in my ear. "Those demons… Did they let you go?"

"I missed you so much," I answer and draw back, my hands sliding into hers. A desperate urgency coils in my chest to beg her to help me escape. But I can't say anything because I sense Elias at my back, and I won't drag my best friend into my nightmare world.

"I heard what happened to Murray. Part of me thinks the dirtbag deserved it, for selling you off, you know? But the other part..."

I nod because I understand her inner struggle. I was experiencing it myself. I stare at my friend, memorizing the cute freckles on her nose, the perfectly shaped eyebrows, the slight kink in her lower lip when she speaks. I want to memorize it all so I have her with me always.

She glances up and over my shoulder when a shadow falls over us. Her expression falls, and I feel her body flinching. She's well aware she's looking at a demon.

"We should go," Elias says, his voice strong without a hint of understanding. Right now, I wish it had been Dorian bringing me out here, as he'd be less 'Terminator bodyguard' and more of a 'flirty boyfriend' type of guy.

Joseline's eyes plead with me, and her hold tightens. "Come to my place, just for a bit to catch up."

"That's not a good idea," Elias answers for me, and I stiffen. People walk past us on the sidewalk, most taking a second glance at the big guy behind me. He looks like a bull in a china shop, and when I glance over my shoulder at him, I notice the unease on his face. He hates it here, it's obvious.

"We're leaving now," he demands as Ramos goes to open the door of the limousine parked a few spots down the road.

"Aria," Joseline begins and draws me to look at her. "I'm worried about you. Are they keeping you prisoner?"

"Not quite, but sort of."

Elias places his heavy hand on my shoulder, and I shake it off. "Give me a freaking second," I snap.

He growls under his breath, which has Joseline backing away.

"I'm fine, I promise. And I'll try to call you more, okay?" My attempt to reassure her fails; her fright is palpable.

Elias takes my arm and draws me toward the car. I stumble back, my hand slipping out of Joseline's. She doesn't move or say a word, but appears shell-shocked and frozen on the spot. Guilt chews on me that I ever told her about the demons. She is a witch with small ability, yet the sight of a demon renders her speechless.

I can't fault her, and I feel awful at leaving her this way. Elias nudges me toward the open door, but I'm furious that he's doing this.

Shoving his hand away, I snarl, "I can get in on my own."

One last look to my friend before I get into the limousine, and deep inside, I know that this might be the last time I ever see her. I want to scream and protest, but what will that get me? Dragged and tossed into the limo, and the last thing I want is for her to worry even more about me.

Elias shuts the door, and I curl in on myself, staring out at my friend as we drive away, leaving behind the life I once had.

CHAPTER TWENTY
CAIN

The morning sun breaks through the trees, and I'm still at my desk poring over more of the library's books and documents for any hint of what Aria could be. This time it's mythical creatures from long ago, most either long extinct or only told of in stories, but so far, I've had no luck finding anything close to being able to manipulate darkness or equivalent to it. I'm starting to wonder if Elias and I had seen the right thing after all. Maybe the darkness I sensed was fabricated from my natural lust for her? I don't know.

Have I misjudged her, and she's really ordinary, like she claims?

But then, it doesn't explain how she was able to resist Dorian's compulsions or find the relic on her own. Coincidence? Don't believe in it. And no one on the living plane can resist Dorian.

Sighing, I lean back in my chair and run a hand over my face. Even though I know I need to leave her alone, her very presence calls to me. Draws me in. It's like a siren's song that only I can hear through every crack and floorboard in this house.

I want her. I know I do. I want her more than I've ever wanted anything in my entire existence, besides my father's throne, but even that dream is fading. Even with all the money and research at our disposal, we aren't any closer to finding another piece of Azrael's harp. It's beginning to feel like a waste of time.

Maybe Dorian was right. Maybe we should focus on rebuilding our lives here instead of obsessing over the past. I never thought I'd say such a thing, but with Aria so close, my focus is shifting. My control is slipping. The temptation to claim her in other ways besides a contract is a driving force, and I wonder why I continue to fight it.

I know she's probably asleep in her room at this early hour, and I shouldn't disturb her, but I want to see her again. Elias had said the visit to her old apartment had been difficult for her, especially when the young witch friend appeared. Imagining Aria hurting brings out the monster in me.

The moment I rise to stand, my cell rings in my pocket. I fish it out and hold it to my ear. "Yes?"

"Mr. Cain."

I recognize Alfonzo's voice right away, even if the last time we spoke was two months ago. Expecting more bad news, my muscles tense.

"We've found it," he says. "The heart."

I almost drop the phone in my hand. Alfonzo's team is one of the many we have scouring the earth for parts of Azrael's harp, and after endless searching, they've actually found another one of the pieces we need.

Excitement surges to the surface, rushing my words. "Where? You have it now? You must send it here immediately."

"Er—" The phone crackles and spits with static, the connection weak. Wherever he is, the service isn't the best, but I still catch the hesitation in his tone. "We know where it is, but we haven't been able to reach it."

My excitement quickly turns to annoyance. I clutch the phone tighter. "What does that mean?"

"... tracked it to… Polar Desert… Antarctica." More static breaks up his sentence, and I growl in frustration.

Antarctica? Shit.

After close to a decade of searching, we'd found the cord in the pit of an active volcano. We knew Gabriel—the flying ballerina—wasn't going to make finding the harp's pieces easy, but an Antarctic tundra? That seems a bit excessive.

"It's meters below the ice… Lost four men…" Alfonzo struggles to give me details through the bad connection. "We have to return… Regroup…"

Fuck. We're so close to another piece of the puzzle now, there's no way I'm letting some snow and ice stop us from getting what we need.

"And you're sure it's there," I bark into the receiver. I glance at the clock on the wall, wondering how long it'll take me to get there if I charter a private plane. Antarctica isn't exactly the easiest place to get to. "You've seen it yourself?"

"Yes, through the robot's camera… But—"

That's all I need to know. "Send me the coordinates. I'm on my way."

The moment I end the call, a knock sounds, snapping my attention to the french doors. Dorian stands there on the other side with his stupid lazy grin on his face. Rage rolls through me as the truth of what he's done with Aria pops into my head again.

He knew we weren't supposed to cross that line with

her. Especially not knowing what she is or what her real purpose is for being here. He *knew,* yet he fucked her anyway. It's what he does.

Since the lock hasn't been fixed from the last time he broke it, he pushes the doors open.

"Don't bother. I'm leaving," I say and shove past him into the library. He's the last person I want to see right now. My focus needs to stay on the next relic.

"Come on. You're not still mad at me, are you?" Dorian asks as he swings around. "Elias I get. The dog's got an alpha complex, but you—"

I whirl on him, shoulders taught. "You're the one who broke the rules."

"Rules?" He blinks. "I'm sorry. I must've missed the community newsletter with the rules about what to do and not do with Aria."

I say nothing. He's trying to use humor to either soften the situation or egg me on, but unlike Elias, I know him well enough to not be swept up by it. Besides, I don't have time to hash this out right now. I need to catch a plane and get to the heart.

Turning, I head for the hall.

"Where are you going?" Dorian calls after me.

"Alfonzo found the heart, but it's too dangerous for his crew to retrieve it. So I'm going to do it myself."

He's at my side a second later, keeping up with my strides. "Shit, really? The heart? Where is it?"

"Antarctica."

"Fuck me."

I slide him a glare as we enter the foyer. "I should be back in three days. At most."

"I'll go with you," he says.

I stop short. "No."

"Wait, why? You're always griping that you want a

break from the monotony. And I think I deserve a vacation—"

"This isn't a fucking joke, Dorian," I snap, my irritation growing.

He pauses for a long moment, staring at me, before shaking his head and trying again in a different tone. More serious. "We should do this together. Elias can stay here with Aria while we retrieve the heart. You and me. It'll be like old times."

He means when we were in Hell, causing a ruckus and not having to worry about the problems we have now. When we were much younger and a lot more naive. So much has changed since then.

"You know I'll always be by your side," he tacks on, and I know he's referencing our failed plans to overtake Hell. We'd agreed to take on my father together, whatever the outcome. And if I ever make it to the throne, he'll be on my right side and Elias will be on my left, ruling alongside me. Together. That was the deal.

"Do you think Elias will be able to watch her?" I ask him.

"Aria? Oh yeah." He waves his hand. "She'll be busy with work at Purgatory. And even if she manages to slip away, Elias's got the nose to track her. He'll find her again in no time."

He doesn't seem worried about it, and he's right when he says nothing escapes Elias. I just hope I don't end up regretting this decision.

"Got a plane ticket?" he asks, and I shake my head.

"Just got off the phone with Alfonzo."

"I'll book it in the car on the way there." Grabbing his heaviest coat from the closet, he shrugs it on and opens the front door. "Sadie! Tell Edwin to bring the car!" he shouts behind us. His voice echoes throughout the house, but it does the trick.

The young servant scurries out of the dining room. "Right away, Master Dorian." Then she disappears just as fast.

In true Dorian fashion, he drapes an arm over my shoulder and guides me out the door, grinning like a fool. The Town Car appears at the end of the driveway, the tires crunching on the gravel as it follows the circle and pulls up to the steps.

"Cain and Dorian, on an adventure again!" he says as he walks around the car to the other side and opens the door. "This is going to be fun."

I shake my head, but a smile creeps across my lips as I join him inside.

After a long, uncomfortable plane ride, we arrive as close to Alfonzo's coordinates as possible. We arrange for two guides to take us on snowmobiles to the exact location. It's a treacherous journey and indescribably cold, despite all the layers of protective clothing we have on. The trek takes us over three hours because of the whipping icy winds, disorienting whiteness of the snow, and the overall icy terrain, but when we see the team's campsite and drilling equipment, we know we've arrived.

Alfonzo steps out of his small, bright orange tent, bundled up in more layers than either of us. As a water elemental fae, the snow and ice shouldn't be as much of a bother to him as it would a human or other supernatural, but even he has his limits and it's ungodly cold here. Dorian and I have Hell's heat running through our veins, acting as a natural insulator, but neither of us would want to stay longer than we have to. Freezing temperatures and Hell demons don't mix well, for obvious reasons.

As my gaze sweeps the camp, I find most of the other tents and machinery abandoned. Alfonzo seems to be the only one left on the team.

Annoyance prickles up my neck. What are we paying them all for?

"Where is everyone?" Dorian asks before I get the chance to. He has to shout over the ruthless wind.

"Gone. The weather's been challenging. Unpredictable. Most had to be airlifted out of here," he replies. His mouth and nose are covered by a thermal mask, but the exposed skin on his cheeks and around his eyes is an unsettling shade of purple. "I promised them that once we found it, they could go."

And they'd run the moment they had.

"But you found it," I press, wanting to make sure we haven't made the trip for nothing. "The heart."

He nods toward a large crane system with an attached drill that's hovering over a massive hole in the otherwise smooth whiteness. "It's meters down, frozen in the ice. I was just able to see it with my camera, but getting to it will be too challenging."

For a normal man, maybe.

Dorian and I glance at each other, thinking the same thing.

"You may go, Alfonzo. Your job here is done," I say.

He hesitates and looks from Dorian to me.

"Your payment will be wired to your account the moment we retrieve the heart," I continue.

He nods again. "Do you need me to show you how to use the equipment?"

"That won't be necessary," Dorian says with a smile.

"We don't need it."

Without questioning it further, Alfonzo moves toward one of the guides and takes his place on the snowmobile.

"Good luck," he calls before the driver hits the gas and speeds off back in the direction we came.

"What about the other one?" Dorian whispers to me, referring to the other guide and snowmobile.

Whether he's human or a supernatural, I'd rather he not know who or what we are. We have too many enemies in and out of Hell, so discretion is always better. "Send him off, too."

As Dorian walks over to the guide and compels him to leave us, despite the danger, I trudge closer to the pit where the heart lies locked in the ice. I wish there was some way I could sense its dark power, like I could with Aria, but these relics are quiet to me. Or I am deaf to them. Either way, it only makes tracking them down all the more challenging. I want to see it or have some way to know for sure the heart's down there—some assurance besides Alfonzo's word—but from where I stand, there's only an impenetrable darkness.

The growl of a motor cuts through the quiet as the guide drives away, and with that, we're alone in the Antarctic tundra.

Dorian comes over to my side and peers down. He whistles, and the sound echoes through the hole. "That's a mighty long way down," he says. "Any ideas?"

"One." I start undoing my coat's zipper and make quick work of peeling off my top layers.

Dorian's eyes widen and he laughs. "Oh, that's what I'm talking about. Now it's a party!" He pulls off his heavy clothing, too.

The second the last piece of fabric is stripped off, the

bitter air bites at my bare skin, stinging and pinching mercilessly. "We are going to have to make this quick."

Also standing half-naked in the snow, Dorian shivers. "Agreed."

I reach into myself and call to my darkness. It's slow to respond at first—stunned by the temperature—but once it awakens, it washes over me and consumes me entirely. Unlike at Purgatory where I was doing all I could to withhold my power, there's no need to keep the demon inside me. Now it can be released completely.

I feel my wings unfurl and stretch out behind me, and I groan with relief. Their width casts me in shadows. It's been too long since I've been me—the true me. I've almost forgotten how good it feels. Almost better than sex.

Almost.

All around my feet, the snow has melted and smoke swirls off my skin, now burning up with the heat of hellfire. Darkness colors my veins and lines my skin, bringing its raw and uncontrollable power with it. I fucking love the way it hums through my body.

Glancing at Dorian, he's changed into his true incubus form as well. Two horns now curve back from the top of his head, and intricate tattoos weave across his shoulders and torso, all demonic runes that give the incubus more power. Pointed ears peek out from silvery white hair, and he grins broadly.

"It's good to be back," he says as he rolls his shoulders and moves his neck side to side, getting a feel for the changes. "Let's go get that heart."

I push off into the air, spreading my wings wide to gain more height before closing them around myself and diving headfirst for the pit, which is just wide enough for me to fit. Yelling with excitement, Dorian runs for it and jumps in after me.

We descend into the darkness together, Dorian leaping across the icy walls on the way down while I fall down the middle. Surprisingly, it's not as cold down here as it is on the surface, but there's no wind and snow pelting us either. The darkness is thick and hard to see through, even with my heightened vision, but it's familiar at the same time, and before we know it, it gives way to a pulsing red glow that seems to thump to the rhythm of a living heart.

Instantly, I throw out my wings and arms to stop myself. The talons at the ends of my toes and fingers embed into the ice wall, holding me in place. Above me, Dorian slides down into a split, gracefully balancing himself without breaking a sweat.

"Do you see it?" he asks.

I can see the beating reddish glow in front of me and what looks like an enlarged human's heart trapped in the ice. Excitement floods me. "Yeah, it's here."

"Quick, let's grab it and go. My balls are turning blue."

Clenching my fist, I punch into the ice and hold my hand there to let the heat of my body melt away its casing. It doesn't take long, and the moment I can, I grab the relic and yank it out. It's slippery and cold against my palm, but the heart-shaped object continues to beat as if alive. I hold it up for Dorian to see.

"We fucking got a second relic!" His voice echoes all around us in the cavern.

"Good, now let's get the hell out of here."

He begins to leap upward the same way he came down, with more poise, balance, and skill than the world's greatest acrobat or gymnast.

As I wait for him to climb out, I look at the heart in my hand and thank our luck that we were able to get it relatively easily. The cold is a pain in the ass, but not unmanageable. Years to track it down, but only seconds to retrieve it.

Once Dorian disappears from view, I launch myself into the air, manipulate my wings to fit the tight space, and fly for the surface. I reach the top just as Dorian crawls out, so I hook my arms under his shoulders and haul him into the sky with me. As the snowy ground becomes farther and farther away, he throws his head back and laughs. Then he grabs the heart from me and tosses it from one hand to the other as we fly into the clouds.

"See? Just like old times, my friend." He chuckles.

Smiling, I beat my wings against the wind and fly us fast toward the landing strip where the plane waits for us, feeling more like myself than I have in a long time.

CHAPTER TWENTY-ONE
DORIAN

After a rough flight from Antarctica to Australia due to the weather, we spend the money and charter a private, more luxurious jet back to the States. Neither Cain or I want to deal with humans at the moment, and a priceless Hell relic that resembles a real-looking heart can't really go through baggage claim, so it's the wiser choice.

To keep the heart safe, we place it in a special box with velvet cushioning, much like the harp's string, and place it on a small table between us. Always in our line of sight.

As we fly across the Pacific Ocean, Cain lounges back in his over-plush chair, eyes closed but not sleeping. Back in his casual human form, his body is too stiff to be fully at rest, while I'm bouncing in my seat with excitement.

Two relics out of seven. It sounds pitiful when I say it that way, but after years of no luck whatsoever, I'll take the victory. Even if it's a small one. I was starting to think we were stuck here for eternity, but it seems like we may have a chance of returning after all. One step closer to finishing what we started in Hell, without Maverick's bullshit offer.

I peek at Cain, who's so still he doesn't even appear to be breathing. For about the hundredth time, I debate telling him about Lucifer's deal and his recruitment of Maverick, but I know it'll be a waste of my breath. For some reason, he refuses to believe any of his siblings would go against him, but what does he expect? Brother or not, their loyalty isn't with Cain—like any demon, they'll do what they need to survive.

Well, any demon but us. Elias, Cain, and I are a rare breed. Our oath to each other isn't something we take lightly.

I decide it's better if I continue to keep Maverick's proposal to myself for now. I'll never take him up on it, and neither would Elias, so it may be best if he doesn't know. It won't change anything.

"What's the plan when we get back?" I ask against the droning silence.

Cain's gaze slides over to me before he responds. "What do you mean?"

"The plan. Now that we have two pieces of the harp, what are we supposed to do with them?"

"I'm not sure exactly," he says, muscles stiff. I would think he'd loosen up after our adventure in Antarctica, but he is wound just as tightly as usual. "I'll want to do some more research before we try anything. Just in case. Maybe check in on the other teams to see if they're any closer with the other missing pieces."

"Just in case what?"

Slowly, he sits upright in his chair and sighs. "We have no idea what these relics are capable of. The harp can open the gates to Hell, so each piece must hold an immense amount of power on its own. There could be deterrents embedded in them."

"Deterrents? You mean like being in an active volcano

or frozen in the ice in the middle of west bumble fuck Antarctica?"

"Technically it would be south bumble fuck, but I'm talking about beyond the location."

"Like what?" I ask. "Like booby traps?"

His shoulder lifts slightly in a half-shrug, the gesture jerky and unnatural. Something's off with him. I've known him for too long and know the difference between normal stressed Cain and something else.

"You never know. Elias did say the string played music to Aria. I'm still not sure what that means, but it's best if we err on the side of caution."

Playing music hardly sounds dangerous to me, but it does make me wonder why I've never heard anything from the thing myself. Why is the harp silent for us and everyone else but is affecting Aria, of all people?

Bringing her into my thoughts resurrects the delicious memories of how quickly things had spiraled out of control between us. I thought I could control myself around her when I brought her to the lake, but knowing she wanted me just as bad as I wanted her—especially without my power influencing her—made it damn impossible to resist. Then to finally have her fully, feel the way her tight pussy clenched around my cock as her orgasm took hold of her… how intoxicating she tasted on my tongue... it is all I can fucking think about.

What surprises me the most was how she was able to keep up with me and my raging libido. If she hadn't had to work that night, I would've fucked her until kingdom come.

Even with the risk of Cain and Elias being mad at me again, as soon as we get to the mansion, I want to see her again and test her limits. Maybe this time I'll take that sweet little ass of hers, too. Unleash my full demon on her.

Shoulders rigid, Cain leans forward in the chair, taking me off guard. He's staring at me with a new fury blazing in his eyes, which are now a darker shade of blue. Almost black.

"What?" I ask, puzzled. Had I missed something?

"You don't fucking get it, do you?" he growls. His fists are balled on the table between us. "Aria is off limits until we can find out what she is and if she's meant to do us harm."

My confusion grows even more, and I look at him. Where is this coming from?

"Her tight pussy? All you can think about? Take her *sweet little ass*?" He mimics my thoughts back to me word for word, and I freeze. How did he know…? Had I said all that out loud? Fuck, it wouldn't be the first time I said shit out loud I shouldn't have.

"Uh…" If I had, I don't understand where his anger is coming from. We'd talked about me and Aria before. I thought we'd squashed it.

He pushes on. "Are you really that dense, or have you forgotten about Serena? We can't let a girl be our downfall again."

I study him for a long moment as my own annoyance prickles. This has nothing to do with Serena and we both know it. It never has. He wants Aria just as bad—hell, maybe more. He's been obsessed with her since the moment she was brought into our home. He just doesn't want to admit it. Even to himself.

I meet his gaze. "You're not afraid of Aria and what she might do to us. You're afraid of what she's doing to *you*. Your pride is getting in the way, as usual."

His eyes widen. He can't believe I had the balls to say that to him, and honestly, I'm just as surprised myself. But it's true.

"I'm furious with myself for letting you have her first," he confesses, the words flying from his mouth without his control. He's clenching his fists so tight now, his fingers turn white. "I kept making excuses. I kept pushing her away."

Holy fuck. Cain is jealous. I can't believe it.

Pressing his lips into a hard line, he continues to stare at me with a mixture of disbelief and anger. He definitely wasn't planning on telling me all that, but now that he has, he isn't holding back.

"Elias was right. You never think. You continue sticking your dick where it doesn't belong. You're irresponsible, careless, and impulsive." He runs a frustrated hand through his hair in a human-like gesture. It's so un-Cain like, it takes me off guard. I've never seen him like this before. He's becoming unhinged before my eyes.

What the hell is wrong with him?

"You should have never touched her," he tacks on, gaze hardening on me.

"Why, so you could?"

He stops briefly, seeming even more flustered than before. "If I gave into temptation like I wanted to, she would have been screaming *my* name the very first night she arrived."

"So what? We're supposed to just wait around until you finally fucking figure out what you want?" I say. "You don't see her as anything but property. You can't even have a simple dinner with her. She finds comfort in me. You scare her. Like that night in the club—"

His chin lifts. "She wasn't afraid."

"Oh? Because it looked that way to me. But what do I know, right?"

Surprisingly, Cain glances away and his voice lowers as his anger fades from his tone. "You're wrong."

Irritation pokes at me. "Of course you don't fucking believe me. When have you ever? Just like with your siblings. If it were up to Maverick and Lucifer, you'd have a knife in your back right now."

"What the fuck are you talking about?" he asks through clenched teeth.

Even though my conscious shouts at me to not say anything, my mouth has different plans. It's time he hears it. I know I'm toeing the line here, but this conversation suddenly feels long overdue.

"Your slimeball of a brother has been trying to get me to come onto Lucifer's side for years. Now he wants Elias, too. Killing you off grants us a ticket back to Hell."

As expected, he's quick to respond. "Maverick? He'd never—"

"Ah, but he would, and he's tried. Not just once, either. He's been sending me messages through the veil and trying to recruit me to Lucifer's side. I've tried to tell you before, but you never fucking listen to anyone but yourself."

I wait for the outburst. Or the argument. But to my shock, it never comes. Instead, he remains quiet.

Then, after a long moment, he says, "You're right. I don't."

I almost fall out of my seat at that. Holy shit. Did he just *agree* with me?

I can't believe it. Is Hell freezing over? It just might be.

"After all the shit we've been through, you still don't trust us?" I ask him.

The muscle in his jaw twitches as he tries to keep his mouth clamped shut, but it doesn't work for long. "No."

Well, fuck.

"I don't trust that you'll make the right decision on your own. Not after what happened with Elias and Serena," he clarifies, but it doesn't matter. His words have already left their claws in me.

"Then why the fuck am I here? Why are any of us working together? We're supposed to be equals in this."

"I know," he says. He washes a hand over his face and heaves a sigh. "I'm... trying."

It's another confession I don't expect. For the first time ever, I find desperation and confusion in his eyes. Two things I never thought he was capable of feeling. It stuns me and gives me more reason to believe that something isn't right here. This isn't Cain.

He grows quiet again as he looks at the box containing the heart. "Are you taking it?" he asks.

Not sure what he means by that, I ask, "The heart?"

"Maverick's deal," he replies. "Are you taking it?"

"Abso-fucking-loutely not. You shouldn't have even bothered asking. Never even considered it for a second."

"And Elias?"

"He doesn't know, but I can guarantee he would've rather ripped Maverick's intestines out his belly button than take that deal."

"It's why Maverick went to you," he replies. "You'd rather not get your hands bloodied."

"You and I both know how hard the stains are to get out." It's a poor excuse for a joke, but a smile flickers across his lips.

"Yes." Cain rises to stand. Exhaustion clings to his expression now. "When we get back to the house, I think we may need to collect a soul. We're overdue, and unleashing our demons without the power has made us..."

"Cranky," I finish for him. He's right. We haven't eaten since before Aria arrived, and it's made us a bit tense. Whether that's the reason we'd lost ourselves for a moment—I couldn't say.

He nods, but uncertainty lingers in his gaze.

"I'll be in the back." Without saying anything more, he turns and walks to the jet's private back room, leaving me alone with the heart in the box.

A heavy fatigue settles over me, and I slump in my chair. That conversation was much more unexpected and draining than it should've been, and I'm not exactly sure why. My temples pound as a headache builds behind my eyes. But instead of dwelling on it, I decide it might be safer to drift off to sleep instead, and that's just what I do.

The weird tension follows us for the remainder of the way home, and when we walk inside the mansion, I'm stiff with unease and nervousness. Jittery. It's like my insides are bouncing but my body is in rigor mortis.

Cain seems to be just as off his game, and I'm starting to wonder if he was right about the heart and booby traps.

With the specialty box in hand, he turns and makes a beeline for the cellar door. "I'm going to put this safely away with the other relic."

"Good idea," I say. Honestly, the farther I can get from it, the better. I can't shake this uneasy feeling, and it's giving me the creeps.

He disappears down the hall.

It's still early in the night, and I debate going to Purgatory since I know Aria is working and Elias is there chaperoning. But with all the strange things going on with me, it might be best if I stay home. I don't want to risk it.

Cain's thundering footsteps rush up the steps. The door slams open, and a millisecond later, he appears again, looking paler and gasping for breath. The box is still in his hands.

His fear and panic freezes me in place. What can rattle a prince of Hell? Not much, that's what.

"The harp's string," he chokes out. "It's gone."

Oh shit.

A ball of lead sits in my stomach. No… That could only mean one thing.

"Aria," we growl at the same time.

"Fuck," I add on for good measure.

"She took it. She must have." He speaks my thoughts aloud, his panic quickly transforming into anger. "It's the only explanation."

I hold up my hands. "Let's not jump to conclusions here…" I start, but as much as I don't want to think Aria could do such a thing, how could it be anyone else? "Maybe Elias—"

"What? You think Elias took it out for a leisurely stroll through the woods?" he bites out.

"Hey, I don't fucking know. I'm just saying that something else could have happened. We don't want to assume—"

He clenches his jaw. "It was Aria. She must be in line with Lucifer. Why else would she want it?"

"What do we do?" I ask him. "Call Elias at the club?"

"No." The word snaps from his mouth with a whip. "Send him a text, but we have to use this time to search Aria's room. And anywhere else she's been lingering. If we're lucky, it's still in this house and we can track it down."

I head for the stairs.

"Wait."

I pause mid-step.

"Search, but don't make it obvious you did so. I don't want her to know we're onto her," he says.

"Why?"

His gaze darkens, the black slithering over his blue irises. "I'm going to make her tell me where it is."

Was he planning on torturing it out of her?

The thought of her hurt makes worry worm through my chest, but if she is working with Cain's father and isn't who we think she is, then there's no other choice. She's played us all for fools.

"And what of the heart?" I ask.

"I'll keep it with me in my bedroom. If she searches for it there, I'll know." His words are ominous, the threat clear.

Nodding, I continue up the stairs, heading straight for the third floor staircase and for Aria's room.

CHAPTER TWENTY-TWO

ARIA

"Give me a Blow Job. Actually, make it two," a brunette with the tiniest skirt in the world asks, and I scribble it down on my notepad.

"Name?" I glance up, but she's already turned away from me and is laughing with her friends, a gaggle of girls all at Purgatory for a bachelorette's night out, by the look of a red-haired woman wearing a black veil and tiara.

"Excuse me." I lean forward and tap the brunette on the shoulder.

She snaps back around to me, wearing a sneer, like I am a gnat in her face. I tense but plaster on a smile. If my presence annoys her, then I am happy to remain for as long as it takes her to answer.

"What is it?" she blurts out, annoyed.

"Your name to allocate drinks to your tab, or you can forget the Blow Jobs." I arch a brow as she narrows her eyes at me.

"I told you already. It's K Payker," she spits. But I know for sure she definitely did *not* tell me that before. She's just being a mondo bitch.

She flicks her long ponytail over her shoulder as she turns, whacking me in the face with it. The back of her dress is hideous, striped in white, yellow, and orange lines, and pulls tight across her back like she's wearing a dress two sizes too small for her.

I seethe and burn on the inside, desperate to shove my fist into her lower back, or better yet, kick the back of her knees with my heels.

It's almost too tempting, but I find the strength to resist. I'm not going to lose my privileges working here for this candy-corn bitch.

I spin around and march across the club on wobbly feet. I'm not sure I'll ever get used to walking in heels. My gaze shifts to the far corner of the club where I know Sir Surchion sits, pretending not to be watching me and doing a piss-poor job of it. Especially since he hasn't moved an inch and has been nursing the same drink for hours now.

I'm not stupid. I know he's waiting for his moment to corner me again, maybe to question me about the orb. So, I make sure to stick to the crowds and avoid his shadowy section at all costs.

Thank God for Charlotte. She'd sensed my discomfort straight away and offered to take that side of the club for the night. I'd rather not be anywhere near him.

Reaching the bar, I slide in between two empty stools and place my notepad on the counter, glaring back at the girls. The way they giggle while staring at a handsome guy strolling past them—it makes me sick.

Gah, pathetic. Could they be any more desperate?

"You want me to spike their drinks so they're sick for a week straight?" Antonio asks. I turn to find him leaning against the counter across from me with a look that says he'll do it in a heartbeat. His short black hair is slicked back today, his black eye patch giving him an alluring look. The guy is handsome, with a ragged, pirate twist.

"I want to say yes so bad, but I also don't want you to lose your job. Besides, the bride shouldn't suffer. It's not her fault her friend is an ass."

"Well, that school of mermaids is inseparable, and if one hates you, they all will," he says.

Well, that's comforting.

It takes me a second, but then I realize... "Wait, mermaids?" I glance back their way. I mean, I grew up loving *The Little Mermaid*. Who didn't, right? But this is not how I pictured Ariel. Arrogant. Cruel. And so fake that even Barbie would be jealous. Let's not forget the most obvious missing feature—the tail.

Antonio shakes his head. "Wow, Charlotte wasn't kidding. You did live under a rock."

"Hey," I snap, "growing up in foster care and being dirt poor doesn't allow for many experiences."

He holds up his hands in surrender. "No judgement here, but you really should pick up a book or visit Storm. Hell, Google it. That works too." Then, as if an idea strikes him, he taps the side of his head. "Here, let me whip you up a drink real quick." Antonio turns toward the back wall before I can stop him, collecting a handful of bottles.

"Would love to, but I'm on duty."

"Hush," he whispers, his eyes twinkling with mischief. "I won't tell if you won't."

I hop up on a stool and swivel around to take in the club's main floor. Charlotte is in the back laughing with a group of men. She has this way of making guys melt in her presence. I don't know how she does it, but her charm comes naturally, while I still haven't mastered walking in heels.

Sweeping my gaze across the room, I catch Elias

watching me from one of the black sofas near the stage where dancers glide up and down poles in the skimpiest outfits. His gold eyes are pinned on me though; he has no interest in the near-naked entertainment just feet in front of him.

He sits with his legs parted, nursing his glass, and winks at me. A tingle ignites in the base of my gut at that small gesture. No matter how hard I try, I can't forget how aroused I'd gotten when he'd bent me over his lap and spanked me.

Part of me wishes he'll do it again.

"Here you go." Antonio places a glass in front of me. The cocktail is a beautiful sunset color with ice and single black straw.

"I can't drink that," I say and glance at Elias nervously. "Elias is watching. What if he—"

"He won't care what you drink." Antonio leans in, resting his elbows on the bar between us. "I once saw him down an entire bottle of whiskey right before sweet-talking one of the local hotties into one of the Red Rooms without a misstep. The big boy can hold his liquor."

My mind halts at the words Elias, hottie, and Red Room. Everything else he says is a blur, and my chest pinches at the thought of him enjoying someone else's company. Here I was thinking he's a loner who spends most of his time in the woods. Not some playboy like Dorian.

I guess I was wrong.

It shouldn't be too surprising. All three of the demons are drop-dead gorgeous in their own ways. They could have any woman they want in a heartbeat.

My own insecurities rise up from their dark hiding places, and I can't help but wonder why any of them had chosen to spend time with me.

Then I remember why—Sayah. They want to know about my gift and use it somehow. That has to be the only reason.

Antonio points to the untouched drink in front of me and clears his throat. "It's called 'A Short Trip to Hell.' Kind of suitable, considering your predicament, hey sweetheart?" He snorts a laugh at his own joke.

I only stare at it, my stomach souring. I can't stop thinking about him with another girl.

"Well, don't keep me waiting," Antonio presses. "Wild berry schnapps, juice, a can of Red Bull, and a shot of Jägermeister. Enjoy, and I'll whip up those Blow Jobs."

Looking over to Elias, who still studies me, I reach for the drink and think *'Fuck it'* before downing it in several mouthfuls.

Fire instantly races down my throat, and I gasp for air. My eyes tear up from the burning. "Water!" I choke and gasp. "Water! Fuck!"

Antonio bellows in laughter and hands me a bottled water.

My throat feels like it's peeling away. Hastily, I gulp down the water—half of it, to be precise. When the coolness squelches the flames in my mouth, I say, "Sweet Jesus, why didn't you tell me that would be like swallowing hot coals?"

"I gave you a straw for a reason."

"You are an evil man!" The fiery sensation climbs up my throat again, and I chug the rest of the water. Shit. I think the drink burned a hole through my esophagus.

Chuckling to himself, he returns to making the mermaids' cocktails.

When I look over to the dance stage again, Elias is gone. I frown. Maybe he's found someone else to take to the Red Rooms this time.

Unfortunately, Sir Surchion's still eyeing me from his shady spot. I shiver at his piercing gaze. I feel it slither across my skin, even when I look away. At least his crow is nowhere in sight.

Antonio whistles along to the seductive song coming from the club's speakers. He truly does love his job, and it's only now, without his hat on and his hair slicked back, that I notice the tips of his ears are pointy. Is he a fae?

He swings his hips to the tune as he places his hand over the top of one shot. A split second later, a small trail of air bubbles rise to the surface. He repeats the process on the other drink, which leaves me baffled.

Setting a tray in front of me, he places the shots on them and smirks. "Here are the Blow Jobs for the fish-girls."

"What did you just do for the drinks?"

The corner of his mouth curls upward. "Deliver those and I'll tell you when you return."

He swings around and goes to serve a couple of patrons sitting along the bar's counter. I hop off the stool and deliver the shots to the mermaids, who are cackling away. When I arrive, no one acknowledges me, so I place the glasses on the table in front of the brunette.

I head back to the bar and sit back on my stool as Antonio wanders over, wiping his hands down the black apron around his waist.

"Another drink?" he teases.

"Haha, funny," I say. "Now spill about your parlor trick."

He picks up a kitchen towel and begins drying recently washed beer glasses. "Nothing in Purgatory is what it seems, sweetheart. Including the cocktails. They have cute names, but everyone knows each comes with a specific..." His lips pinch to the side as his gaze drifts to the black ceiling. "How do I put this? It gives those who drink them... *benefits*."

I scrunch up my face, not understanding.

"Think of it like tiny bursts of magic spells that are mostly harmless and give people a small buzz. I can whip up a five-minute love elixir, a sprinkle of arousal here and there, or an icy drink that can instantly calm your worries. Stronger ones can be tricky, but I've become quite the whiz at adding hair loss to the Hair of the Dog. Whatever people want, I offer. Best thing about it is that my creations never come with a hangover."

I'm certain my mouth hangs open. He spells the drinks, but the patrons know and willingly enjoy them.

"What about my cocktail?"

"It's a relaxant. How do you feel?"

I blink at him, and well... he has a point, but that doesn't mean I like it.

"The effects are never strong enough so someone loses control of their inhibitions. I'm careful that way."

As I look out to the room where most people are enjoying a drink, I realize that Purgatory is so much more than a club. It's a place where people experience desires and fantasies. It's an escape from reality, and people buy into it.

"What's the Blow Job cocktail do?" I ask him next.

"It pumps a boost of confidence into the drinker."

So fish-girl needs help feeling confident amid her so-called friends? Well that says a lot.

"I'm impressed," I add. "I've heard fae have strong and unusual powers."

"Oh, I'm not fae," he bites out with disgust twisting his tone. "Fae are arrogant, black-hearted assholes who believe they're too pretty for this world. If it were up to me, I'd have them banned, but of course that's up to Cain, and unfortunately, those blond-haired bastards have too much money to be ever turned away."

"So?" I lean forward, arms on my bar, captivated to find out what his story is. "What are you then?"

He eyes me. "I'm a pirate, of course. Don't you see the eye patch?"

I laugh this time. "Okay, that might have crossed my mind."

Setting down the glass he's been drying for too long, he shrugs. "I'm nothing special. A plain old elf. Born in Austria where many fae live and take elves as their house slaves."

I'm sorry, but did he say *slaves*? "You're still joking, I hope."

"Nope." He points to the eyepatch. "This is how my master punished me for refusing to drop to my knees and please him. He took my eye. And I then took my chance and ran away. Never looked back. Got out of the country and came here to this small, woodsy town in the middle of nowhere special. Figured he'd never look for me in Glenside, Vermont. The rest is history." Despite the sad story he tells, he smiles gloriously, like he's proud of the moves he's made and the life he leads now.

I'm angry for him. "I can't believe a fae did that to you."

"It's the past, and this—" he points to his eyepatch again — "is a great conversation starter. Has even gotten me a few dates." We both see someone approaching the bar, and he nods at me before heading over their way. "Back to work."

I'm up on my feet again and collecting empty glasses on tables. The next hour goes by slowly, so Antonio has me help him unstack the dishwasher and take the garbage out to the cans in the alley behind Purgatory.

Outside in the dark, I drag the heavy bag of trash down the narrow lane. Crates are stacked up against one wall, along with empty cardboard boxes. I peer up and down to find it completely empty. I'm the only one out here. Alone.

My stomach flip flops. Could escaping really be this easy? A quick glance at the door, and hesitation coils inside me. An emotion I don't understand, because why would I want to stay under the thumb of three demons? So, I drop the bag of garbage and decide it'll be best to head left, toward the main street.

Then I run.

ELIAS

I watch her at first from within the shadows of the alleyway. My little firefox took the first chance she got to run. It doesn't surprise me, though a deep burrowing disappointment settles over me. I came out here for fresh air, so to spy her hot little ass wiggling as she darts right past me elicits excitement. My animal rouses, skin pricking with the urgency of a hunt, and I lunge after her.

The click-clack of her heels on the pavement echoes all around me. She hasn't mastered walking in the things, let alone running, so I close the distance within seconds. That's when her gaze whips over her shoulder and she spots me. Her eyes grow wide with terror, and in that look, the hound in me rejoices.

There's nothing like fear right before a catch. The look of it. The smell of it. The taste of it. I'm not even in my animal form and I'm practically salivating at the thought of pouncing on her. Of making her mine.

Panicked, Aria tries to speed up her pace but misjudges

her next step, tripping and landing roughly on the blacktop with a loud grunt. A bit disappointing, really. I was hoping to draw it out a little longer, but it's not even close to an even match. Especially running on unsteady legs.

I stalk closer as she scrambles to sit up. The sharp scent of blood hits my nose, and I look down to see her knees are scraped from the fall. Not terribly, but just enough that I see a gleam of red. I'm not sure why, but extreme fear always makes blood taste sweeter. The temptation to sink my fangs into her is there, but I can't. I won't. Not when Cain wants her unharmed... and I'd much rather sedate my primal needs and hungers in other ways with her.

I loom over her. For some reason, she appears smaller to me now. Petite, harmless, delicate. I know my height is unexpected, even for some, but next to her I look like a monster.

And maybe I am.

"Where are you running to?" I ask her as she looks up at me with those huge, doe-like eyes. "You know you won't get far."

Her chest heaves from her failed escape attempt, her breaths short, but I haven't even broken a sweat. "Are you going to kill me?"

My head tilts at her question. It isn't one I expected she'd ask. "Do you want me to?"

She shakes her head.

I smirk. "Good, because I have no plans to. At least not today."

She stares at me for a long while as if she's unsure I'm telling the truth. Then she glances at the deserted alley around us. She hadn't even made it to the sidewalk. We were still secluded behind the club, next to a stack of crates and shipping pallets. The reek of sitting garbage and stale water lingers in the air.

"I'm going to have to tell Cain you tried to run again tonight," I say. "He's not going to be happy."

"Please don't tell him," she rushes, suddenly nervous. "I really like this job. He'll never let me out of the house again. I can't—"

I hold up my hand to stop her. "I won't. You don't have to worry. But this will be the one and only time I keep a secret from him. And that means, as much as I enjoy the chase, you won't try running off again."

She doesn't reply, and in her silence, I hear her doubts and fears. She doesn't want to promise me anything, especially not trying to earn her freedom. If another perfect moment presented itself, she would take the risk.

Hesitantly, Aria shifts to tuck her legs underneath her butt, but the move brings her face inches away from my groin. I'm always uncomfortable in clothes—they're too restrictive for my size, and pants are the worst. If I have to, I usually wear something loose fitting. Tonight, I chose sweatpants, despite the upper-class dress code for the club, but the problem is that it leaves very little to the imagination.

And from all the excitement from chasing Aria, my dick is pretty much on full display, protruding and defined through the gray fabric. And her sudden closeness only makes it worse, stretching the material to stand at full attention.

When Aria realizes where she is, she jerks back, her cheeks flaming with a blush. But then she does the oddest thing. She peeks up at me through those long, dark lashes, and her tongue skims over her bottom lip.

The images in my head go straight to the gutter. Her hands wrapping around my cock as her tongue tastes me.

Me guiding the entire length into her slick, hot mouth until it hits the back of her throat… I mean, how could I not think about it?

Heat spreads over my skin, and lust pulls at my core. What I wouldn't give to make those visions come true right now.

As I stare down at her, something passes over her gaze. It's something my beast recognizes too.

Untamed sexual hunger.

"I…" Taken off guard, her voice trails off, and she starts to stand. I take her arm and help her up. She doesn't back away from me though, and the look in her eyes reminds me of her startled expression after our spanking session. When she wanted so much more, and I left her hanging. Yeah, I was an asshole—still am—except right now she has me by the balls because I fucking want all of her. And she knows it.

"You were saying?" I urge her, smirking.

Her hand is on my bulging cock suddenly, and I groan, taken by surprise. She has this ability to leave me stunned every time we are together.

"You sure that's what you want to do?" I hiss as my cock pulses with arousal.

She nods. "Are you afraid?"

I throw my head back and laugh at this temptress, but she's not letting go of my erection either.

I grab her by the back of her neck and draw her to me. "Be careful. You push too much and there's no going back."

"If I remember correctly, you started something you couldn't finish the other day."

Oh, so this is her revenge plan. I'm game. "Do you like what you feel?"

I expect her to pull back any second now and walk away, teasing me as payback, but she doesn't. She remains locked in place, the heat of her touch burning through my clothes.

"Well?" I press.

Her chin dips in a nod.

I huff a laugh. "Nothing like Dorian's cock, is it?"

She swallows roughly, and I'm fixated on the movement of her throat. "No."

That's fucking right. Not even close.

I run her hand over the front of my pants to really emphasize what I'm packing underneath. Her hand trembles in mine. And there she is, the shy girl I know is inside there behind her bravado.

"Shit..." she hisses under her breath.

Dorian may be a sex demon, and he may have fucked her first, but he's got nothing on me when it comes to size. I'm the one who can make her wildest fantasies come true. And the look on her sweet face says she knows it, too.

Before I have a chance to form another thought, she grabs the waistband of my sweats and wrenches them down. My cock pops free from its restraint and bobs in front of her.

I didn't expect such boldness from her. She's normally so innocent-looking. Inexperienced. I definitely didn't take her as a sexual vixen, so her behavior surprises me.

Am I complaining though? Nope.

Even though Aria's seen me naked before—during our very first encounter in the woods—and she's just touched me, the sight of my cock seems to surprise her. It only inflates my ego more, and I smirk.

"It looks to me like you want to take it for a spin."

She crouches down in front of me in response, and my stomach clenches with need.

Fucking hell. The simplest of gestures has my pulse galloping. I'm all riled up.

Her fingers wrap around my shaft and grip me tight. Anticipation buzzes through me, and like before, my thoughts run away with all my self-control. Her mouth comes down, her soft, full lips encasing the head as her tongue tastes me for the first time.

Every muscle in my body seizes at once. A growl vibrates in my chest as she takes more of me inside. Slowly. Gently. As if she's savoring me or testing her limits. I'm not sure which.

"Aria..." Her name comes out in a deep rumble as she brings my cock out of her mouth and takes it in again, going deeper, sucking, teasing. It drives me insane to stand here and do nothing but let her explore. Her mouth feels so fucking good, but I'm not the kind of guy who does soft and slow. It's not my style.

I want more.

She continues to draw me in and out with the most subtle moves of her head while one hand strokes me at the base of my shaft. She goes so deep this time, I feel the curve of her throat, and I'm shocked she's able to take me so far without gagging. It only turns me on more.

"That's it. Open up that throat of yours. Take it all," I tell her and tilt my hips so I hit that sweet spot at the back of her throat again. When her tongue runs along the bottom of my dick, lapping it up, she looks up at me again to show me she has no problem doing as I ask. "Good. Hmm... Fuck yeah. Just like that."

She takes me all the way to the hilt, closing her lips around me, and the warmth and tightness of her mouth makes my head whirl. Delicious tingles spread over me, and all I want is for her to take me deep like this over and over again.

The aggressive part of me wants to take over. What she's doing is absolute torture, and she doesn't even realize it, but I'm hovering on the edge. Of course, I don't want to hurt her, but I need more than this slow shit.

I decide it's time to really put that sassy mouth of hers to the test.

"Have you ever had your throat fucked before, Aria?" I ask her as I push my fingers through her hair. I use my hold on her to yank her off temporarily and tilt her head back so she's looking up at me instead.

Excitement lights in her eyes. She likes being handled this way. Rough.

I should have known from her reaction to the spanking. It makes sense.

With the same naive expression she'd given me before, she shakes her head no. But I know now it's only a ruse. An act she plays. There's a sex fiend hidden under all that fake innocence. It just needs to be unleashed.

"Would you like to?" I ask next.

She leans forward and lets her tongue circle around the head of my cock again. Teasing me.

I tangle both my hands into her hair this time and force her to look at me again. "You have to say it, Aria. I have to hear you say it."

"Yes," she breathes. Her gaze is foggy with lust. "I want you to fuck my throat, Elias."

Shit. She's just said the magic words.

I use my grip on the back of her head and crouch down to kiss her. Hard. And she parts her lips without hesitation. Our tongues wrestle, the desire between us growing to a dangerous level. Just when it's about to erupt, I break the kiss but keep my grasp on her to hold her in place.

Her hands clutch my thighs as I guide my dick back into her hot mouth. Another growl of pleasure vibrates in my chest. I move slowly at first, testing the waters and her comfort with my size, but it's not long before her nails dig into my flesh, urging me to go faster.

Taking her silent cues, I pump my hips, loving the feeling of her lips sucking me, her wet mouth surrounding me, and her tongue massaging me all at the same time. She moans and gurgles, the sounds of her own pleasure rocketing through me. I speed up.

"Fuck yeah. That feels good. Shit." Every curse I can think of springs from me. With each thrust, I feel the back of her throat. Her one hand finds my balls and squeezes them, and I bend my knees to really ramp things up.

I thrust into her, and she takes it all. It's so fucking hot watching her on her knees, taking every goddamn inch of me, I just can't take it. It's mind-boggling.

When it comes to sex, I've always been a marathon kind of guy. Not a sprinter, if you know what I mean. I can last for a long time, but something about this and the feel of Aria's mouth on me has my climax rearing up much sooner than expected. When her beautiful dark eyes roll up to meet mine and I find that animalistic hunger there again, I lose it. I thrust to the very back of her throat one last time, pushing myself to the hilt again, and hold her there. My entire body trembles as my orgasm slams into me. I pulse inside her and her neck works to swallow everything down.

As I pull out, I tug her head back once more and lean down to kiss her with just as much fervor as before. This time she tastes salty and sweet, and I can't believe she not only took that throat fucking like a champ, but she swallowed me all down.

For about the thousandth time since this girl walked into our lives, I wonder who the heck she really is. She's a marvel.

Both gasping for breath, we separate, and I take in the

delectable scent of her arousal. Knowing that she enjoyed that just as much as I did has my cock twitching, yearning for another round. But instead, I pull up my sweats and gently wipe any spit from the sides of her mouth with my thumb.

"You're amazing," I say.

"You know it," she teases even as she blushes and her wide-eyed, almost virginal demeanor clicks back in its usual place. But I'm no fool.

After I help her stand and assess the minor scrapes on her knees—they're just small flesh wounds—she leans into my side and smiles. Before I know it, I'm draping an arm across her shoulders and guiding her back into the club so that she can patch herself up and finish her shift.

And hopefully I can find a way to get the damn image of her sucking me off out of my head.

CHAPTER TWENTY-THREE

CAIN

My blood boils.

Dorian had no luck finding the missing relic in Aria's room, so she must have hidden it somewhere else. I've been pacing all night, searching the whole damn mansion with Dorian, but like every time before, the relic is silent to me. The only darkness I feel is the sweet hum of Aria's hidden power, lulling me to give into temptation.

Elias hasn't been much help. The moment he returned with Aria, he headed into the woods. Something about needing fresh air or some other bullshit, while Aria rushed straight for her bedroom.

Dorian and I both searched her room multiple times, only to come up empty. I should've confronted her the moment she stepped into the house, but I was hoping to have found it by now. The only other place she could have stashed it was Purgatory. Unless she already passed it to Maverick or Lucifer somehow…

My head pounds with all the possible scenarios, each one worse than the last. My brother's betrayal, and now

Aria's, jabs at me. I don't want to believe it, but how could I not?

I pace back and forth in front of the parlor's fireplace, waiting for her to wake up. The thought of barging into her room crosses my mind, like it's done a dozen times before, but if there's one thing I've learned about Aria it's that she doesn't buckle under threats. That's why I need to take a different approach. And that means calming the fuck down.

Unfurling my fisted hands, I exhale loudly and march over to the dining room. My sights lock onto the glass carafe filled with red wine. I lick my lips, my throat suddenly feeling as dry as the desert.

Since the flights back from Antarctica, I've felt strange. When talking to Dorian, I couldn't stop my true thoughts from spilling out, and the things I said... Well, I surprised even myself. And Dorian seemed off, too.

I'm starting to think it has something to do with the harp's heart and the magic it possesses.

I need to research more. See if I can find out anything about Gabriel potentially placing magical safeguards onto the relics to prevent them from being found. But first, I need to find the missing relic. The string. Or, as the story says, a lock of Eve's hair, the very first human woman ever created.

Another wave of anger rolls over me. I grit my teeth, burning up. Maybe Elias is onto something with running through the woods to release his wild side. Our time in Antarctica showed me that it's been too long since I just let go.

Fuck. I pour wine into a glass and drink it down in three gulps before filling it once more. A fruity taste lingers on my tongue, and it makes me wonder if this is how Aria tastes. Then I think about Dorian rutting her, and how it shouldn't bother me as much as it does. But I can't stop my hands from shaking as images of them together bombard me. It's torturous.

I've never hated and wanted someone so much in all my existence.

"Hello?" Aria's soft, faint voice comes from behind me.

I stiffen at first, then turn as she strolls in to join me. A small smile tilts her lips as she walks along the opposite side of the table. Despite her innocent look, my instinct pushes me to lunge at her and demand she give me the relic, but I hold back. I'm jittery with anticipation, and my thoughts are a jumbled mess. There's a war raging inside me, and I'm not sure what side of the line I should be on. Both feel like they'll lead to my undoing.

Swallowing down a breath, I square my shoulders and let a guise of calmness wash over me.

"Wine?" I offer her, gesturing to the carafe that's now half empty from my own indulgences.

She shakes her head, her gorgeous dark hair falling perfectly around her face. She's beautiful and dangerous. I see that now.

"I try not to get drunk before eight a.m.," she says as she studies me. Her sarcasm is cute, and I find myself huffing a laugh before I register what's happening and clamp my mouth shut. I've never in my life thought of anything being *cute* before. The word is nauseating.

Something is seriously wrong with me.

She wanders over to her chair at the end of the table, wearing a pair of skinny jeans, a T-shirt, and an oversized cardigan sweater, somehow looking just as delectable in comfy clothes as she did in that high-slit red dress.

"Is... everything okay?" she asks with worry tingeing her tone. But not for herself. Worry for me.

"Yes," I say too quickly, but then correct myself. "Well,

no, actually. It's not." I place my glass of wine on the table and lick a drop from my lips.

"What do you mean?"

"Sit. We need to discuss something."

She arches a brow at my request yet does what is asked of her. I move to join her, but hesitate. Being too close can lead to problems—more than I already have—so I remain standing with my hands clasped on the back of the high-back chair.

She looks up at me, hands in her lap.

I should demand she tell me where the relic is, force her to tell me why she took it, but the words stay locked in my chest, refusing to come out. All I can do is stare at her—at the delicate curves of her pink lips, the way she rubs them together nervously as she watches me with just as much intensity. It's mesmerizing.

I bite my tongue, heat engulfing me suddenly, and that same strange sensation from the plane crawls over me once again.

"You okay?" she asks, forehead wrinkled with concern. "You seem... different today."

"I'm fine." Even if my heart pounds faster, kick-starting my adrenaline. I rub the side of my face and straighten myself, unable to get comfortable in my own skin. *Get it the fuck together.*

"So where did you and Dorian vanish to the last couple of days?" she asks in an attempt to break the building tension.

My grip tightens on the chair as I struggle to speak. "We had business to attend to out of town."

"Oh."

The relic. Ask her about the relic.

"Did anyone else bother you at Purgatory last night?"

Fuck. I've lost control of myself again.

She fidgets with the hem of her cardigan, then looks up at me. "It's nothing I couldn't handle."

I don't like that answer because it implies something did happen, but before I can ask, she adds on, "I like it, though. It keeps me entertained."

"That's good then."

"Is that really what you wanted to talk to me about?" she asks.

I hesitate. "Not exactly."

Her gaze is scrutinizing. As if she's trying to figure me out. "Are you sure you're okay?"

"I've got a few things on my mind."

"Like?" she asks immediately, her response lightning fast.

I grit my teeth and try to force the words out of my throat. They struggle to come. "Like... you telling me... where the relic from the basement is?"

She grows rigid, eyes darting to the door then back to me. Contemplating running, maybe?

But a moment later, she eases in the chair. "That string thing in the box? In the basement? How should I know?"

Her lie is as smooth as butter, but I can still see through it.

"This isn't a joke, Aria," I say. "You have no idea what you've taken."

"I don't know what you're talking about. I didn't take your *precious*."

Oh, she's good. She looks behind her at the kitchen door, her face a mask of indifference. I can tell she's used to lying and covering her tracks.

"You were the last person to be seen with it. How exactly did you find it in the first place, anyway?" I ground out.

Her gaze narrows on me. "I didn't take it. What would I want with a string?"

"Aria," I growl. She keeps deflecting my questions, and my annoyance builds.

"Maybe you need to do another search for it in the basement."

"Tell me where the relic is," I demand, losing grip on my control. "I don't appreciate being lied to. I want to know everything. Everything. Like why you thought it was okay to fuck Dorian."

I freeze. That's most definitely not what I intended to say. But just mentioning them together has my chest flaring up like it did on the plane.

Her eyes widen in shock. She hadn't expected that from me either. "Is that what this whole thing is about? You're jealous?"

I pull back. "You're mistaking me for someone who cares."

She laughs at me. *Laughs.* Hell, I've smited demons for less.

"Why else would you ask me that question?" she asks. "I've hurt your pride."

My hackles bristle, and blood speeds through my veins. She drives me insane with her challenging words, constantly pushing and pushing me. Dorian had said something similar on the plane, about my pride getting in the way, and fuck. It's looking more like they are both right.

Heat scales up the back of my neck. I'm no longer thinking straight. The earlier urge to resist her has morphed into something else. Instead, I want to prove them both wrong. I want to give in completely. To dominate her.

Stepping closer, I reach out and grab her by the back of

the neck, tired of constantly fighting my desires. "If I cared, I would have already kissed you long before now."

Her chin lifts and her breaths turn short and quick.

Moving at the same time, our mouths clash, and we kiss like we have something to prove. I slide my tongue into her mouth, probing her, tasting the sweet allure I've been starved for. Each lick and brush of her lips awakens every nerve in my body.

She moans against my mouth, her hands reaching for my chest, her fingers roaming under my shirt, gliding over my sculpted muscles. Her touch is on fire while my cock hardens to the point of pain.

"You're insufferable," I whisper against her lips. She answers by kissing me with even more fervor than before, and I groan.

Holding back is not going to work. I've had enough of that. All I can think about now is taking her completely, mind, body, and soul. Nothing else matters.

I grab her arms and pin her between my body and the table, our kiss never breaking. My erection presses into her stomach, and she grinds herself against me, making delicious sounds that have me drowning under her spell. I'm getting wrapped up so fast, I've forgotten myself. Suddenly, I can understand why Dorian lost himself so easily to her. She's intoxicating.

But even this isn't enough. I need more. My hands sweep over her hips, then her ass. She shifts so that I'm nestled in between her legs, and something primal ignites in me just at the thought of fucking her right here. Right now.

I break our kiss, our faces inches away, both of us breathing heavily.

"Get on the table," I command.

The look she gives me is filthy and so damn sexy, I'm

going to enjoy every second of fucking her and making her submit.

She lifts herself onto the table, legs spread wide, and I take my place back between them. The moment I reach for the button to her jeans, a thunderous explosion comes from the main foyer of the house. Dust rains down on us.

I spin, pushing myself in front of Aria to face the entryway. She flinches against my back when another smashing sound erupts, and we both stare toward the house's front door. Thunderous footsteps rush inside, but I smell the intruders before I can see them. Wet dog hair. The air reeks with it. Then a piercing howl rings throughout the house.

Werewolves!

I swing toward Aria, pull her off the table, and start nudging her toward the kitchen door. "Quick. Go to your bedroom. Use the elevator in the kitchen. Lock the door and don't leave no matter what you hear."

She blinks up at me, her cheeks paling and eyes wide.

Seeing her scared has me tensing, my heart pounding. And at that moment, I struggle to believe this girl works for my father. The fear is genuine—I recognize the look of it—and those in Lucifer's command fear nothing.

"I won't let anyone hurt you, but you need to run." I twist her around by her shoulders and push her forward.

She doesn't need to be told twice and bolts across the room, then vanishes behind the kitchen door. Knowing she's gone does little to comfort me, but I spin on my heels and storm out of the dining room.

In the entryway stand at least ten mutts, still in human form. I spot the moon emblem from the werewolf biker gang on each of them. Fury bleeds through my veins. How dare they come into my home and break down the door.

Better yet, how the fuck did they find out where we lived?

Had the man I'd killed in Purgatory been that important to warrant barging in here and demanding revenge? He seemed like nothing more than a mouth breather.

But when four additional wolves burst into the house, a trickle of doubt clings to the back of my mind. This isn't about punishing me for killing one of their packmates. This is meant to be a slaughter.

A werewolf with shaggy black hair moves forward, chest sticking out, heaving for breath. The Alpha, maybe? Power changes hands so many times in packs as the wolves constantly challenge each other, it's hard to keep track of such things.

"You're in my home," I growl just as Dorian leaps down from the top of the staircase and lands halfway down the steps with a thump.

"Thought I could smell dog," he snarls, his body already morphed into devilish form. Horns, his torso covered in intricate tattoos, and his hair a stark silver.

"You butchered our Alpha," the wolfman mutters, eliciting growls from the rest of the pack, all of them stepping forward in unison. So, it looked like the bastard with sticky fingers at the club was actually their Alpha. That's unfortunate. Then this must be the pack's second-in-command. "Eye for an eye! Give us the girl and we are gone!"

Them mentioning *my* girl, Aria, infuriates me. Every muscle in my body tenses, my wings itching to come out. The heat of Hell snakes across my skin, flooding me with power. I'll rip out his tongue for ever suggesting such a thing.

Dorian barks a laugh, then tilts his head back and mimics a wolf's howl. Fuck, I love fighting with him by my side. He makes it even more exciting.

"No one touches our property," I say, my voice deepening. "Turn with your tails between your legs and get the fuck out of my home, or you die like your pathetic Alpha did."

"Fuck you!" The head wolf holds my gaze, never backing down, while several of his men exchange worried looks. This bastard will be the demise of his pack.

"Wrong answer." Instantly, darkness fills my veins and lines my skin. My demon erupts out of me just as I throw myself toward them. My shirt tears as my wings push out and stretch to their full length.

Dorian releases a war cry and catapults himself into battle alongside me.

This is what I miss about our days in Hell. The constant battles that consumed our days, the streets running fresh with blood, the smell of death in the air. The exhilaration is addictive.

The wolves come at us, and we clash spectacularly just as Elias appears behind them in his massive animal form, all black fur, sharp yellow teeth, and glowing eyes. He's naturally bigger than any werewolf I've ever seen, and when he snarls, most of the Mooners force their own change. Elias charges through them, swinging his head and sending men and wolves flying.

Perfect. Now this is the kind of fight I can enjoy. The three of us battling through the carnage. Like old times.

Chaos explodes around. I launch myself at the asshole who demanded Aria, untamed fury buzzing in my veins. These wolves have no idea who they've challenged today. But it'll be a choice they'll never make again.

I slam into him, and we both hit the ground hard, my fists pummelling into his face even before his head smacks into the marble floor. Someone else crashes into my side.

My wings unfurl, and the sharp talons on the ends spear into the wolf's chest. He cries out.

I boot him backward while I elbow another bastard in the head. The second-in-command is on his feet in the next second and coming for me again. These bastards are resilient with their ability to heal quickly. But that just makes it all the more fun.

I swing out when something sharp bites right into my calf, teeth sinking into flesh and bone. Pain jolts through me, and I buckle. Twisting, I see a massive brown wolf attached to my leg. A bloody cut zig-zags across his muzzle.

The second-in-command holds up his hand, which has sprouted fur and claws, and with one quick swipe, his nails slice across my chest. I roar, the pain fueling my rage. My wing cuts across the air, hitting him before he can strike again and throwing him clear across the foyer.

I drive a fist into the brown wolf's head to get him off me, but he's locked there. At the same time, two other men crash into me. I'm pushed onto my back, the air knocked out of my lungs.

There's no place for fear in my heart, not when everything inside me burns with fury.

Punches and teeth tear at me, but I've fucking had enough of playing. I was enjoying the fun, but not anymore. A blaze skips down my arms, my Hellfire igniting, and I shove my fist into the wolf's head once more, his fur singing, burning in seconds.

Howling in pain, he releases my leg and begins morphing back into this human form. Seconds is all it takes for me to whip upright and cast a fist into one man's chest, breaking bones. He gasps and falls backward, while the third man recoils from my approach.

I leap to my feet and snatch him around the throat, then

hurl him across the room where he slams into the wall before collapsing into a heap to the ground.

Dorian is painted in blood. It runs down his face, but he smiles through it as several wolves bolt outside of the mansion.

"Wolves? More like pussy cats!" he shouts at them as they flee.

With eyes like the flames of the underworld, Elias races after them. The hound in him can't resist the hunt and chase.

I charge back into battle, over the dead already sprawled across the floor. None of them will be leaving here alive. I'll make sure of that.

Let it be known that any fool who wants to face us in our home will meet the same brutal end.

No one messes with what belongs to us.

CHAPTER TWENTY-FOUR
ARIA

Boom.

I flinch at the deafening cacophony coming from downstairs. It sounds like the house is falling down around us, and I don't even know what the hell is going on. By the howls and cries, I'm guessing there's an ambush on the demons. I can't help but think it might be related to the incident at Purgatory. Cain killed a werewolf, so is this retribution?

Crossing my bedroom, I triple check the chair shoved up under the door handle. It makes me feel secure, yet at the same time I feel cornered. What if the demons lose? Will I become wolf food? Surely no one can defeat a demon, right?

I pace to the window and stare out into the morning sunlight. I hate that I can't even jump out of the window without breaking my neck if it comes down to it. It's a damn fire trap in here. If only Cain hadn't taken my rope after my failed escape attempt.

The thought of Cain brings back his words about the string relic. He knows it's me. He *knows.* I'm not sure what to do about it. Or how he hasn't killed me yet. Instead, he kissed me.

I hug myself and keep pacing. I can't just admit I took it. It's not like I can be like, "Hey, I wanted to put it back, but oops, it accidentally merged with another relic I stole."

Fuck! I'm in trouble.

I head to the wardrobe and reach into the back where I tucked my satchel with the relics behind a rack full of clothes and within layers of thick blankets, making it undetectable. If anyone searched in here, they clearly missed it.

Threads of music whisper in my ears, soft and melancholic, and it relaxes me.

With the satchel in hand, I flop down onto my bed and cross my legs, then dig my hand in and pull out the relics. A single touch and the orb vibrates lightly in my hand, the music picking up in tempo. But something's changed. The mercury that once flowed inside the orb has changed color to a pale silvery turquoise, which is beautiful. But what does it mean?

I curl a finger around the golden string attached to the orb. It's melted right in there. The only way to pull it apart is to rip it off, but considering these have magic attached to them, I don't want to tempt fate any more than I already have.

But if Cain owns the string, he has to know what it is. Maybe I need to come clean. They might know the best way to separate them without causing any damage. Then they can get theirs back and I'll keep mine.

Sure, they'll be pissed, but what other choice do I have? It's only a matter of time before they find them or I cave under the pressure. They might even start torturing me. I shiver at the thought.

It might be easier if I reveal it now before it comes to

that. Maybe it'll lessen any punishments. I mean, it was an accident, after all.

My shadow presses against my chest, and I don't hesitate letting her out.

Find out if it's clear out there, I whisper in my mind.

The moment Sayah slips out of me, the song grows louder in my mind, the orb vibrating faster.

Sayah doesn't seem to care and slides across the floor and under the door. I turn my gaze to the relics, wishing I understood them better.

"What are you?" I ask as I trace a finger over its cold, smooth surface.

Moments later, Sayah returns and passes me images of an empty foyer covered in blood splatter. She slithers up the wall, waiting for me to make a decision on what to do next.

"No demons, either?" Her dark head swivels in a no.

Man, I hope they're okay.

I wait on the bed for another ten minutes. Still, it stays deathly silent downstairs. The more I think about the relics, the more I realize that being truthful with Cain may be the better solution. They are always going to watch me, aren't they? Maybe by doing this, it'll lead them to trust me.

And that's when I'll make my move to get out of here.

The thought of leaving squeezes my chest, but this twisted relationship I am finding myself in with the demons is only going to end one way, isn't it? With me in Hell.

Up on my feet, I wrap my oversized cardigan tighter around myself, then stuff the relics into one of the large pockets. Together, they are only the size of a tight fist and fit into my pocket easily. I glance over at a mirror and can't see the bulge in my pocket easily. So, with a quick nod for Sayah to follow, I go and remove the chair from the door.

I poke my head outside into the hallway and find no guards. Had they joined Cain in the fight?

Still no sounds.

So, I slip out of my room and on soft steps, quickly hurry toward the staircase. Sayah mimics my movements like a true shadow should, just in case.

A faint drumming sound crackles over my mind.

It comes so abruptly that I lose my footing and trip over my feet. I crash into the wall and freeze on the spot. Fear clings to me as I look back down the hallway, except I'm alone.

Heart pounding, I'm not sure what I just heard. I know it wasn't the orb.

I straighten myself. The relics continue to hum in my pocket to a tune. Heat radiates from them and warms my leg. A tingle races down my thigh and to my toe, twitching.

Oh, crap. There's another relic, isn't there?

I don't need this. There's already enough danger going on.

I exhale loudly. I need to just ignore its call. Why in the world are these demons collecting dark relics anyway?

Sayah glides along the rug, going straight ahead and past the staircase like she knows where I'm being called from. The shallow drum beat echoes against my eardrums, mingling with the relic's song. Like they were always meant to go together. And that sends shivers up my arms.

Sayah disappears to the second floor, our tether stretching out as the distance grows. I call out to her in my mind, but there's no response.

"Shit!" I mumble under my breath. There's no way I can hide *this* from Cain.

Quickly, I chase after her, hurrying down the steps and following the sharp turns down other corridors. If I remember correctly, Dorian's room was on this floor, but she's bringing me to the opposite side of the house, to a part I've never seen. Coldness clings to the air here. Every window has been covered by heavy curtains, blocking out the sunlight, and scratches adorn the walls as though someone had tried to wrangle a lion.

My pulse races with fear, but I track Sayah down to one of the rooms. Our dark cord dances underneath the door jamb as she moves about inside. As much as my stomach churns with worry, I press an ear to the door.

More stifling silence.

The orb and cord begin to buzz louder in my pocket. As if responding, the drums pound faster. I feel the boom of them in my chest.

With a shaky hand, I push down on the bronze handle and the door swings open. I freeze in the doorway, half expecting someone to greet me. But there's no one.

The whole room is encased by bookshelves, with a single narrow window flooding the room with light. A regal four poster bed draped in crimson and gold sits in the center, reminding me of something out of a classic romance novel. There are books everywhere here, and while they pique my interest, I'm a lot more curious in what Sayah has discovered.

Who's room is this? Another guest room, or one of the demons'?

Sayah hovers near a black round box that sits alone on a shelf, and I can't help but be reminded of how I found the string in the basement. I reach over and open it.

The sight of a pinkish organ has me drawing back at first, grimacing. Then I lean in to take a better look. It's heart shaped, and I'm not talking about all the Valentine's

Day crap, but like a real human heart. Eeek. Why would anyone make a relic look like this? It glints under the sunlight as though it's made of glass.

Gingerly, I reach over and touch the item. It's no bigger than the orb, the surface steaming hot. And with it comes a strange sensation that races up my arm and over my body. My stomach tingles and my thoughts sweep to the three demons, at how much they've affected me, how I can't seem to say no to them. I see each of their faces in my mind, all gorgeous and deadly and completely irresistible in their own way. But I know it's more than that… I'm starting to feel drawn to them in other ways too.

I tell myself it's wrong, but I can't help it, apparently. The urgency to see them and tell them the truth burns through me.

I draw my hand away, and for that split second, clarity divides the fog in my mind. The emotions that clog my thoughts fade as if in response to me no longer touching the relic.

I blink at the relic. "What are you?" Its effects are quick and strong. If this belongs to Cain, it might explain his strange behavior this morning. His emotions flip flopping all over the place. Though he wasn't holding it… so what does that mean it affects me differently to the demons?

A bang sounds outside like someone shutting a door. I leap away from the shelf, but when a scraping sounds, I whip back around to see the box holding the heart slipping off the edge.

Instinct has me lashing out my hands, and I snatch the relic falling out of the box and rushing for the floor.

Stumbling for balance, I tuck it against my chest, holding it safe, while my own heart slams into my rib cage. That was too close. If the thing smashed, the demons would never forgive me.

My thoughts float to the demons once more, to an image of all their hands on me at once, touching, exploring, stroking, and heat pools in my core. Desire spirals through me instantly.

No!

The heart is influencing me again. I try to fight it, pushing those sexy thoughts to the back burner, and focus on inspecting the object in my hands. To my horror, I find the golden string from my pocket has somehow snaked out and merged with this relic during the fall.

"For fuck's sake. Seriously?"

As tempted as I am to rip that cord from the heart, I only have one option here now, don't I? I have to come clean with Cain, because I don't want to destroy his relics while trying to get mine back.

This is just great!

I call Sayah back to me, and she does so quickly, almost as though she senses the deeper mess we've dug ourselves into. I don't waste a moment and stuff the third relic into my sweater pocket with the other two. Hurrying out of the room, I zoom toward the stairs, hoping I can find Cain and speak to him.

I come to an abrupt stop at the top, my stomach twisting in horror. At the bottom, half a dozen bodies lay in puddles of blood. All dead. Red paints the walls and ceiling, and the place reeks of wet dog and decay.

Carnage. Utter carnage.

Bile hits the back of my throat, and I cover my mouth to stifle a scream from escaping.

A groaning sound comes from the parlor on my right, and with my thoughts flying to Cain all bloodied and gasping for his last breath, I race down the stairs. Carefully stepping around the dead, I enter the room and skid to a halt again at the sight before me.

I can't move, can't breathe, can't even make sense of what I'm looking at. Cain grips a man by the throat, their faces inches apart. The victim's mouth is gaped open, and he makes desperate whimpering sounds.

A grayish energy lifts out of his mouth, and Cain inhales it. He isn't looking my way, but the slurping sound he makes raises all the hairs on my body. Like at Purgatory, his skin is lined with black veins, but this time he has enormous goddamn leathery wings jutting out of his back.

I don't know where to look... at him draining the soul of that poor sucker, or the way his wings stretch out, almost spanning the width of the room.

The world tilts sideways. This is too much to take in. Terror slides through me, squeezing me into an invisible strait-jacket. A gasp escapes my lips.

Cain jerks his head in my direction, eyes completely black. His feeding ends, and his mouth twists into a grimace as his wings pull tight against his back. I was just kissing this man—no, this demon—but now I see that's exactly what he is. A Hell monster who drains the life out of people.

At that exact moment, I know I've made a very, very big mistake coming to see him.

I'm racing before I can think straight, right out the front door. All I can picture is Cain holding me like that and sucking out my soul the same way.

The vicious wind collides into me. But I can't stop, not when... I gasp in fright at what I've just witnessed.

"Danger," the joined relics sing in my mind in their beautifully sad song.

I spin around just as a screech comes toward me. A huge crow sweeps through the air, coming right for me. I scream and swing back around, then I slam right into someone so hard, I'm thrown backward onto my ass.

Someone tall and solid as a rock stands before me. Someone I don't recognize.

He reaches down for me, but I shove against him. "Get away from me!"

Except the asshole is too fast, and he snatches my arm, hauling me to my feet. "Sorry, but you're coming with me."

"Run. Run. Run," the objects continue to sing like I'm not trying.

I shove a hand against his chest. "What's going on?"

"You've got sticky fingers, and now it's time to pay up."

My mind races too fast to make out what he's talking about at first. I glance back at the mansion to call for help, but the brute drags me away so viciously, I stumble and fall onto my knees. Several feet away, a black van pulls up on the path right in front of us.

His meaty hand seizes my arm and wrenches me forward.

I scream and slam a fist into his arm to release me, bucking against his grip.

As the back door to the van slides sideways, I scream. But I'm shoved into the empty compartment. I roll inside across the metal floor and turn back to escape when I catch a glimpse of a massive black wolf sprinting down the driveway from the mansion, kicking up gravel with his unnatural speed.

Hope flutters in my chest. It's Elias! He's coming for me!

The man's gaze whips over his shoulder, and once he sees the hellhound barreling towards us, he jumps inside with me and yanks the door shut. He bangs on the driver's seat and yells frantically, "Go, go, go! Get us the fuck out of here!"

The skid of tires erupts and we roar out of there, me thrown to the other side, my face hitting the floor. I yell and try to brace myself as we sway all over the place. I wait for any signs of Elias descending on the van to rescue me, but there are none. Under the roar of the vehicle's engine, I can't even hear his thundering footsteps anymore.

My stomach flips with fear. I'm really on my own.

Tears blur my vision and I wipe them, staring at the front of the van, past the metal barrier that divides me and the front.

Someone is glancing back at me from the passenger seat, and at first all I see are gleaming white teeth, the bright light from outside silhouetting his features.

"Sit back and enjoy the ride. It will take a while."

Only when I hear the voice and squint to see the man do I realize who just kidnapped me. The realization sends shivers down my spine.

Sir Surchion. The fucking asshole who I stole the orb from.

CHAPTER TWENTY-FIVE
ELIAS

Shit!

I bolt behind the unmarked van as it speeds down our driveway, when the ragged gash in my thigh from that werewolf attack quickly makes itself known and slows me down. The distance between Aria and I increases and increases. My heart thunders in my chest, and emptiness swallows me. I couldn't get to her in time.

What the fuck just happened?

A seizing pain laces through my quad muscles, and I groan. The werewolf must have gotten a bigger bite out of me than I originally thought.

The van containing Aria becomes just a black speck among the shadows. When it whips onto the road that connects to the main one leading back to civilization, I know it's gone, and my gut twists.

I snap around and unleash a howl filled with menace and sorrow. A wind brushes past, away from me, and combs through my fur. Of course, the wind isn't blowing in my favor so I could catch a scent. It's never easy.

I rush back to the house, growling under my breath.

My heart beats furiously, and I charge into the mansion, past the broken door to where I find Cain shaking off his demon form. Wings knitting into his back, skin taking on a human-like glow, eyes blinking back to blue, making him look normal. Though the splatter of blood over his arms and clothes tells a very different story.

"Aria! Where the fuck is she? She saw me in my real form and ran," he growls, his voice deep and voracious.

"Now this was fun!" Dorian emerges from a side room just then, topless and wiping blood off his torso with a towel. When he catches Cain's panicked look, his cheery expression falters. "What did I miss?"

"It's Aria," Cain says. "She's run off."

"Fuck, really?"

In a heartbeat, I suck in a ragged breath, and with it, I call back my hellhound. He drags through me like barbed wire, hating to be tucked away. Bones stretch, my body contorts, fur vanishes into my skin; the transformation takes mere moments before I stand upright as a man.

"They took her," I say, a snarl hanging off my last word.

"They? Who?" Dorian turns to me and scans my naked form, raising a brow. "Pretty sure we got all the rabid mutts."

Cain bursts past me and darts outside to the middle of the circle driveway. His movements are frantic and fast. It takes me by surprise. When I glance at Dorian, even he looks stunned at first.

"I didn't see who took her," I tell Dorian, then I swing around and follow Cain outside into the front yard, Dorian on my heels. "A black van pulled up out of nowhere. They grabbed Aria and threw her inside. I wasn't fast enough. I tried, but I couldn't reach her."

I press a hand to the deep bite on my thigh and curse this realm for slowing our ability to heal. If we were in

Hell, this would have been mended by now. My rage spikes, but sitting here fuming isn't going to fix the problem. We are too far gone for that shitshow.

"You're kidding me." Dorian's mouth drops and he runs his hand through his hair over and over. "Just now, they took her just now?"

"Yes!"

"Who the fuck were they?" Cain whips around. "Did you see the number plate? What did you smell on the air? Something, Elias, we need something to find her." His frantic demeanor is contagious. Even Dorian starts pacing.

"It happened so fast. I came around the corner as they threw her into the van. I was upwind from the breeze so I didn't catch their scents." I think back, wracking my memory over every second that passed. "No number plate, the windows tinted too dark to see the driver. The man who snatched her had his back to me, but he was bald. I barely got a glimpse of him because I couldn't stop staring at Aria."

"Was she hurt?" Cain asks. "Did it look like they harmed her?"

"Not that I could see in those few seconds."

"Had to be those fucking werewolves," Dorian growls, his shoulders rising, muscles twitching in his neck. "They wanted Aria from the start. It has to be them."

"A bird," I blurt, the memory of the black feathery thing popping from my memory. "There was a crow that flew right after her like it meant to scoop her up."

Cain freezes, his eyes widening in realization.

Dorian hops down the steps. "What? Do you know what that means? A crow?"

"Fuck." His eyes flash from blue to black once more as his demon side takes over. He looks between the two of us, and his voice turns into a deep rumble. "I have a pretty good idea where she is."

ARIA

When the van stops and the door slides open, I recognize where I am immediately. The back of Sir Surchion's antique store. The warehouse.

Of course, he brought me back to the scene of the crime.

Sayah crashes against my ribcage, afraid of what's to come, while the joined relics in my pocket vibrate. In my head, their beautiful sad song sounds more like a lament now than before. An ominous warning that makes acid churn in my stomach.

I'm dragged out into the mid-morning daylight. The bald man who'd thrown me into the van holds me by the arm as the driver—another hulking guy with tattoos scrolled across his neck and arms—jumps out. They both leer at me.

"The guys didn't say she would be such a lamb," the driver says. That's when I see the familiar moon emblem patch on his jean jacket. Baldy has one on his vest, too. They're from the Full Mooners. I don't remember either of them from that night at Purgatory, but that doesn't mean much. That night was a blur. "I was expecting more of a fight from her."

"She is quite a doll, isn't she?" Baldy muses. "But we're not being paid to ask questions, so let's just finish the job and collect our payment."

So, Sir Surchion hired these werewolves to kidnap me?

Was the gang's attack on the house also part of his plan? I was starting to think so.

"All in due time," Sir Surchion insists as he rounds the front of the vehicle. "Aria and I have a few things to discuss first."

Hearing my name on his tongue makes a shiver skate over me. I don't remember ever telling it to him.

When he sees my wide eyes, he smiles. "I know quite a lot about you, Miss Aria Cross. And we have much to talk about."

My body ices over. He not only knows my full name, he knows *about* me. Does that mean he knows about my powers and Sayah? Or about my parents and what I am? Either way, this can't be good.

But still… I can't help but want to ask a million questions about who the hell I am.

Sir Surchion gestures us toward the warehouse's back door, and the bald werewolf's grip tightens on me. I tug against him, but he pulls me along like I weigh nothing. "Let me go, chrome-dome. You're all going to regret this."

He growls at me, showing teeth.

His friend laughs.

Sir Surchion holds open the door, and I glance over my shoulder for any signs of Elias's glowing yellow eyes or black fur among the shadows. When I see nothing, my heart sinks. Maybe the demons aren't coming for me after all.

The guards push me inside, and I stumble into the dank and musty warehouse. Sir Surchion strolls ahead of us down the aisle. As we pass the packed shelves and priceless antiques, a squawk sounds overhead. I peer up to see Mordecai on the open rooftop window, his black eyes fixed on me.

He swoops down and glides inches from my head,

forcing me to duck before finally landing on Sir Surchion's shoulder.

Fucking rat with feathers.

Sayah continues to ping-pong inside me, demanding out, but a shadow can only do so much. It's obvious I'm not going to be able to fight my way out of this. I'll have to wait for the right moment to flee. Maybe use her as a distraction if I have to. It was my only chance.

At the front of the large building, beside the shop's door, his two monster hounds perk up. Their nostrils flare as they take in my scent. Or maybe it's the werewolves they smell, because when they bare their fangs our way, the Mooners growl back. Fighting for dominance or whatever it is canines do.

As long as they don't start peeing on each other.

"Brutus, Joel, these are our guests," Sir Surchion says to them. His voice echoes in the vast space. "No need to get testy."

The hounds sit back in obedience, but their eyes follow our every move, bodies rigid.

"Here. Put her here," Sir Surchion demands, pointing to a spot on the floor.

The tattooed werewolf joins his buddy by seizing my other arm, and together they force me onto my knees in front of the old man. Then they step back to form an intimidating wall behind me.

"Not feeling so brave now that you're not all dressed up with a demon holding your hand, hm?" Sir Surchion asks as he peers at me from over his circular purple lens. Mordecai cackles as if laughing at me.

"Just you wait. They're coming for me." I lie, but I wish it were true. But then, a new thought forms. If there's no way to escape with those two meat-head wolves around to track me down, I could have them turn on Sir Surchion instead. I'll have to be clever about this.

What was that saying from Abraham Lincoln again? A house divided… can hopefully help get my ass out here? Something like that.

"Your little plan with your Mooners didn't work. It didn't even slow them down," I say.

I hear the wolves behind me breathing heavily.

I keep going. "The demons killed them all. Didn't even break a sweat while doing it, either."

Sir Surchion frowns, disappointed. "The werewolves knew what they were getting into. They wanted a chance at revenge for the one murdering their Alpha, and I knew where the demons were hiding out. Well, Mordecai did." He strokes the bird's head, and he bristles his feathers in appreciation. "We helped each other, you see."

They had an arrangement, he means. But for what—to bring me here? All because of the orb I stole? There had to be a million other things in this shithole shop that were worth more money than a bunch of musical, macabre-looking objects.

Both the demons and Sir Surchion were obsessed with these relics, but I couldn't understand why they were so special.

As if they sense me thinking about them, the relics' song grows louder in my ears. I feel their weight in my pocket.

"They'll come for me," I repeat, trying to convince myself that all the time we've spent together meant something to them. At this point, I don't even care if it's because they own me. If it means them busting through that door and saving me, I'll take the bruise to my ego.

Sir Surchion leans close to my face, and his lips curl up into a sickly sweet smile. "Oh, I'm counting on it."

He snaps his fingers, and the two guard dogs jump to their feet. With a swift wave of his hand, they're off, launching for the door we entered through.

A snort of laughter. "It's going to take more than two mutts to stop three Hell demons." Elias alone would eat them from breakfast.

"Trap," the relics sing on cue. My eyes drop to my pocket, but when Sir Surchion's gaze falls too, I quickly snap my attention up, hoping he didn't notice.

He slowly straightens again. "You're right," he continues, "but if you didn't know, the Full Mooners have a pretty large pack. And I doubt they've killed them *all.*"

Oh crap...

The relics were right. This was about to be an ambush.

Suddenly, a hand slaps with the side of my face so hard it topples me over. I fall onto my ass. My eyes water from the sting, and I taste blood on my tongue. The inside of my mouth has a new gash, and I press my palm against my cheek. Anger floods my veins. The bastard hit me!

Sir Surchion stands over me, hand raised as if to strike me again. "That's for breaking in and stealing from me," he barks. Mordecai swoops off his shoulder at me, and I fall back. Throwing my hands up to shield my face last minute, the bird's sharp talons rake across my forearms, slicing into me before he flies to the rafters. "And that's for being a cat person."

Blood trickles down my arms, and I clutch them close as the pain rolls over me. It's so stunning, I lose my voice and am left gasping for air.

Sir Surchion paces away from me, only to whip back around and stride back. Rage contorts his face. "You stupid girl." He spits the words and stretches his fingers toward me. "Give me the Orb of Chaos. Just tell me where it is."

"I don't have it," I bite back. "You have the wrong person."

A vein pops out of his forehead as he struggles to remain calm, but he looks like he's bound to erupt like a volcano at any second. Even his face is cherry red. His head snaps up to the werewolves, and he says two words that spike fear in me. "Strip her."

"What? No!" I shout.

Calloused hands grab me again and yank me back to my feet. I fight wildly, bucking, kicking, and putting all my strength into getting the wolves to let go.

"Search every inch of her. If it's not on her now, then at least we get a bit of a thrill," Sir Surchion says.

No. No. No. No!

Panicked, I keep punching, giving all I've got to wrench their grips off me. Against my hip, the relics' buzzing increases tenfold. Their song rises in volume, urgency, and power, making my heart shake to the thundering bass and vibrato. The tattooed man grabs my sweater and pulls it, but I turn and aim my knee for his groin.

"Fuck off," I snap, but he twists last minute and I miss his nuts.

His fist flies at my face and clips me right under the eye. Excruciating pain laces up my face, feeling like it's about to crack open. I stumble backward into the bald werewolf's chest, clasping my face.

Oh my fucking god, it hurts so much. How the hell do guys stand being punched like this and keep fighting?

One of them clasps my jeans and wrenches. The button and zipper pop as the material is tugged down my hips. The room tilts around me from moving so damn fast.

Sir Surchion laughs maniacally, and I just want to rip his eyes out for enjoying my pain.

As Tattoos continues to manhandle me, he pulls at my

sweater, patting me down, touching my breasts like a disgusting prick. I fist his vest and drive my knee right into his balls, hard, this time meeting my mark.

He groans, clutching himself, and drops to the side like one of those fainting goats. For good measure, I kick him in the guts and smile as he coughs and hacks.

Suddenly, a thick arm locks around my neck, pressing me against his body while squeezing my throat.

I struggle for air, digging my nails into the brute's arm. A threatening growl rumbles in my ear, and fear leaps down my spine. This isn't how I want to die. The entire time, Sir Surchion studies me with mirth in his gaze, loving this.

"If you don't play nice with me, there are consequences," he says.

I use the last of my breath to choke out my thoughts. "Fuck you, you sadistic assho—"

He gives the man behind me a quick nod, and my words are cut off by an excruciating sharpness in my shoulder. I scream. The pain is blinding and burns like hell, as if someone just buried a handful of searing fireplace pokers into me.

Eyes blurry with tears, I realize Baldy has bitten into me, his mouth now elongated into a wolf's muzzle. His razor-sharp fangs are buried deep into flesh and muscle, scraping bone.

I thrust against him, the pain unbearable, and my knees buckle. Just as fast, he tears himself away, leaving a ragged mess of blood and flesh. My head spins, and for a moment, I lose sense of everything around me.

When he releases me, I fall to my knees, unable to hold myself up a moment longer. Tears sting my swollen, cut cheeks, but I can't stop crying. I've never felt anything so horrific. Every movement, no matter how small, hurts.

"Now tell me. Where is the orb?" Sir Surchion pushes.

I can't even form words; the pain has stolen my voice.

"I'm waiting!" he bellows.

Only a whimper spills past my lips.

Ferocious barking erupts from behind us, and my heartbeat falters. An even louder snarl follows, like the roar of a lion, followed by the dogs' squealing yipps of defeat.

My pulse gallops. Please let it be Elias!

And Cain, Dorian—please let it be them outside!

A choir of wolf howls echo throughout the warehouse, and terror replaces any ounce of hope I had left. Seconds later, the gruesome sounds of fighting break out. Tearing, shouting, banging, growling. My chest tightens at the thought of any of my demons hurt.

A screech has me looking up. Mordecai sits on the open window again, peering out. He shrieks again at his master, who turns pale.

"Quick!" Sir Surchion orders someone over my shoulder, sounding panicked, but I don't dare turn. Looks like the battle outside isn't going the way he'd hoped.

"Find the orb!" he keeps barking.

I feel the chill of the air kiss my torn and bloodied shoulder. The relics shake so violently in my pocket now, I don't know how they've not seen them yet.

It takes me a second, but I notice Sir Surchion's gaze is no longer on me. Instead, he's looking at the floor… at a growing black shadow that's elongating from my feet, across the floor toward him, all on its own.

But not just any shadow. *My* shadow.

Sayah! No!

I try to call her back, but she continues to stretch out before me, her form darkening and becoming denser before my eyes. My lungs squeeze. For some reason, breathing is becoming harder, and my head whirls from the lack of oxygen.

Even the werewolves freeze in place, now staring at my secret being exposed without my doing.

Come back! I shout at her through my foggy thoughts. *What are you doing?*

Somehow, she's able to keep ignoring me and raises off the floor, reminding me of some kind of evil spirit creature. Made for horror movies. Even though we're still attached by a dark cord, she looks nothing like the shadow I've known most of my life. No, she's something else entirely.

Her head swivels my way, and she blinks, revealing two bright red eyes.

Holy fuck.

"Another demon!" Sir Surchion yells, but fear makes his voice tremble. "She's one of them!"

Her opaque arm lashes out and collides with Sir Surchion's chest. He's lifted off his feet and thrown across the room, slamming into a shelf with such force it rocks back and forth. I leap back as collectables spill and crash onto the ground. Then, the massive structure falls forward, right on top of him. The resounding boom echoes throughout the warehouse.

Reddish-orange wisps of power spiral around my body and through the tether binding Sayah to me. I can't even process what's happening because my stomach spins with nausea, and I'm left gasping for air that I can't seem to take in. I may have lost control of her, but her actions seem to be affecting me. And not in a good way. The more solid Sayah becomes, the weaker I feel. My entire body tremors, and I'm icy cold all over.

She's draining me.

Sayah takes a menacing step toward the fallen shelf, but

colored spots dance before my eyes, and the world sways around me.

Just then, the warehouse door bursts open, sunlight pouring inside, but I can't see who's won the fight outside, the demons or the werewolves. Despite my resistance, the darkness creeping into my vision takes over. And the last thing I remember is the sweet relics' song humming in my ears like a lullaby as I lose myself to unconsciousness.

CHAPTER TWENTY-SIX
CAIN

As another wolf lunges for me, I grab it by the top and bottom jaws and use all my strength to rip its muzzle in half and then off its face. Warm blood splatters across my neck and forehead, and I throw the body on the ground with a thud. This may have been fun at first, when the wolves attacked the manor, but now it's just irritating. Aria is in that warehouse.

After changing back into our demon forms, we hurried to the heart of Glenside where everyone knew Sir Surchion's antique shop sat. That's when Elias had caught Aria's scent on the breeze, and we followed him to the back of the warehouse. The ambush came only seconds later—another two dozen Full Mooner werewolves jumping from rooftops and crawling out of their hiding places in the shadows. Fucking pricks.

Much like our clash with them at the house, this fight itself wasn't an even one, but with every second that passed, every wolf we killed, we were being kept away from Aria. A werewolf biker gang and the collector? Now I had no doubt they were working together in this, and from the looks of it, Sir Surchion was using the wolves to buy time.

Aria's scream echoes from inside the metal building, and my body tenses with a deadly combination of rage and fear. We have to get in there.

Gaze whipping to my left, I see Dorian crouched low, hand frozen mid-punch in front of a man's bloody, beaten-in face. Hearing Aria's cry has paralyzed him, too. He glances at me and we exchange knowing looks, then search for Elias among the carnage. In his massive beast form, he snatches a man between his jaws, chomps down, and shakes his head viciously, painting more blood across the blacktop. A silver wolf sneaks behind him and latches onto his already wounded hind leg, and Elias snarls, baring yellow fangs and kicking out. The wolf is thrown off and slams into a pile of trash cans with a loud bang.

The ground is littered with naked bodies from the fallen Mooners. Dorian finishes off his opponent and stands. Only a few werewolves remain alive, but seeing their fallen pack members, they turn tail and race down the alley in retreat. About damn time.

Once we're alone, I let my wings fold into my back and shake the rest of my demon off until I'm in my human skin once again.

As Dorian strolls to my side, his horns recede, the platinum leaves his hair, and the tattoos fade away. Elias's change looks more painful with his hurt leg, but he gets through it, standing there butt-ass naked seconds later with a chunk missing from his thigh.

"Do we have a plan?" Dorian's question is directed to either of us.

"Get Aria out. Kill anyone in our way," Elias growls, still riled up from the fight. His eyes glow ominously.

Dorian glances at me for a final word, but I only nod. I'm thinking the exact same thing.

"Works for me," he says with a shrug. "What are we waiting for?"

Boom! A loud crash sounds from inside the warehouse. The ground shakes under our feet.

We exchange fearful looks.

Not wasting another second, I run to the building's heavy metal door and power kick it open. It swings violently, crashing against the wall, and the three of us shoulder our way inside the dark building.

The first thing we see is Aria on her knees at the end of the aisle, her clothes torn and hanging off her body, blood matted in her hair and covering her neck and arm. In front of her is the black outline of a shadow. No, a monster, standing upright like its own entity. Ruby-red eyes shine as it looks at us.

What the fuck is that?

It's nothing like the shadow I thought I saw shifting around Aria's room when we first met. This is new and fucking incredible!

Aria collapses on the spot, and my chest seizes with dread. At the same time, the dark creature shrinks and slides across the floor, zipping into Aria's unmoving body.

Two men barrel toward us, both wearing the werewolf gang's emblem. Elias lunges for them immediately, another snarl ripping from his throat.

"Cain, the relics!" Dorian says, pointing toward the front of the warehouse. And there they are—the gold cord, the heart, and…

There's a third piece lying there beside Aria. A glass orb filled with silvery-blue liquid. I freeze, my heart thundering. Is that… the eye?

Not only had Aria stolen our relics, but she had found the harp's eye as well?

As Elias battles with the two werewolves, Dorian rushes for Aria and I charge after him. He falls to his knees next to her and gingerly lifts her limp, unconscious body into his lap, frowning deeply.

"She's covered in blood but still alive," he whispers, assessing her wounds. She's deathly pale, and her face is badly swollen and bruised. There's a nasty cut under her eye and claw marks up her arms, but nothing is as bad as the missing chunk of flesh from her shoulder. "Those bastards bit her."

I don't know what to feel at the moment. My heart tugs seeing her like this, but at the same time, the sting of betrayal is there since now I know for a fact she took the relics. I should be furious with her. I should kill her on the spot. But I only feel confusion and a deep ache in my chest when looking at her in Dorian's arms, and I'm not sure why.

The thud of two more bodies hitting the floor sounds from behind us, and a moment later, Elias appears on my right, wiping blood from across his mouth with the back of his hand. I don't need to turn around to know he's finished them off.

"Shit," is all he says, and I'm not sure if it's from the sight of Aria's mangled body or all of the relics nearby. There are shelves and shelves of them. Then Elias searches the space around us. "Where's the old man?"

"The gutless weasel probably ran," Dorian replies.

"Let's get Aria out of here." That's the most important thing. "You get her. I'll grab the relics."

As Dorian stands, he cradles her to his chest. I crouch down to collect the eye, string, and heart. I still can't believe that not only had she been able to find all three, but she'd gotten them to merge, just as they've been designed to do.

A sudden flutter of air whacks into me, along with a dark feathery wing. Needle-like claws spike into my arms, and I curse and jump back. That's when I see the damn crow hastily descending in front of me.

I try to grab the thing, but the little shit is slippery and manages to swoop back up, just out of my reach.

Light catches on something it carries in its beak, glinting. I jerk my gaze down to the ground and find the relics gone.

"Sonofabitch!" I lunge after it as it zigzags higher to an open window in the ceiling. It perches there and peers down as if mocking me.

There is no way that thing will steal my keys to get back into Hell.

Summoning my demon's power again, my wings unfurl. I test them, about to take flight. "We need to get that fucking bird!"

Gently, Dorian lays Aria back on the ground, and both he and Elias spin to find the easiest way up. But before they can move, a thunderous roar responds from behind me, shaking the whole damn warehouse.

Goosebumps ripple over my skin, and I twist around. "What the hell now?"

An enormous dark figure rises up from a fallen shelf, lifting it as if he weighs nothing. Fiery orange eyes burning like an inferno find me. When the monstrous creature steps forward, I realize what I've come face to face with. It's a fucking dragon.

This beast before me is the color of night, scales glinting a silvery gray. Bat-like leathery wings span outward, throwing us into shadow, and steam rises from its flaring nostrils.

All three of us stand frozen at first, staring at the monster standing so tall, it almost hits the lofty warehouse ceiling.

That's when the crow swoops down from the window and lands on the dragon's shoulder.

"I think we found the old man," Elias says, sniffing the air that starts to reek of fire.

"Shit, I had no idea he was a dragon," Dorian murmurs.

On two feet, Sir Surchion unleashes another earth-shattering roar, his breath blasting into us. It smells putrid and is scorching hot. All these relics he collects, all his treasures, make so much sense now. Dragons love their shiny objects.

"Get Aria now," I hiss under my voice to Dorian.

He hurries to her side again, but before he can scoop her up, Sir Surchion's glowing hypnotic eyes narrow on us. He swings his head into another nearby shelving unit and knocks it over. We dance out of the way as everything comes crashing down around us.

Then he steps forward, one of his massive clawed feet now creating a wall between us and Aria. He sucks in a tremendous breath, his chest expanding, and I know what's coming next.

"Shit!"

Fire blasts from his gaping mouth, his body leaning into the attack.

No time to think, we're scrambling in every direction to escape the inferno. Sure, we like heat as much as the next demon, but our powers are weaker on this plane. Our ability to heal is slowed, and dying is a real possibility. Only if we die, our souls are lost. We cease to exist.

I throw myself behind another shelf, the blast of fire slamming into it. Flames lick the sides, crackling and spitting. The heat is unbearable, and that's saying a lot coming from me. I don't move or I'll end up turned to ash.

Fury lances through me that the asshole ambushed us. How the hell didn't we know his true form? The clues were there—always collecting shit, greedy as hell, and was his accent Romanian? Hindsight's 20/20, but that doesn't help us now.

But right now, I just need to get my hands on Aria and the relics. I'll deal with him later.

When the fire flatlines, a savage growl rumbles through the warehouse.

I throw myself out from my hiding spot just as Dorian and Elias burst out of theirs. We exchange quick, intense looks, proving we're all thinking the same thing. This is fucked up.

We bolt for the dragon, but when a darkness rises over us, along with an intense gust of wind, we're forced to stop short. The dragon's wings spread out once more as he rises off the ground. The ceiling of the warehouse groans as its panels open up like a box, sunlight drenching us.

Clutched in the dragon's claws is Aria. She's slumped, unconscious, and the bastard carries her away from us. The crow beats its wings, escaping too, still gripping our relics.

My heart clenches with dread.

Dorian lunges toward them, scaling the shelves, while Elias races down the aisle, jumping up on stacked crates. Knowing I'm faster with my own wings, I push against the ground and launch into the air, but the moment the dragon meets the sky, the roof lowers again, caging us in.

"No!" I bellow after them as I watch their shadowy figures disappear into the clouds. A sharp ache settles in my chest, right over my heart, knowing I failed to keep my promise to her. I told her I'd never let anyone hurt her, and now, not only is she unconscious and bleeding out, but she's been stolen from us by Sir Surchion.

He has Aria *and* our relics.

But not for fucking long. I'm seething.

I roar, the sound raw and primal on my throat, my whole body shuddering. This isn't how it's going to end.

"Dorian, Elias," I shout once I touch down on solid ground again. They jump to meet me and come to my side. "Looks like we're going dragon hunting."

THANK YOU

Thank you for reading Playing With Hellfire

Start reading book 2 in the Sin Demons series.
Hell In A Handbasket

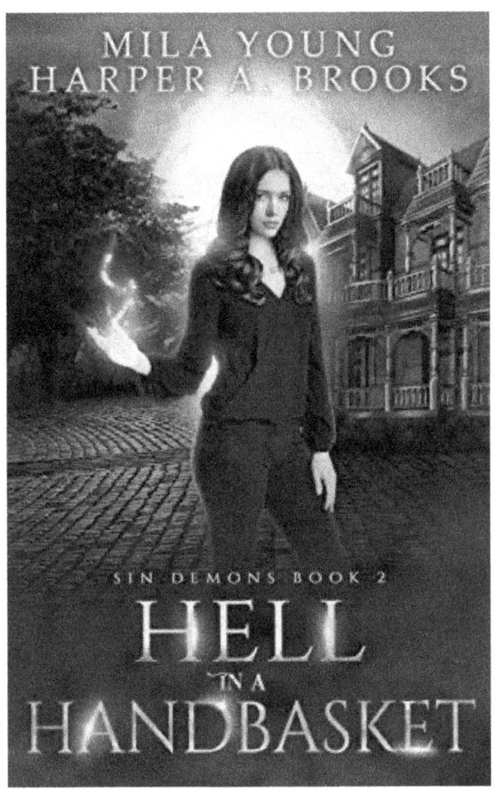

ABOUT MILA YOUNG

Best-selling author, Mila Young tackles everything with the zeal and bravado of the fairytale heroes she grew up reading about. She slays monsters, real and imaginary, like there's no tomorrow. By day she rocks a keyboard as a marketing extraordinaire. At night she battles with her mighty pen-sword, creating fairytale retellings, and sexy ever after tales. In her spare time, she loves pretending she's a mighty warrior, walks on the beach with her dogs, cuddling up with her cats, and devouring every fantasy tale she can get her pinkies on.

Ready to read more and more from Mila Young?www.subscribepage.com/milayoung

For more information...
milayoungarc@gmail.com

ABOUT HARPER A. BROOKS

Harper A. Brooks lives in a small town on the New Jersey shore. Even though classic authors have always filled her bookshelves, she finds her writing muse drawn to the dark, magical, and romantic. But when she isn't creating entire worlds with sexy shifters or legendary love stories, you can find her either with a good cup of coffee in hand or at home snuggling with her furry, four-legged son, Sammy.

She writes urban fantasy and paranormal romance.

RONE AWARD WINNER
USA TODAY BESTSELLING AUTHOR

Want to read more from Harper A. Brooks?
Subscribe to Harper's newsletter and get *Halfling for Hire* for free! http://BookHip.com/MCBDCN

Join Harper's reader group for exclusive content, sneak-peeks, giveaways, and more! www.facebook.com/groups/harpershalflings